"What do you want, Joseph? What do you want from me?"

The air between them became hot and thick with a palpable lust. Joseph licked his lips. He was imagining what it must be like to consume a woman's entire breast.

"I want to make love to you."

She leaned forward and took his hand. Together they rose from the table and walked out into the parking lot.

"You'll be gentle with me, won't you? I haven't been with anyone since my husband and I divorced five years ago. You'll take it slow, won't you?"

They were almost to her car. She pulled out her keys and opened the car door.

"Promise you'll be gentle with me."

"No," Joe said.

His huge, powerful hands clenched tight around her throat....

SUCCULENT PREY

WRATH JAMES WHITE

LEISURE BOOKS NEW YORK CITY

To Mom.

A LEISURE BOOK®

December 2008

Dorchester Publishing Co., Inc.
200 Madison Avenue
New York, NY 10016

ISBN 10: 0-8439-6164-3
ISBN 13: 978-0-8439-6164-5

The name "Leisure Books" and the stylized "L" with design are trademarks of Dorchester Publishing Co., Inc.

Printed in the United States of America.

10 9 8 7 6 5 4 3 2 1

Visit us on the web at www.dorchesterpub.com.

ACKNOWLEDGMENTS

Special thanks to Brian Keene, Ed Lee, and Jack Ketchum for support and inspiration. Thanks also to my ex-wife Rosie who was with me through the writing of this and put up with the weirdness. And to Zondria, my biggest fan, who was also with me through the writing of this and who was always supportive and encouraging and helped me get through the rough patches.

SUCCULENT
PREY

Part I

Chapter One

Joey tasted nickel and copper. Blood. His mouth was filled with his own blood lying thick on his tongue. He tried to spit it out but the duct tape strapped across his face made it impossible. He had no choice but to swallow it, gagging as a wad of blood and phlegm slid down his throat in a warm lump. Joey tried hard to keep from crying. He'd been crying for hours and it had done him no good. The fat kid seemed to enjoy his tears.

Why me? Why is he doing this?

It was a pointless question with no answer that would have made a bit of difference. He was suffering and he would continue to suffer and there was nothing he could do about it.

At first he had been confident that his parents would rescue him and punish the fat kid. He was sure that as soon as they realized he hadn't made it home from school they'd be kicking down every door on the block looking for him. But that had been many hours ago and no one had come for him. Now he was afraid that no one would ever find him; that he would die down there in the dank basement.

The rusted fiberglass-on-steel tub in which Joey lay

was rapidly filling with blood. Joey splashed about in a river of red, slipping farther down into the tub. He'd heard that you could drown in three inches of bathwater and wondered how many inches of blood were already in the tub. He knew he was bleeding to death. His flesh had been split open like overripe fruit and was leaking in a steady sluggish drip down into the large bathtub.

Joey didn't know how many times he'd been stabbed and cut. Slashes crosshatched his thighs and buttocks, many of them going clean through to the bone, yawning wide like toothless smiles filled with bleeding pink gums. He could see the red muscle fibers and stringy sallow fat boiling up out of one particularly deep wound in his upper thigh. Luckily his genitals had been spared the fat kid's attentions. His anus, unfortunately, had not. He'd cut him there too and then he'd done worse. Joey tried his best not to think about that pain.

Several times now the fat kid had come, dipped a glass into the tub, filled it with Joey's blood, and brought the glass to his blubbery lips to drink. His squinty little eyes would flutter in absolute ecstasy as he gulped down the red liquid, making sickening smacking noises. Even through the pain Joey found amusement in knowing that he had pissed himself in the same tub from which the fat kid was drinking.

Time stalled as Joey slipped into and out of consciousness. The basement was a perpetual night, an endless nightmare from which he could not awaken. The windows along the tops of the basement walls were spray-painted black. Faint glimmers of light leaked between the cracks in the frames and cast eerie shadows on the damp walls. The only genuine illumi-

nation came from the fluorescent light at the bottom
of the basement steps and that was only turned on
when the fat kid came down to play. Joey was beginning to fear that light. In the dark he was alone. Safe.
Whenever the light came on the pain started all over
again.

Joey's throat was raw and hoarse from the agonized
shrieks that had torn their way up from his belly and
out into the moist, stagnant basement air. Even after
the fat kid covered Joey's mouth with duct tape he
had continued to scream at every thrust and slash of
the knife, scalpel, sharp steel pins, and needles. Not to
call for help, but to drown out the pain with noise.

Joey lost track of how many times the fat kid came
down to torture him or drink from his wounds. The
image of the teenager's chubby cheeks splashed with
Joey's blood, his eyes glazed and sparkling with
hunger and lust, made chills dance along Joey's skin.
He wondered if the kid was a vampire. Vampires were
supposed to be thin and beautiful and this kid was all
lumpy and misshapen with pimples exploding all over
his acne-scarred face, but he had drank an enormous
amount of blood. Only a vampire could have drank
that much blood without getting sick. But if that kid
was immortal then he was fucked because that meant
he'd have to look like that forever.

Maybe he just thinks he's a vampire? Joey wondered. Or maybe he *is* a vampire but just a different
kind than the ones in the movies. An uglier kind.

The basement door creaked open again and sunlight spilled down the stairs, illuminating the cobwebs
and rat droppings and chasing away the cockroaches
that had come to lap at the blood splattered around
the outside of the tub. A few tepid rays of sunshine

struck metal and cast their gleam farther into the room. Joey's eyes followed the sun rays back to their reflection in the stainless surgical steel and he shuddered.

Several cruel-looking implements were laid out on a metal table a few feet from where Joey lay bleeding. Razor-sharp scalpels, knives, and needles, arranged the way surgeons did on TV—in order of practical use. They were all stained with Joey's blood.

The basement door closed again and the lone fluorescent light at the top of the basement steps flashed on. The bulb was broken and flickered continuously, casting eerie shadows around the room. Joey cringed as the fat kid came back down the stairs, backlit by the strobe-lighting fluorescent bulb. He was just one great malformed shadow.

The fat kid was naked. His pale flesh was stained with Joey's blood, including his short, fireplug-shaped cock, erect and straining beneath the weight of his low-hanging gut. Joey began to whimper as the kid's gore-streaked smile came swooping down at him and he felt those clammy hands and blubbery lips, that slimy wormlike tongue, and blunt little teeth worry at him, probing and digging into his wounds, ripping them wider. He began to scream against the duct tape sealed tight to his lips as he was turned facedown in the tub and he felt the pain lance through him again in rhythmic thrusts, drawing more blood.

Joseph Miles woke up with his heart thundering in his chest, his lungs sucking in air and forcing it back out in rapid bursts. His old scars screamed as if they'd just been made. His eyes slid back and forth, sweeping the room, looking for the fat kid. He reached out and stroked the large powerful forms of Hades and Beelzebub, his guardians, nestled beside him in the bed, one on each side. The rock-hard muscles coiled beneath their fur reassured him. They would've torn that fat kid to pieces. Anyway, he was locked up now. He'd never hurt Joey again. Still, Joey was grateful for his two guardians.

He squinted against the harsh invasive glare of the morning sun lancing through the cracks in his vertical blinds and tried to will the clouds to shield him from it. Hades and Beelzebub did not appear to mind the sunlight nearly as much as he did. Joey found that surprising. Weren't monsters supposed to fear the light? That's what the books all said. But the fat kid had snatched him off his bike in broad daylight and Hades and Beelzebub loved the sun. They lay snoring steadily in the warm morning light.

Their heavy rumbling breaths vibrated through the mattress like a revving engine. Joey could still smell the meaty steel-and-copper scent of flesh and blood in each exhalation. He cringed, remembering their last meal.

Joey stared at the two massive beasts, admiring their fearsome jaws with the savage, lethal-looking canines. Their mouths could easily have crushed the largest bones in his body. Their necks were as thick as his waist and their legs and shoulders were broad and muscular. The combined weight of the two monsters was nearly three hundred pounds, three times his own weight, and with them lying on the blanket he was trapped beneath it, unable to move.

Beelzebub was the first to notice that the young boy had awakened. He leapt up and ran to the head of the bed where he began happily licking Joey's face. Hades woke up next and soon Joey was being covered in saliva as the two huge beasts showered him with affection. Joey hugged them, running his hands over the smooth black fur coating their muscular bodies, and began to cry. He knew that if anyone found out what they'd done they would destroy the two beasts and he'd be alone again. Defenseless.

It had been over a year since Joey had been attacked and nearly killed. That's when his parents had brought home the two monsters to protect him. For the last six months Joey and his friend Mike had been teaching the two predators how to kill from a book they'd ordered from *Soldier of Fortune* magazine on building prey drive and a Schutzhund video on bite work. Using a dummy they'd made of old clothes, they'd taught the two dogs to leap up and rip out a man's throat on command, how to dive for a man's legs and crush his ankles or rip off his quadriceps or hamstring muscles with their massive jaws to bring him down, how to rip open a man's belly and tear out his intestines. They were learning quickly. Joey had been dying for a demonstration of their abilities.

Right up until Hades and Beelzebub split little Mikey like a wishbone, Joey had been confident that he could call the dogs off before they went too far. The fountain of arterial red that splashed his face moments after giving the attack command had proven him wrong.

He had been standing next to Mikey in the park. They both had their shirts off and Joey kept catching Mikey staring at the scars on his chest and stomach from where he had been attacked. He knew that Mikey was about to ask him about them, that he would have to remember that horrible night spent in

Damon Trent's basement tasting his own blood. The last thing Joey wanted was to remember. He whistled and pointed at his friend. The two rottweilers turned in unison, baring their fangs. Hades was the first to attack.

Mikey had his arm wrapped in a bite sleeve made from a stolen leather jacket and two thick pillows, but Hades ignored it. Mikey's eyes widened in fear as the massive beast charged. He held out the bite sleeve and she dodged it as if it were a gun, just like she'd been trained to do. She went straight for his throat.

Joey couldn't help but be impressed as he watched that thickly-muscled instrument of destruction launch herself into the air like a missile, leaping nearly three feet off the ground, her fangs bared. Her jaws clamped onto Mikey's throat and she brought him down to the park floor in a cloud of dust. She began thrashing and jerking her head from side to side, snapping Mikey's neck and tearing his esophagus to shreds. Blood erupted from the boy's throat and soaked the animal's snout. Blood from Mikey's punctured carotid artery and lacerated jugular sprayed all over the ground and doused young Joseph in a shower of red. He licked his friend's blood from his lips and a shiver vibrated down to the root of him, giving him an instant erection.

Beelzebub was just seconds behind his sister. He dove into Mikey's stomach and began ripping and tearing at his abdominal muscles, burrowing his way to the boy's organs.

Joey's legs trembled. His jaw fell open and his eyes widened in shock. He reached out his hand toward the dog but hesitated. Something about the sight of the blood, the torn flesh with the white bone and pink-and-purple organs gleaming through, the sound of muscle and tendons being ripped by those merciless fangs, transfixed him. It was so horrible . . . so beautiful.

The boy stood frozen, staring as Hades attempted to tear Mikey's head from his shoulders. Joey tried to shut out the rattling whistle coming from Mikey's mangled throat as the boy continued trying to suck air into his lungs even as Beelzebub tore into him. Joey clapped his hands and yelled for the dogs to stop.

"Down! Down, Hades! Down, Beelzebub!"

When Hades unclamped her jaws from Mikey's throat the boy's head was twisted at an acute angle. There was little doubt that his neck had been shattered. His pupils were fixed and dilated and his chest had ceased its rise and fall.

Joey looked down at his murdered friend and began to cry. He hadn't meant to kill him. His sorrow rained down on him like a summer storm. He was relieved by the immediacy and intensity of it. Joey knew a lot about serial killers. He'd read about them, had almost been killed by one, and had an irrational fear of becoming one, becoming like the perverted freak that had kidnapped him and carved him up in his basement. But he was relatively sure that serial killers did not feel remorse for their victims. As long as he could cry he was sure that he was normal, even if his tears were more for the two massive rottweilers than for his dead playmate. He knew they would be put to sleep once the police found Mikey's body and figured out what had happened.

Two days later the dogs were destroyed, but not before Joey had taken them back to the park to watch them feed on Mikey's remains.

When they arrived at the spot where the attack had taken place the boy's savaged corpse was still lying in a heap on the park floor just where Joey had left it. Only now it was seeping fluids other than blood and myriad insects had begun making a meal of him. Joey found himself becoming aroused as he watched the two dogs bite off and devour huge chunks of the boy's flesh. He masturbated to his first climax as Hades devoured Mikey's genitals, adding his own virgin seed to the blood-soaked earth.

Chapter Two

Ten Years Later . . .

Joe sat in his art class staring at the nude model posing unenthusiastically atop a wooden stool. Her breasts were much smaller than what Joe preferred. Her hips, ass, and thighs were likewise barely existent. She was proportioned very much like a prepubescent girl rather than a grown woman. Not at all the type of woman that normally roused the beast. But something about her was getting to him. Her big, vulnerable, doelike eyes, the seductive smirk turning up the corners of her thick lips or the way they seemed to be constantly puckered as if blowing a kiss. Something about her was arousing him. And that was just not good.

Years ago a psychiatrist had suggested painting as therapy to help Joe deal with the trauma he'd been through. They thought it would be good if the shy young boy learned to express himself creatively. Since then Joe had used his art as an outlet for his fantasies, but as his fantasies had begun to twist and pervert he'd had to hide his work from those who wouldn't understand it. He was now beginning to think this art class might not have been a good idea. It was hard to hide your art in a room filled with thirty other students.

Joe's hand trembled as he dragged the paintbrush over the canvas. More and more red found its way into his palette as he imagined ripping the waifish model open and tasting her insides. It was just one more sign that he was starting to lose control of himself.

Earlier that day he'd received a call from his father reminding Joe of how much he was paying for his education and that he'd better not be out partying all night and getting shitty grades like he had his first year in college.

"Don't piss away your chance to make something of yourself by going out every night chasing those college sluts. There'll be plenty of time to dip your wick in those split-tails after you get your education. College ain't all about beer bongs and toga parties, boy. Don't fuck this up! I can barely afford to keep you there now. I'd be retired now if it weren't for you—you're the only reason I keep working. But you'd rather get drunk and bang every coed slut you see. Young, dumb, and full of cum. You'd better control that shit this year, boy! Don't let your grades slip again. You hearin' me, boy?"

Joe listened halfheartedly. Loans and government grants were paying for his education; all his dad did was send him spending money. He could easily replace that eighty dollars a week with a job. Even McDonald's paid more than that. But something about talking to his father always made the beast hungrier. His dad always pissed him off and the anger seemed to trigger the lust.

Joe's hands whipped frantically back and forth across the canvas. His palette was now almost completely red, white, tan, and pink. Blood, bone, and flesh. He was painting the model from the inside out. He was also panting hard and staring at her so intently that she began to shiver as she stared back. Joe could feel eyes on him, in back of him. He could hear them gasp at the mayhem on his canvas. But he couldn't stop painting. An erection was tenting his pants as he slashed at the canvas with his brush. Finally, the model snatched up her clothes and ran out of the room, breaking the trance Joe had found himself in. The room went completely quiet. Joe could still hear his own breaths coming hard and fast like a steam engine at full speed. He struggled to get himself under control even as he became aware of the stares of his peers—and the professor. She was the first to break the silence.

"Uh . . . Joseph? That was a pretty intense session there. Do you mind if we take a look at your canvas?" The professor was another starving waif with no appreciable nourishment on her gaunt frame. Her skin hung loose against her bones as if someone had already sucked out all the muscle and fat. The bones in her face stuck out prominently and her eyes were sunken back into her skull. Her dried nest of blonde and gray hair hung in a tangled mess down to her shoulders and her hands were perpetually stained with paint. She had always reminded Joe of a walking, talking skeleton.

Joe said nothing. He watched stoically as she lifted the canvas from the easel in front of him. The rest of the class was closing in on him, stepping from behind their own easels and crowding in tight to stare over his shoulder at his masterpiece. The canvas dripped with red. There were gasps all around.

"This is some very passionate work, Joseph. What inspired you to create this?"

The woman's voice trembled. She'd be calling his counselor the minute class was over. They'd have his ass on a psychiatrist's couch by the end of the week and once they found out everything else that was in his head they'd stick him in a straitjacket and toss him in a padded room. He had to say something to dissuade them from thinking he was crazy, but he couldn't focus. The proximity of his fellow students was making his mouth water. The air was thick and humid with the smell of warm, young flesh. He stared from one to the other, not looking at their faces but at breasts squeezed tight into little T-shirts and blouses, nipples pressed against the fabric, naked thighs sticking out from beneath shorts and skirts, bare arms, necks, even the shaved calves at the bottom of a pair of Capri pants were arousing him. Joe wanted to scream. Worse yet, he wanted to attack.

"I don't know. I-I'm sorry."

"No, don't be sorry. This is wonderful work. An artist should be passionate. Raw bleeding passion is what makes an artist and if this is what you have inside of you then you should do quite well. It reminds me of Francis Bacon." The art teacher smiled at him, laughing at his obvious embarrassment. Joe tried not to be insulted by her delight over his discomfort but he felt as if he was being patronized, even mocked.

Joe looked at the canvas again. It did look a little like something Francis Bacon would have painted. He looked back at the art teacher's forced smile and now recognized it as little more than an attempt to reassure him. She was not ridiculing him. Not baring her fangs.

"Thank you," Joe whispered sheepishly.

"It really is an intense piece."

Despite her praise, Joe could still hear the nervousness in her voice and smell the fear in her perspiration. His nostrils filled with the scent of her arousal. Luckily she did absolutely nothing for him sexually.

His classmates continued to gawk at his work, some praising, some condemning, others casting nervous, disgusted glances his way. Finally, the model, who'd run out of the room, came back. All eyes turned to her as she tiptoed back into the room with a robe wrapped around her and her shoes in her hands. The slender woman looked over the teacher's shoulder at the canvas with her big, nervous, watery, doe eyes and then at Joseph. She shuddered. An insecure smile crept tentatively onto her lips, testing the waters before splashing across her face.

"Is this me? Is this how you see me?" Her voice was small and timid but there was something sultry in it too. Her eyes locked with Joe's as if challenging him.

"Yes. That's what I saw." Joe averted his eyes. Ashamed.

"I like it. It scares me. Nothing's ever really scared me before."

"Then you can keep it."

"What? You can't give this away. At least let me pay you for it."

"No. It's yours. You inspired it. You should have it."

The model looked down at the canvas again with the angry slashes of red ripping through the pinks and tans and she shuddered once more.

"I inspired it?" she whispered, awed.

"Yes."

"Then let me take you out to dinner or something to pay for it."

Joe looked up at her with that carnivorous lust still brimming in his eyes.

"I don't think that would be wise."

The girl's mouth opened and then shut again. She wandered out of the room holding the canvas in front of her at arm's length, just staring at it. Everyone else got up and slowly filtered out of the room behind her. Joe quietly gathered up his things and left as well.

He was so aroused that he almost sprinted across campus to get back to his dorm room to masturbate. It was late and he was hoping that his roommate would be out at one of the bars or something so he'd have a few moments alone.

He was barely through the door before the phone rang. It was his father again. He was drunk and in the mood to confess, to unburden his soul.

"Look, son, you know I love you, don't you? You're the only good thing in my world and I don't want you to turn out like me. That's why I'm so hard on you, boy. I just don't want you to wind up like me. I don't think it's in you anyway really. You're too soft. Do you know what I am, son? I've done terrible things, boy. Really awful things. Not even your momma knows about it. But I think you should know . . ."

"You're drunk, Dad. Go to sleep."

Joe hung up the phone and climbed under the covers. He didn't quite feel like masturbating anymore.

He slept for two hours and when he awoke there were three messages on his answering machine. They were all from his father.

"Joey? You there boy? I shouldn't be saying all of this on a damned machine. Answer the phone! I've got to tell you about that kid Damon, the one who attacked you when you were little. Joe, pick up the phone!"

Joe pressed the button to erase and the next message came on.

"Look . . . that Damon kid . . . I knew him. I . . ."

Joe erased that one too.

"There were a lot of women . . . and kids. I couldn't control myself. It was like . . . an addiction."

Joe hit ERASE and pulled the phone cord out of the wall. He plopped down in front of the computer and opened a book to read. It was a zoological text called *Perfect Predators*. Joe smiled as if laughing at some private joke.

Chapter Three

There are some cultures that believe you can only know God by examining his works. Not by reading a book or listening to the superstitious ramblings of some hypocritical child-molesting priest, but by watching his movements in nature. It followed logically from there that to know what God wants you must look at those creatures who lack the will to do other than what nature had intended of them, those creatures programmed by nature to act solely on instinct.

Joe liked to study animals, particularly the predators. It helped him to understand the natural instincts that drove human behavior. Joe had many questions about so-called aberrant behavior in humans. Could it be that what we called aberrant behavior was in fact the natural state of man? Was there an instinct to kill? An instinct to rob, rape, maim, and destroy? In animals Joe saw every act that man had proclaimed criminal and sinful performed with startling regularity. In nature there was homosexuality, incest, patricide, matricide, infanticide, war, robbery, rape, necrophilia, and cannibalism. In countless nature documentaries Joe watched with interest as baboons murdered chimpanzees, ate their own young, and stole food from one another. He watched dogs raping their own mothers, and lions attacking and killing other male lions and murdering and cannibalizing their offspring. Joe didn't feel like such a monster when he looked at the behaviors God appeared to favor. God was apparently a lunatic.

Joe flipped through the pictures of the big jungle cats in his zoology book and felt a stirring kinship. They all enjoyed their positions at the top of their respective food chains. Yet man alone sat uncontested atop the global food chain, the superpredator. There was nothing on earth on which man did not prey in one way or another, either for food, clothing, medicines, hair products, jewelry, good luck charms, or merely for sport. Yet man had no natural predator—except man himself.

Joe stared in admiration at a picture of a sleek jaguar pouncing on a gazelle and smiled, imagining what it must feel like to take that first bite and taste the flood of warm blood from a lacerated artery fill your mouth. He turned the next page to a photograph of a baboon crushing the skull of a small chimpanzee. The pain and terror in the monkey's eyes excited him. He imagined himself as the baboon, his jaws clamping down on the skull of a young coed, his sharp canines piercing her brain. Joe squirmed uncomfortably in his seat as his erection swelled.

The hunger in his belly merged with the hunger in his loins to form something dark and murderous, awakening the predator coiled in his gut waiting for the scent of prey. He looked at his sleeping roommate across the room, tucked beneath the blankets, snoring softly, and his stomach growled at the prospect of fresh meat. The monster was ravenous tonight.

Joe turned with effort away from the still form of his roommate and closed the zoology book. He flicked on the PC and pulled the monster out of his shorts, taking it firmly in hand. He was sick of studying. It was time for a break. He went online and quickly found his favorite website. He clicked on the icon at the bottom of the cannibal sex site and brought up a page labeled "The Preparation of Human Flesh For Human Consumption." He began to read as he masturbated in long languid strokes to the descriptions of dismemberment and cannibalism.

For the best taste, choose *very* firm breasts with large nipples (half an inch or more in length) that stand up high on a girl's chest. Large breasts (36C to 40DD) with fat marbled into the meat make the softest and moistest cuts, so easy to chew you can almost eat them raw. The breast should be sliced off close to the rib bones, thus leaving some muscle under the breast meat. Serve sliced thinly cut diagonally, with or without the nipples intact, in sauce. If she is lactating you can use the milk to create a delicate cream sauce.

Joe began to salivate. He scrolled down further on the Web page as he stroked himself energetically, casting an occasional glance over at his sleeping roommate, hoping the guy wouldn't suddenly wake up and interrupt him. It would be a shame to have to kill him, although now he was certainly in the mood for it.

If the girl is to be cooked alive, she should be given several enemas and starved for at least 1–2 days prior to serving. She should be flushed out thoroughly (through both her anus and her urethra), all body hair removed (except her head hair, if the head is to be used for decoration), and the body washed down completely. Before starting, a painkiller should be administered. A strong alcoholic beverage is suggested, as it tends to improve the taste of the meat. If you are thinking of marinating the meat in wine then you might consider using that wine as the anesthesia to begin the marinating process.

Once the girl is properly anesthetized, with a very sharp knife carefully open her belly from just above her vagina to her sternum, not slicing too deep. Unlike venison or beef this meat is best served rather gamy, rich with the taste of fear. You want the girl to be alive right up until you cut off the first tender slice of this most choice and delicious meat.

"Yes!" Joe exclaimed breathlessly, shuddering with ecstasy as he reached up to pinch his nipples and slather his palm in saliva. Joe desperately wanted to know what the flesh of a living, breathing woman tasted like. He wanted her to be conscious and aware, watching as he tore the meat from her bones. He reached back down and took his erection in hand again, delighting in the slick feel of his own saliva as he jerked on his blood-gorged penis.

You may decide to leave the uterus intact as this can be stuffed. Rinse out the body cavity with clean water, rub the inside with butter and herbs. Core out the anus and stitch shut. Stuff her belly if desired with rice or stuffing mix, and sew the incision shut. Weigh her after gutting and stuffing and calculate her cooking time by the following rule: Barbecue 15–20 minutes per pound, and oven roast @ 375 degrees for 25–30 minutes per pound. Few girls will live longer than 1 hour while cooking since she will die as soon as her heart starts to cook.

Joe knew that most of the stuff on the site was bullshit. No one could survive the torturous ordeal of being vivisected long enough for you to cook them alive. Still, like all good pornography, it was all about the fantasy. He closed his eyes and tried to imagine himself as a chef serving up fresh girl meat. He felt the orgasm building within him as he imagined the aroma of freshly cooked flesh and tried to envision what the look in the woman's eyes would be as he peeled off bits of her flesh and devoured it before her as her heart boiled in her chest. He drooled and his cock tingled and swelled even more as he read further down the page. His erection was now so hard that it felt as if the skin would burst. Once again he looked over at his roommate to make sure he had not awakened. One of the boy's legs was now sticking out from beneath the covers. Joe had to restrain himself from going over to take a bite out of it. He turned back to the computer screen but continued to cast sidelong glances at his sleeping roommate as his engorged organ began to pulsate and the first drops of precum dribbled from the swollen head.

Joe pinched his left nipple hard as he continued to masturbate, then he reached down and slid a finger into his rectum to massage his prostate. He read frantically through the rest of the page as he neared climax.

His legs kicked straight out in front of him as the monster leaped up and shot a long arc of semen up onto the computer screen. His entire body jerked convulsively as he ejaculated again and again in what seemed an unending stream of liquid white, and visions spiraled through his mind of succulent human flesh cut lovingly from the breasts, thighs, and buttocks of a woman bred for her meat.

What the hell am I becoming? Joe wondered as he continued to pant breathlessly, still quivering from the powerful orgasm.

Joe used a tube sock to wipe his semen from the computer screen. He then licked his fingers clean of his still living fluids, imagining it was the blood of prey. Joe turned off the computer and crawled into bed with his erection still undiminished. He masturbated three more times before he finally drifted off into sleep. He was getting worse. It was time for another reprogramming session.

Chapter Four

The walls of the room were barren, painted a neutral antique white. The laminated wood floor was scuffed and scratched. A solemn crucifix hung in the center of one wall with the tortured and bleeding effigy of Christ affixed to it. The entire room seemed to perspire, the floor to heave as if breathing heavily as the combined lusts of a roomful of sex addicts boiled the air and raised the humidity.

Joe sat with his huge shoulders slumped forward, his tremendous arms resting on his thighs, his head nestled in his oversized hands, and his eyes boring into the sacrificial lamb seated directly across the room baring his soul for group consumption. There were seven of them crammed into the little room in the basement of the church, swapping titillating tales of sexual excess for the purpose of therapy, eagerly devouring each detail of one another's sex lives. Joe had no idea how this was supposed to make them better. It seemed like he'd been coming to these meetings for years.

His hunger roiled within him like a living thing clawing at the lining of his stomach. He'd eaten a full breakfast so he knew that it wasn't physical. He'd masturbated twice before leaving the house too. Sometimes that took the edge off his appetite. Not today. Today the only thing that would assuage his carnivorous lust was fresh meat. He needed help. He was having a harder and harder time resisting the temptation to feed. Everywhere he looked there seemed to be meat ripe for consumption. He was hoping this therapy session would at least calm his hunger long enough for him to make it through his classes.

Among this bizarre assemblage of predator and prey he should have felt right at home, but even here he had to maintain his secrets. He was more of a predator than any of them would ever have realized or been comfortable with, and as much a victim as the little man with the nervous eyes and bruised face. They were all victims here, victims of their own addictions, prey to their desires.

Joe had been coming to these meetings almost every day since he started college last year. He was now beginning his sophomore year at the local university where he was enrolled as a psychology major. The irony of that always made him laugh. *Physician, heal thyself.* He had started coming to Sex Addicts Anonymous after he'd gotten hooked on the sex and swingers club scene. He spent so much time in the sex clubs last semester, waking up nearly every night with a strange woman—or in some cases, strange couples—in his bed that he'd nearly flunked out of school. So he'd come here to get his life in order. But now his addiction had mutated and he wasn't sure they could help him anymore. The problems of the other confessed addicts almost seemed pedestrian in comparison to the monster raging within him.

"I wound up drunk in an alley giving a blowjob to a stranger."

His name was Frank. He had a busted nose, a black eye, and a huge gash on his forehead. It was a common sight. They were all pretty much used to it now. He always came into the group session with a new bruise or cut. Joe wouldn't have been as interested in hearing about Frank's sexual exploits were it not for the violence that always accompanied the passion.

Joe had heard all of Frank's stories before. Each day was just more of the same. Yet another variation of the "Meet boy, fuck and suck boy, get the shit kicked out of him by boy" theme. The only thing that ever changed was the order of the events, the severity of the attacks, and the size of the attacker's cock. Frank was a homosexual who had a thing for straight men and often risked an ass kicking to get one. He enjoyed telling his lascivious tales of sex and battery even more than the rest of the group enjoyed hearing them. This was not so much therapy as group catharsis and cathexis. He spit it out and they sucked it up.

In the beginning they would try to outdo each other. Each of them would tell their most extravagant tales of sexual hedonism. Mary was a housewife who had affairs with strangers almost daily, claiming to be addicted to the taste of semen. Tom was her male equivalent. He cheated on his wife with male escorts and loved to feel cum on his ass. Jane and Billy were a couple who were hooked on meeting people on the Internet and having sex with them after months of cybercourtship. Sam was addicted to pornography and masturbated eight to twelve times a day and often in public. Malcolm heard voices and exposed himself to women in parks. He was still young, only nineteen years old, but well on his way to becoming a rapist and probably a serial killer soon afterward. He was the only one close to being as fucked up as Frank or Joe himself. But no one knew how disturbed Joe was. Joe didn't share.

Soon they were all rushing through their confessions, eager to get to Frank's latest adventures, and he never disappointed. He knew they were counting on him. Far from curing the dysfunctional little man, they were enabling him, feeding his addiction as much as he fed theirs. Joe often wondered what would have happened if he shared some of his own experiences with the group. He was pretty sure he could have outdone Frank.

Joe wasn't sure if it even made sense for him to come to these Sex Addicts Anonymous sessions anymore. He had progressed way beyond just your average sex addict.

"What happened next, Frank?" Mary, the session leader/counselor, asked with the appropriate concern on her face. Joe knew that half the people in the group went home and masturbated to the confessions they heard at these sessions. Sam, occasionally, didn't bother to wait until he left the room.

"Well, he had the most enormous cock. I swear it was almost a full ten inches and I was gagging on it and loving every minute of it. He came all down my throat and then pulled his cock out of my mouth and came all over my face. Then he got mean." Frank paused and looked down in his lap where his hands lay clenched tightly. No doubt hiding his erection.

"What did he do?" Everyone leaned forward in

their chairs. Their own addictions drew them into the tale, hungrily searching for that salacious tidbit to momentarily assuage the hunger burning in each of them.

"He smiled down at me and told me how beautiful I looked with cum on my face, which I thought was kind of nice. But then he started calling me a filthy cum-sucking faggot. He punched and kicked me until I almost passed out. The funny thing was that while he was kicking my ass I noticed that his cock was getting hard again. After he'd beaten the shit out of me, busted a couple ribs and broke my nose, he pulled my pants down and raped me, anally. No lubrication at all. It had to have chafed him as much as it did me. What was even weirder was that I kind of enjoyed it."

Nothing surprising there, Frank, Joe thought. Everyone knew that the effete little guy, who came in every week with his face looking as if it had gone through a meat grinder, was a hardcore masochist. He just hadn't admitted it to himself. If he could just admit it then he could start finding safer trade in S&M clubs before he ran into someone who might really hurt him. Someone like Joe. He was already imagining what he would do to the petite little man if he were ever to get him alone.

"So how does that make you feel now, Frank?" Mary asked, her voice full of false concern. Mary was almost as indiscreet in her desire to hear about Frank's exploits as Sam, who already had his hand in his pocket, jacking off unselfconsciously.

Mary had been a regular attendee at these meetings longer than anyone and seemed to wield no more control over her addictions than the rest of them. She propositioned Joe after almost every session. He knew that she'd already fucked nearly every straight guy who'd ever set foot in this place in the seven or eight years she'd been coming. Joe also knew that it drove her nuts that she hadn't had him yet.

Joe kept his body in excellent condition. Working out was as much of a compulsion for him as fucking. His face was hard and lean with a squared-off jaw and dark blue eyes. His friends had jokingly called him Clark Kent back in high school because he looked like he should have been on the cover of a Superman comic book. Mary wasn't Joe's type, though. She was a skanky trailer-park slut. Too skinny, with no ass and small tits. She looked like a drug addict, which she had been until she'd switched addictions. Frank was just about to reply to her question when Joe interrupted him.

"I fantasize about biting women's breasts off and eating them."

That shook things up. Everyone stared at Joe with mouths agape as they tried to compose the proper healing response to such a perverse admission. It was the first time Joe had shared with the group and they didn't want to discourage him, if only for the promise of a new fetish to feed on. This beat every one of Frank's rough trade encounters in Polk Street leather bars, except maybe the one where he got fist-fucked by that biker with his arm lubed with motor oil. It certainly shamed Mary's confessions about fucking the neighbors' husbands and masturbating with fruit and household appliances, even the time she'd put peanut butter on her clit to get head from her Great Dane.

Joe got up and left before they could respond with

their trite little twelve-step slogans, though it would have been curious to know which one they could have whipped out for cannibalism. That was the one addiction none of the books addressed. Joe knew. He had already checked.

Joe jogged the distance from the little storefront church where the SAA meetings were held back to the campus to hit the gym before classes started. When he walked into the weight room it was already packed. The track team was in there doing their morning strength training. "Muscle equals speed!" he heard Coach Truman yelling as he built his athletes into physical specimens that looked more like middleweight boxers than sprinters. Joe stared at their elegant bodies in a trance. He'd always had a fetish for large round buttocks and no one had a meatier, more finely formed gluteus maximus than a sprinter. Particularly the African-American ones who seemed to be genetically gifted with the type of round meaty asses he loved.

They all wore those tiny running shorts that exposed the bottom half of their enlarged glutes. Their thighs were finely sculpted and shimmering with a sheen of sweat. It was almost too much for Joe to bear. He watched the women's sumptuous asses bounce by as they walked from one piece of exercise equipment to the next. He felt like a lion lying down with sheep—and he was getting hungry. An erection was straining in his sweatpants and he had no real way to conceal it. It didn't matter how many girls noticed his arousal and giggled or sneered in disgust. It was worth the sight.

Joe began his workout with 500-pound squats, grunting and straining his way through four sets of ten. Then he loaded nearly a thousand pounds onto the leg press for another four sets that left his legs quivering from overexertion. He finished off with hamstring curls and quadricep extensions before hitting the showers.

Even in the locker room the sight of the men's naked flesh was arousing him. Joe wouldn't have called himself gay. What he felt when he looked at the male athletes' thick muscular thighs and tight well-sculpted asses, their heaving pectoral muscles, and even their thick cocks dangling limply between their legs, was something far more visceral. He didn't want to fuck them. He wanted to eat them alive. To rip their supple flesh from their bones, taste the warm blood and meat as it washed over his tongue and down into his belly.

Joe finished his shower and removed a fresh change of clothes from his backpack. He shrugged quickly into his jeans and T-shirt before running off to class. He could hear the guys whispering at his back as he left the locker room. They all thought he was a pervert. But they knew better than to say it to his face. Joe was not exactly a small man.

Chapter Five

The tweed-wrapped and bow-tied professor busily scribbled on the huge blackboard at the front of the lecture hall. Flashes of multicolored young flesh whisked by as students hurried to take their seats. Smooth chocolate browns and tans. Creamy whites and yellows. Joe tore himself with effort from the entrancing glimpses of bare arms, slender necks, and naked thighs and calves to give attention to the names the professor had scrawled across the board.

Andrei Chikatilo. Ed Gein. Gary Heidnick. Jeffrey Dahmer.

"All of these men are murderers. Signature killers with a very unique signature."

Joe recognized the connection between those four names before the professor even spoke and he immediately perked up, suddenly very interested. They were not just serial killers. They were killers who had at least partially cannibalized their victims. Each of them had tasted human flesh. Many on more than one occasion. Some, like Dahmer and Chikatilo, were famous for it.

"All of these men murdered, butchered, and ate their victims."

A shudder ran through the lecture hall like a group wave, followed by a moan of utter revulsion. Joe smiled. This is what he had come here for. He'd been delighted when he'd seen the course offerings for criminal psychology. It had taken a fight to get into the class due to its overwhelming popularity but as soon as he had read the title of the course—"Abnormal Psychology: Serial Killers and Why They Do It"—and seen who the professor was, he knew that he had to sign up.

Joe knew many more names he could have added to the professor's list. Ed Kemper, Albert Fish, Issei Sagawa, even Ted Bundy had engaged in mild cannibalism. It was a common final stage in the evolution of the serial killer. Some of them just got there sooner than others. Some were caught before it ever advanced to that stage. But Joe's theory was that all serial killers, if not apprehended first, would eventually escalate to cannibalism. It was a progressive disease and he feared that he himself might have been infected.

Professor Locke was one of the leading authorities on forensic and criminal psychiatry. He had worked with the FBI back in the late eighties, developing serial killer profiles in their Behavioral Sciences Unit. He had authored many books on serial murderers, sex and cannibal killers specifically, before he came to end his days teaching the next crop of psychiatrists and criminologists. He was the reason Joe had come to this school.

"So, why do they do it? Any thoughts?"

Joe's hand crept slowly into the air before he'd even fully decided to raise it.

"Ah! The football player. You have a theory?"

"Actually, I'm not in the athletics program. I'm a psychology student."

The professor peered over the top of his thick bifocals at the enormous young man in the front row, looking him over with new interest. The kid was huge. He was at least six feet five inches tall and nearly 260 pounds, all of it apparently muscle. He would have been a terror on a football field.

"Well, let's hope you are not wasting your talents. Tell us, what do you think makes them do it?"

"I think it's a disease. Not just a mental deficiency but a contagious, transmittable virus."

Everyone in the room began to giggle, including the professor. He held up his hand to silence the other students.

"No, let's hear the boy out. Go ahead."

Joe hesitated but couldn't hold himself back.

"I think it's a progressive disease that in its initial stages may manifest as only the need to inflict pain and humiliation but eventually builds to murder, mutilation, and finally to necrophilia and cannibalism. It may in fact be the very disease that spawned the werewolf and vampire legends. Perhaps it's transmitted through saliva or blood, like with a bite or a scratch just like those legends say. Maybe even through semen or vaginal secretions like AIDS. Perhaps you're most susceptible to the disease during childhood and it has a long incubation period, maybe decades. That could explain why most serial killers are in their late twenties and early thirties. And why almost all of the really violent ones experienced some type of trauma or abuse as children. I think that at some point in their youths they exchanged bodily fluids with another killer or perhaps just a carrier and they acquired the contagion themselves."

"That's a very interesting theory, son. Very interesting. I'm not sure it has any merit, but I'll tell you what. Why don't you pursue that. Research it and turn something in to me at the end of the semester. Everyone has to do a paper for his or her final grade anyway and this is what we are here to try and find out this semester: what makes these monsters do it. You convince me of that one and you are guaranteed a 4.0."

Joe was encouraged by the fact that Dr. Locke hadn't shot his theory down completely. The man seemed to be honestly intrigued. Perhaps he was on to something after all. But Joe wanted more than a perfect grade. He wanted the professor's help in isolating the serial killer virus and finding a cure.

Joe sleepwalked through the remainder of his classes that day. His desire had reached a feverish intensity and he was having a hard time concentrating. His head swiveled like a gun turret as students passed in shorts, tank tops, and miniskirts, a buffet of luscious bodies whose every movement was a maddening temptation. He could smell the sweat on their skin, the musk of recent sex between a woman's thighs, the coppery twang of menstrual blood, the acrid bleachlike aroma of semen drying inside them, the humid sweat beading beneath the hairy scrotums of the jocks. The most maddening aroma was that of their youthful spirits. Joe could smell their souls burning beneath their skins like an unseen inferno as furious as a forest fire. He wanted to tear into their flesh to get at it. To devour that energy and make it his.

With effort Joseph Miles wrenched his eyes from the heaving bosom of a passing coed. Joe could almost see the light of her soul swirling like a rainbow and exploding like a nuclear blast. It made him dizzy just looking at it. The scent of it was even more radiant, like fruit and wine and meat and blood all combined into one delirious fragrance. Life. He wanted to taste it so bad it made his stomach cramp. He was so thirsty for the taste of her blood that his throat felt parched and dry. His saliva felt thick and tacky in his mouth.

A riot of emotions swirled through Joe's mind. It had only been recently that his passions had taken such a morbid turn. Before it had been enough to fuck anything and everything he could get his hands on. But lately the normal suck-and-fuck rituals had begun to bore him. His typical fantasies of multiple sex partners had turned to blood-soaked orgies of torn and ravaged flesh. He could no longer even masturbate without imagining biting into a woman's tender buttocks or engorged breasts. He knew there were places on the Web where he could talk freely about his desires, where they were appreciated. He had sought them out when he first discovered his predilection for the taste of human flesh. He'd been surprised when he'd discovered how many professed cannibals were out there stalking cyberspace for human prey and even more surprised when he discovered that there were women and men who sought these cannibals out, offering their bodies for consumption. All he could think about now was going online to seek solace in his fellow perverts.

Chapter Six

There was a cybercafe just off campus where a lot of the students hung out. Joe often went there to surf the cannibal sex sites with the hope of finding others with his unique fetish and perhaps someone with whom he could assuage his hunger. The Long Pig Message Board was his most frequent stop. "Long pig" was the name given to human flesh because it was said to taste like pork. Joe had never tasted it before except for a few harmless nibbles here and there, but he knew that it wouldn't be long before he indulged himself. The hunger was increasing exponentially with each passing day.

Many of the people on the site claimed to be willing cattle. The site was filled with flowery romantic fantasies written by these long pigs about feeding the appetite of their dream lovers. All of them were eager to serve as meat for the hunger of human predators, or so they claimed. Joe wasn't so sure that any of them did anything more than fantasize.

They would post long descriptive appeals for a chef to prepare their flesh to be eaten alive or roasted on a spit and then the supposed cannibals would write them back with lascivious details of just how they would cook and consume them. Sometimes they would swap e-mail addresses, presumably to hook up offline. But since the same "long pigs" would be back the very next day tempting someone new, Joe presumed that it was all bullshit. Occasionally, however, a few of them would disappear and never return. Joe liked to think that those had been the real deal and had finally fulfilled their fantasies; that they were now digesting in someone's stomach, happy and content, if somewhat diminished.

The only problem with the long pigs available online was that they were almost exclusively male. In fact, he had only seen one female on the message board in the entire time he'd been frequenting it and she had been an obvious fake; getting off on the fantasy of being consumed but too terrified to try it for real. Joe was so worked up today that he didn't care. He began posting long descriptions of how he'd rip apart a long pig with his own blunt little teeth and consume them piece by piece. He could feel someone reading over his shoulder as he typed and hear their gasp of astonishment.

"Oh, my God, that's sick!"

It was the voice of one of the girls from his mythology class. She was the type of bubbly airhead that had probably been a cheerleader in high school and had blown half the male faculty for better grades.

Joe ignored it. Even when the girl brought a couple of friends over to read what he had written and they began to speculate on his sanity, Joe continued to tap away at the keyboard. That was the only problem with the cybercafe. No one minded their goddamned business! Still, Joe didn't want to go on his roommate's computer during the day. The guy would have a heart attack if he knew the kind of person he was really living with.

On the message board Joe went under the screen name of SuperPredator and was fairly well-known. He was a regular. So much so that he had begun to think of himself more and more in terms of his on-line persona, a voracious ultrapredator at the top of the food chain above even other human beings. He finished his long post and hit SEND. The replies came almost immediately.

A man calling himself "Meatforthetable" was the first to respond.

HEY SUPERPREDATOR! YOUR APPETITE SEEMS PRETTY LARGE BUT I THINK I CAN FILL IT. I'M SMALL AND PRETTY LEAN BUT I'M LARGE IN ALL THE RIGHT PLACES. I'VE GOT AN 8" COCK AND A NICE PLUMP REAR LIKE A YOUNG TEENAGED GIRL. COME AND GET ME! He left his e-mail address at the bottom along with a link to his website where he promised there would be pictures.

Next was the tease. The woman who called herself "SweetFlesh" sent a long sweaty reply that sounded as if she'd written it with one hand.

HEY SUPERPREDATOR! I HAVEN'T HEARD FROM YOU IN A WHILE. I WAS STARTING TO THINK YOU DIDN'T LIKE US ANYMORE. I TELL YOU WHAT BABY, IF YOU'RE REALLY AS HUNGRY FOR LONG PIG AS YOU SAY THEN YOU'D LOVE SOME OF MY SWEET TENDER MEAT. THAT MAN MEAT IS TOO TOUGH FOR A REAL CONNOISSEUR LIKE YOU. YOU NEED SOME OF THIS NICE TENDER GIRL FLESH. I'VE GOT DD BREASTS WITH BIG FAT NIP-PLES, WIDE HIPS, AND THICK THIGHS, AND A NICE BIG FAT ASS. IT WOULD TAKE YOU A MONTH TO EAT ALL OF THIS.

She'd obviously forgotten that she'd once sent him a picture of herself and she'd been a petite Filipino woman who, to her credit, did have huge breasts but was far from having voluptuous hips or a "big fat ass" as she claimed.

Joe knew it was all bullshit, but it was getting him violently aroused. He decided to check out Meatforthetable's website.

When he clicked the link at the bottom of the message he was surprised to see a familiar face pop up on the screen. Frank. The same guy he'd earlier been speculating about devouring whole as he spun out yet another tale of sex and abuse at the SAA meeting. It was a nude photo and Frank hadn't been lying. He did have a pretty big cock and an ass that was fatter and rounder than most men, sort of like that of a woman. Joe sent him an instant message and he responded with undisguised enthusiasm.

HI SUPERPREDATOR!

HI FRANK.

Pause.

DO I KNOW YOU?

YES. YOU KNOW ME. WOULD YOU LIKE TO KNOW ME BETTER?

YES, BUT I'M SORT OF NEW TO THIS. YOU WON'T KILL ME, WILL YOU? I JUST WANT YOU TO BITE ME, TO HURT ME. YOU CAN EVEN BITE OFF A FEW PIECES IF YOU WANT. I JUST DON'T WANT TO DIE.

I WOULDN'T KILL YOU, FRANK. WE'RE OLD FRIENDS. I JUST WANT TO BITE INTO THAT SWEET LITTLE ASS OF YOURS.

WHO ARE YOU?

I'M SUPERMAN.

Chapter Seven

Joe had set up an apartment down in one of the seedier areas of town, far away from campus. A commercial district filled mostly with warehouses and retail stores. It was nearly desolate at night. He had intended it to be his art studio. The tiny room was cluttered with paint and canvas. One or two finished paintings hung on the walls amid the countless unfinished ones. He'd found it more and more difficult to paint lately. It was supposed to be therapeutic, but letting his imagination roam like that only seemed to make the monster hungrier. Luckily, he'd soon found other uses for the old apartment. It was perfect for little clandestine affairs.

Frank arrived just after midnight, wearing baggy jeans and a tank top. Clothes that he could easily slip out of. He smiled wide when Joe answered the door.

"Oh my God! I was hoping it would be you!" His eyes lit up like an orphan on those rare Christmas mornings when Santa Claus did not forget him.

The small man with the bruised and battered face and the nervous, desperate eyes of a cornered animal, tiptoed gingerly into the dingy hallway. Joe slammed the door behind him. They both stood in the ancient vestibule eyeing each other greedily.

"Superman," Frank whispered softly in appreciation, as he looked the big muscular college kid over from head to toe. He fell into Joe's arms and tried to kiss him. Joe shoved him back against the wall and pinned him there with one arm.

"Uh-uh. I'm not that way."

Frank looked frightened but he was excited.

"I didn't think you were gay, but then why am I here?"

"To be eaten."

Joe produced a small slim scalpel and Frank's breath quickened.

"You . . . you said you wouldn't hurt me."

"No, I said I wouldn't kill you and I won't. But there will be pain. I'm sure you'll like it, though. Jack off if you want. Get the endorphins going. You'll enjoy the pain once your adrenaline starts racing."

Joe unbuckled Frank's jeans and dropped his pants. Frank's cock was hard as granite and glistening with a sheen of precum. Joe wanted to slice it off and eat it but he held himself back.

The frightened little man took his eyes off of the scalpel in Joe's hand for a moment and looked at his surroundings.

The walls were all cracked, with paint peeling from them in long sheets. Everything was covered in cobwebs and dust and the hallways were all dark. There was a reception desk with a shattered mirror in back of it and an overturned chair covered in rust and dust.

"What is this place? Does anyone actually live here?"

"This is nowhere. Now turn around!" Joe commanded.

The small man turned to face the wall. He leaned his face against the drywall but left his hands free so that he could stroke himself as the man he'd known as SuperPredator online and simply as Joe at the SAA meetings began to cut Frank's trembling buttocks. Frank shot a hot stream of semen all over the filthy wall and down onto the cracked tiles at his feet as the huge muscular man sliced off a chunk of his ass.

Joe was overwhelmed by sensations as he brought the glistening blood-wet meat to his lips and slurped it into his mouth. Just as he'd expected, he could taste the little man's soul as he devoured the small sliver of life, absorbing a small piece of him and assimilating it in his stomach, becoming one with the diminutive masochist. He could taste the little man's fear and pain and ecstasy vibrating on his tongue like he'd just licked a coke spoon. He could feel Frank's life marrying with his own, surging through his blood like rocket fuel, and was surprised when he found himself suddenly gripped by his own orgasm as the tender meat slid down his throat. His body jerked and bucked as if having a seizure. Frank looked up at him in awe. He couldn't believe the man was cumming just by tasting him. They both collapsed onto the hard dusty floor, panting heavily.

"Oh my God! That was incredible!"

"You should go now, Frank." Joe's breathing was still heavy, but his voice was cold and hard. He didn't look at Frank as he spoke, but rather stared straight ahead into the shadowy lobby.

"What? You want me to leave? You're not going to fuck me? You don't want another taste?"

"If you don't leave now, I'll never let you leave. Do you understand? This is the only chance I'm going to give you to save your life. Leave now and never come back here." He was still not looking at Frank. His body was tense now and his erection had come surging back to life.

Frank wanted to take the man's cock down his throat. But something in Joe's voice let him know that staying there any longer, getting the SuperPredator aroused again, would have been a death sentence.

Frank gathered up his clothes and scampered out into the street, stumbling as he tried to run and step into his pants at the same time. He slid his underwear up over his wounded ass, wincing from the pain, and hopped down the street with one leg in and one leg out of his jeans and the blood saturating his boxer shorts. Joe slammed the door behind him.

The next day Joe went online again and was instantly assaulted by instant messages from Frank begging for a repeat performance. He logged off and left the café. He had to stay away from the Long Pig Message Board for a while. It was easier to cure an addiction when there was no supply. Eating that one slice of flesh from Frank's buttocks had been the most intense sexual experience he'd ever had and he wanted more. Much more. He knew now that whatever was wrong with him was beyond his control and that if he saw the little man again he'd probably murder and eat him. He had to get more serious about finding a cure. There was no way SAA could handle this problem.

After a quick shower, Joe caught the BART train back to campus. He kept his head down, trying not to make eye contact with anyone as he made his way across campus to the university library. He was afraid that his eyes would betray his thoughts. There was a small piece of gristle between his teeth from his recent appetizer. He worked at it with his tongue, trying to worry it free. Each time his tongue brushed the miniscule piece of flesh a fresh tingle went through his loins.

Chapter Eight

The library emptied out as even the die-hard medical students and political science majors finally returned their dusty old books to the shelves and dragged their tired minds back to their dorms. Joe had heard it said that when you slept your mind let go of all logic and structure, all sanity and order, for the madness of dreams. Joe wanted anything but madness. He was actively trying to fight it off. He was convinced that he was onto something, something that would explain the insatiable hunger roiling within him.

Joe knew that he was not a monster. Not by choice. Maybe none of the others were either? Not until they were altered by whatever sickness had infected him. If it was a disease, not a disease of the mind but a true physical virus that was somehow transmitted from one person to the next, then it could be cured. There might be an antidote.

Piled before him were three stacks of books four feet high that encompassed nearly two centuries of rape, murder, and superstition. Joe poured through the tall stacks until the moon had traveled from one side of the sky to the other. He knew that the librarian must have been dying of curiosity. She had seen him there every night for over a month scouring through books on serial murder, vampirism, and lycanthropy, doing computer searches on war criminals and mob mentality, sexual fetishes, and cannibalism. He knew that she must have been curious to know what it was he was working on, but she had only asked him once and when he hadn't replied, she'd had the good sense to avoid further inquiry. It was a good thing too. She had just the sort of ass he liked, plump but firm.

More than once, Joe had masturbated sitting right there in that library, imagining tearing into her voluptuous buttocks with his teeth and devouring the tender flesh in huge gulps. He'd hid his frantic hand movements behind an unabridged dictionary and sprayed his semen from neurosurgery to nightingale. Then he'd left quickly, sure that she had noticed. When he returned the next day she smiled politely and gave no indication that she was aware of having been the star of his gruesome masturbatory fantasies.

Just last week he'd even painted her portrait. He'd composed several sketches of her, stealing glances at her generous buttocks as she scuttled back and forth between the rows of dusty books. When he'd gotten home that night he'd let out his pent-up sexual energies onto the canvas. He'd masturbated several times as his passion boiled over and his paintbrush whipped across the canvas in violent slashes of reds, whites, and beiges, mixing his own blood and semen into the paint. When he was done he'd hidden the portrait away in his little apartment across town along with all the others. Anyone seeing it would have immediately recognized his obsession. Even in the abstract she looked like meat.

It was past three o'clock in the morning when

Joe's eyelids would no longer remain aloft and his head came crashing down into the middle of Colin Wilson's *Criminal History of Mankind* with a thud that echoed loudly throughout the empty room.

"Okay, you. Time to let the monsters rest for a night. Go home and get some sleep now."

Joe nodded and rose from the table where he sat behind a mountain of books. He eyed the pleasantly plump librarian's large breasts with interest and saw her shudder beneath the heat of his gaze and cross her arms over her breasts as if to protect them from more than just his eyes. Embarrassed, Joe gathered up a few books to check out and stumbled toward the desk. He had an erection bulging in his pants and he'd seen her eyes zero in on it before he could cover it with a hardbound copy of *120 Days of Sodom*.

The librarian walked behind him, not wanting to feel his voracious eyes crawling over her ass, as Joe staggered toward the front desk. Not that she had a particularly nice one in her opinion. It was far too large and her hips were too wide. And not that she thought herself particularly attractive. Emma Purcell hadn't felt attractive since she'd turned forty and her breasts had drooped and her ass had spread, but something about the way Joe stared at her made her fear that he might rape her or worse. She didn't know what it was but she preferred to have him in clear view at all times.

Maybe she was just reacting to the fact that the man had slowly worked his way through every book on deviant sexuality and serial murder in the entire library and was now apparently branching out into monsters and werewolves.

When he checked out his morbid little books and left, she sighed audibly and crossed herself, asking God to forgive her for the moistness spreading between her thighs at the thought of what such a powerful young man could do to her.

Joe walked down the steps and out the front door of the library into a waiting cab. He stuffed the armload of books onto the backseat then jumped in and directed the driver back toward the dorm.

The temptation to cruise through the Tenderloin for street prostitutes was overpowering and it took a supreme act of will to tell the driver to turn right on Sixth Street instead of left, but Joe knew that there would be nothing up there to stop him from indulging his appetites. It would be like a morbidly obese woman trying to diet at Baskin Robbins. Where he was going was more like the supermarket. At least there would be somewhat healthier choices available even if he were not inclined to make them.

He pulled up in the crowded parking lot and looked around to make sure he didn't recognize any of the cars. The last thing he wanted was to be spotted by one of the other students or worse yet a faculty member. There was no way of being sure. He obviously didn't know everyone at the university but at least he didn't see any cars belonging to anyone in his immediate acquaintance.

Joe listened to the crunchy sound of the gravel crackling beneath his feet as he walked across the parking lot. He sniffed the night air and tried to pick out the smells of sex from the pungent stench of urine, exhaust fumes, cigarettes, and alcohol. He tried to hear the pants and moans above the sound of techno dance music emanating from the small storefront. He was losing himself. In his anxiousness to get inside the club he'd left his library books back in the taxi. He'd have to try to track them down in the morning. But for now, the hunger was fully upon him, demanding his absolute attention.

Joe flashed his ID and paid his twenty bucks. He reached down and readjusted his cock, which had swelled until it pressed painfully against the coarse fabric of his jeans and rubbed against his zipper. The monster was awake.

He stripped off his shirt and unbuckled his pants, freeing the raging monster from its prison of denim. After handing his clothes to the topless coat-check girl with the pierced nipples who was so skinny you could see rib bone through her chest, the massive sophomore began to make his rounds through the club. Almost immediately he spotted a woman who seemed plucked from his darkest fantasies. He knew that he was going to do something bad tonight.

She was absolute perfection, a tall voluptuous Spanish beauty with long flowing hair that hung down to her ample waistline. She had catlike almond eyes, full rose-colored lips, and cinnamon tan skin like some delicate pastry. None of these attributes were what caught his eye, though. She had thick hips and thighs and a deliciously plump and luscious posterior that jiggled as she walked, awakening the monster's hunger with each step she took. It was more beautiful than water to a dehydrated desert traveler. Joe swallowed again and again as he began to salivate uncontrollably.

Joe had seen her there before. Usually she was with some queer boy or another and once she came in arm in arm with a six-foot lesbian. She was an absolute fag-hag but he knew that she was not gay herself. Though he'd seen her tonguing that Amazon's clit in one of the orgy rooms, he'd also seen her in a threesome with two jocks he recognized from college. He'd masturbated in a corner by himself watching the two basketball players lubricate their latex-sheathed erections and fuck her in one hole after another as she moaned and quivered in ecstasy, looking as if she was in heaven. He watched as they both climaxed and then left her just short of her own orgasm, laughing and high-fiving as she cursed at them. They dressed and left, still chuckling over their own good fortune. He'd followed her out to the curb and watched as she angrily fought against the tears threatening to spill from her eyes, finally losing after a valiant struggle. Joe had wanted to go to her then, but something had held him back. The hunger was not as strong then and she hadn't seemed like prey. She'd seemed like someone that he could have fallen in love with. A whore with a heart of gold.

Now, as she strode past him, Joe watched the seductive sway of that exorbitant ass as if in a trance. His lust was at a fever pitch and even the memory of her heartbreaking tears seemed to fuel his desire. He felt the hunger surge within him, driving steel through his loins. Her ass was perfect, the most beautiful, sumptuous buttocks he had ever beheld. His salivary glands went into overdrive and Joe wiped the drool from his mouth repeatedly as he stalked her through the sex club, that ass drawing him irresistibly toward it.

The club was called The Backdoor and it seemed the perfect setting for a woman with an ass that looked like God had shed a teardrop that slid down her back, nestled just above her thighs, and became flesh. This was the place where couples came to put spice back into their marriages by swapping mates or picking up a spare for a threesome. Singles came here looking to be a part of a ménage à trois or a random orgy. It was rare that two singles met in a place like this. But Joe was not interested in having to suck off some dude just to get some quality time with his wife, not when he could get exactly what he wanted out of this voluptuous princess.

Some might have called her overweight, those woman-hating faggots in the fashion industry for instance, whose standard of beauty is based upon the breastless, hipless, thighless, assless physiques of pre-pubescent boys. They had no appreciation at all for true femininity. For them womanhood was something to be suppressed, strapped down, starved away, and hidden beneath layers of clothing and shame. It was obvious that this woman was having none of this. She was proud of the gifts nature had imbued her with. It showed in the fit of her clothing, the tilt of her head, and the swish of her hips. To Joe she was the very essence of sensuality, her every curve dramatically enhanced, her sexuality exaggerated to pornographic proportions. Her ass looked as if someone had taken two beach balls and shoved them down the back of her jeans. Perfectly round and absolutely enormous! Joe was transfixed by it.

It jiggled and bounced maddeningly, wobbling high on her lower back as if it were waving to him. He wanted her so bad that it hurt. He could see the radiance of her wild spirit shimmering in her sinews, in her skin, fat, and muscle. He could smell it scorching the air. Her flesh was alive with the energy of life. Joe smirked as he thought about all those misguided spiritualists and religious zealots who mistakenly believed that the soul was some separate entity imprisoned in human flesh. But he knew better. Spirit is flesh. Inseparable and indivisible. He had tasted it himself. He reached down and began stroking himself as he followed her from room to room.

All around couples, threesomes, foursomes, and more, fucked, sucked, spanked, and masturbated with what seemed an overabundance of energy. Only sex addicts came to these types of places and any true addict would have sex for as long as sex was available regardless of hunger, thirst, fatigue, pain, or discomfort. Of all people, Joe should know. His own addictions had led him beyond the limits of sanity and morality. Just as it was now leading him through a sex club with his throbbing hard cock pointing the way like a divining rod.

The Spanish woman stopped abruptly and her rotund buttocks continued to jiggle for several seconds after the rest of her body had ceased movement. Joe felt both elated and disappointed now that her ass had stopped its bewitching dance. He could now catch up to her, but he could no longer delight in her salacious movements. If all went well, he reminded himself, he would have far more to delight in soon.

"Uh . . . hello?" Joe reached out and tapped her on the shoulder, feeling foolish as he drooped his shoulders and bowed his head in an effort to appear smaller and less intimidating. But Joe was enormous. There was no way he could look anything *but* intimidating. He had gotten very adept at playing the gentle giant, however. Every year on the news he'd heard about people getting mauled to death for being dumb enough to try to pet polar bears and grizzlies because the things were so cute. He figured he could look at least as cute as a grizzly.

When she turned around Joe was stunned by how young and innocent her face appeared. She had pudgy cheeks with deep dimples, full bow-shaped lips, and large timid eyes with thick heavy eyelashes. The body of a whore with the face of an angel. Her breasts were tremendous, every bit the equal of her remarkable ass. She was a goddess.

She turned to him and smiled. Joe was loath to lose even a moment's sight of that blessed ass but he found the beautiful smile spreading on her angelic face worth the loss.

"Yes?" she asked, smiling wider.

Joe didn't know what to say. He was so excited that the words spilled out before he could give them order and finesse. It was his lust, the monster throbbing between his thighs, putting the words in his mouth. His prey-drive guiding him through the necessary social niceties.

"I-I love you. You are the most sensuous woman I have ever seen. I want to worship you forever," Joe said.

I want to eat you alive! he meant.

The woman's smile faltered a moment as she examined his face to see if he was serious. She knew that while some men found her irresistible, even more just saw her as a fat chick. His expression looked so timid, though, so fearful of rejection, that she was immediately convinced of his sincerity. This gigantic muscle-bound man, with the body of a Greek god and the face of a movie star, was throwing himself at her feet.

"You mean that, don't you?"

"I have never seen a more perfect woman than you."

She reached out and ran her hands over his mountainous pectoral muscles, his thick shoulders and biceps, over his rippled abs and down to the erection throbbing at his center. Without pants or underwear his massive organ bobbed in the air, pointing directly at her.

"My God! What a beautiful cock!"

"Thank you," Joe said timidly. Blushing noticeably.

She caught the thick slab of meat in her hands and began stroking it, barely able to fit her hand completely around it as she pulled him closer until her breasts rubbed against his stomach. He was so tall that his cock went up between her cleavage as she closed the distance between them. She knelt slightly so that her breasts lined up perfectly with his genitals. She began sliding his cock up and down between her breasts. Joe shuddered, feeling like he was about to explode.

"What's your name, handsome?"

"Joe. J-Joe Miles," he stammered as he tried to keep himself from orgasm. He didn't want to cum like this. He wanted that ass. Its image was still burned into his mind even as he tit-fucked her between those huge double-Ds.

"Good to meet you, Joe," she said, still rubbing his cock. "My name is Alicia."

"I want you, Alicia."

Her knees went weak.

"Well, we are in the right place for love now, aren't

we?" she said, gesturing around at the orgy rooms filled with urgently fucking couples. There was a pain in her. It was obvious that she had long ago convinced herself that sex was all she was good for.

"No," he replied. "We should go someplace more private. This isn't the right place for you. You deserve more."

He was saying all the right things. She slipped back into the blouse she'd been carrying around with her.

"Okay then, Joe. You lead the way."

Joe retrieved his pants and shirt from the coat-check girl and they walked out of The Backdoor and into the parking lot to catch a cab.

"So, who are you, my handsome stranger? What do you do for a living?"

"I'm a student. A psychology student at the university."

"And what is this then, some kind of research?"

"No. Not at all."

"Well, I've never been to college. But I've always been interested in people and what makes them tick. I've seen sides of the human psyche that most people don't even have the stomach to read about, all kinds of perversions. Shit you couldn't even imagine. From grown men who dress like babies to women who like to be pissed on and humiliated."

"How the hell do you meet people like that?"

"I work at a fetish store on Folsom. We sell everything from leather, to latex, to iron shackles, to vibrating butt plugs, and adult diapers."

"I know the place. I've been in there once or twice."

"Really? Now what is a nice college boy like you doing in a place like that?"

"The same thing I was doing at The Backdoor. The

same thing you were doing there. Trying to make life a little more intense, a little more worth the effort. We go through so much just to take the next breath, just to wake up each day. If life is just work, eat, sleep, repeat, then it ain't worth it. Is it?"

The beautiful Spanish woman suddenly turned away from Joe and looked out the window of the cab. When she turned back her eyes were sad, full of ghosts.

"No. There has to be more than that. There's so much pain everywhere. Something has to make all that pain worthwhile and sex is the only thing strong enough to justify all the shit we go through. You know? Pain is so strong that just a little bit of it can fuck up your whole day. You could be at fucking Disneyland having the time of your life and then you get menstrual cramps, or some asshole calls you fat, or you see something that reminds you of how fucked up your childhood was, and that quick, your entire day is ruined. You just want to roll over and die. Sex is the only thing strong enough to make you forget about the pain. I mean you can fuck when every muscle in your body is sore if the sex is good enough. You can lose yourself in it. At the moment of orgasm nothing else exists in all the world but your pussy and his dick."

"Yes. Yes." Joe felt as if he was at church listening to religious testimonials, hearing all his deepest beliefs reaffirmed. He slowly unbuttoned her blouse and ran his hands over Alicia's breasts, squeezing her hard nipples until she gasped. He leaned down to kiss her throat and could not restrain himself from biting her shoulder as he felt the passion build in him. He could taste the very essence of her in the salty perspiration glistening on her moonlit flesh. Her soul was so alive. It had known such pain and such ecstasy. It was like tasting a dozen people rather than one. This was a woman who had lived. Her life was full and rich, tragic and passionate. Joe wanted to feel that life filling him.

"Hold me, Joe. Make the pain go away. Make it all go away."

Joe watched as she unzipped his pants and pulled out his engorged penis. He pulled her close to him, hugging her tight while she stroked his cock and wept quietly. When he released her she smiled at him and then lowered her thick satin-soft lips down to his manhood, sliding the entire organ down her throat. Her tongue twirled around the head of his cock as she bobbed her head up and down on it, bringing him so maddeningly close to orgasm that he almost broke her neck trying to wrestle free of her mouth before he came. When she looked up at him with concern and a tinge of fear from the rough treatment, he kissed her passionately and reassured her. He unzipped her jeans and slid a hand down her pants into the moistness between her thighs.

"I don't want to cum that way. Not yet. I want to give everything to you. I want to make you cum a dozen times. Then I'll cum."

Joe always knew the right things to say to a woman. His predatory instincts were perfectly in tune with his chosen prey. She relaxed and smiled at him. Of course it could have just been the fact that he now had her clitoris swollen to the size of a grape and she was just seconds from cumming herself. Joe had a feeling that the taxi driver was beating off in the front seat. He could hear him breathing heavily.

He didn't mind, though. Joe wasn't shy; he just pretended to be to set the ladies at ease. It was stupid, really. How many truly shy guys would've been walking around a sex club with their dicks in their hands, beating off while following a beautiful woman from one room to the next? A shy person would at least have put his cock back in his underwear before he tapped her on her shoulder and introduced himself.

Joe kissed his way down her cleavage and sucked on her swollen nipples. He shuddered at the taste of her skin, imagining biting through to the tender fat and muscle beneath. He wanted her now. Joe pulled away quickly, breathing hard as the hunger raged inside him. He was having a hard time controlling himself. He liked this girl with eyes like a wounded child. He didn't want to hurt her but the monster was awake now and it was off the chain.

They pulled up to the old downtown apartment building and Joe paid the taxi driver.

Joe and Alicia walked into the building and quickly took the elevator upstairs. Joe made her turn toward the wall as they stood in the elevator so that he could stare at her ass and rub his hands over it.

"You like that, don't you, baby?"

"I love it. It's the most beautiful thing I've ever seen."

The doors opened with a whoosh that filled the musty elevator with the acrid smell of urine and cat hair.

"The old lady next door has about a dozen cats that piss and shit on everything. Please excuse the smell."

"Just as long as your place doesn't smell like that," she said, looking uncertain.

How could he live in this hovel? she thought.

He bent and kissed her deeply, crushing her breasts against his rock-hard stomach as he sucked the breath from her throat. She had forgotten all about the smell by the time he unlocked the door to his apartment.

Joe scooped Alicia up into his arms the minute they entered the apartment and carried her into the bedroom, kissing and biting her neck, lips, and cheeks.

"Whoa! Slow down, killer."

"What?"

"Let's get to know each other a little, okay?"

Joe didn't understand. Just minutes ago she had seemed ready to fuck him right there in the cab and now she wanted small talk?

"What do you want to know?"

The beautiful Spanish woman looked him up and down. He was nearly perfect, she thought to herself.

"First, why did you pick me? I mean, there were better-looking women there than me."

"No, there weren't. I've never seen a more beautiful woman than you," Joe said, dropping his eyes down to her feet and sweeping them back up again to her face.

Alicia knew that she had a pretty face. Ever since she'd been a kid she'd heard over and over again how irresistible she'd be if she lost some of that fat.

Alicia noticed one of Joe's paintings on the wall. It was a portrait of the librarian with her back turned and her enormous buttocks filling the canvas.

"Did you paint that?" she asked, looking around at all the paint and canvas that littered the floor of the apartment.

"Yes. She's beautiful, isn't she?"

"What are you, a chubby chaser? You got a thing for big mammas?"

"I like all types of women. Why do you think you aren't attractive?"

"Look, man, I know why guys go after girls like me. You think maybe you'll get more out of me in bed. You think I'll try to overcompensate for my weight by being a freak for you and letting you treat me like a whore and you know, you might be right. I'm sure I fuck better than most of those skinny bitches. But it's not because I expect you to love me. I don't expect to ever see you again after tonight. I fuck because I enjoy it. I want to fuck you because you're gorgeous and you have a big dick. Now, why do you want to fuck me?"

"Because I like your ass. I *love* your ass! And I like the way you walk. You walk like a woman who's sure of herself, who knows what she wants and what she can get. I like your beautiful eyes and your sexy lips. I like the way you look at me. There's so much pain in your eyes. It makes me want to make you happy. It makes me want to do anything for you."

For a moment Joe thought she was about to cry. There was so much more he could have added but he didn't want to scare her off.

"Yeah, I've been hurt. I've been hurt a lot."

"Let me kiss it and make it better."

Joe ran his hands up into her hair and drew her close. He kissed her so deeply that he stole her breath.

"My God!" Alicia exclaimed as Joe laid her on the bed and ripped out of his own clothing. His body was a work of art. His abdominal muscles were stacked like masonry bricks beneath a chest like two concrete slabs. His arms were knotted with thick venous muscles and his penis was swollen. Alicia licked her lips and again dove for his huge cock, sucking it down her throat with practiced ease. Joe shuddered with pleasure and allowed himself to enjoy the wonders of her talented tongue swirling around the head of his bloated organ and then down between his balls. He was dangerously close to cumming when he pulled her back. She stared at him with her thick bee-stung lips pouting like a spoiled child.

"But I wanted to taste it! Don't you want to cum in my mouth? I want to drink you down."

"I want to taste you first."

Joe pushed her down and gently removed her clothes. Alicia could hear his breath quicken every time another inch of flesh was unveiled. She had never had a man show so much appreciation for her body. She had fought for years to grow comfortable with the extra pounds she carried and she was finally at the point where she believed herself to be sexy. She'd never had a problem getting a date. There were plenty of men who loved her generous ass and double-D breasts. But she'd never seen a man who seemed to literally worship her body the way Joe did. He licked and sucked every inch of her as he unwrapped her. The nape of her neck, dragging his tongue down between her cleavage as he removed her bra, flicking his tongue across her nipples and licking her belly button as he removed her shirt, kissing the crease where thigh met pelvis and then working his way down her leg to her toes as he slid off her jeans.

Alicia quivered and trembled as Joe sucked on each toe and flicked his tongue over the soles of her feet, then worked his way back up the opposite leg, kissing and nipping at her calves with his teeth, sometimes gently, sometimes enough to make her cry out. He turned her over and kissed and sucked the back of Alicia's thick meaty thighs, biting into the tender flesh so hard it brought a gasp and tears to her eyes. Joe then rubbed his face over her buttocks, purring like a kitten. He slid one hand up between her thighs and into that warmth and wetness before biting down hard on her ass, drawing blood. One finger was already circling her clitoris as the other thrust its way inside of her and Alicia found that she did not mind the pain so much. In fact, it seemed to accentuate the pleasure.

Joe lowered his lips to the crack of her ass and began to lick and kiss it as he continued to finger her clit. Alicia shook and moaned. She began to thrash and convulse with a tumultuous orgasm when he wriggled his tongue into her anus. Joe nearly came himself. Her ass was truly luscious.

Working his tongue from her asshole to her clitoris Joe had his face wedged completely between Alicia's buttocks, lapping up the steady stream of juices as she came again and again. Alicia was almost completely spent when Joe rose up with his erection in hand and began easing it into her asshole, which was now well lubricated with his saliva. She'd never had anal sex with a man she'd just met before. Usually that was reserved for those long-term serious relationships and she'd never done it with a man so well-endowed. But then, she'd also never had her asshole eaten out like that before either, so she was now more than willing to go along with just about anything.

There was not nearly as much pain as she'd been expecting when he first slid himself inside her and by the time he began thrusting deep into her she was feeling nothing but ecstasy.

Joe could feel his control starting to slip. He hadn't wanted to stop licking her asshole. He'd wanted to chew it out, to gnaw his way up inside of her. He'd wanted to tear into that magnificent ass, to feel each tender morsel slide across his tongue and down his throat. He'd had to stop in order to prevent himself from eating her alive. The pleasure of his dick in her ass was nothing like the pleasure he imagined from her ass in his stomach.

Moans, gasps, and cries of pain and ecstasy rose to a crescendo as Joe pounded into Alicia's exquisite asshole and bit down on the back of her neck and shoulders. He reached around and beneath her, back up into the wetness between her thighs to masturbate her to orgasm. It didn't take long. He withdrew his pulsating sex from her rectum just before his own orgasm tore through him and turned her around to bathe her face in his seed. She opened her mouth and stuck out her tongue to catch every drop of him. She lapped up every drop of it, raising each breast to her lips to lick Joe's cum from her nipples. Joe knelt down and licked the rest of it from her cleavage then rose to face her and kissed her deeply, letting his seed slip from his mouth into hers. She swallowed and moaned appreciatively.

"Mmmm. You are delicious!" she said, smiling.

"Do you want to play some more?" he asked.

"Oh yes!"

Alicia was ecstatic at the prospect of getting to sample more of the beautiful college boy who looked like a young Christopher Reeve on steroids. Joe reached around and withdrew the leather restraints from under the bed.

"Let's play," he said as he strapped her in. She hesitated for only a moment before giving in.

Joe pulled her arms behind her back, still kissing her shoulders and neck. He fastened the restraints around Alicia's wrists, cinching them tight and then affixing them to the thick chain attached to the leg spreader wedged between her calves, pausing to gnaw and suckle at the tender fat that hung from the back of her arms. He then leaned down to buckle the leather cuffs around her ankles and lock the ankle restraints to the leg spreader. When he was done he forced the ball gag into her mouth and strapped it around her head, locking it into her jaw. Then he knelt back down to suck at her nipples.

The gag stifled Alicia's moans, but even with the ball wedged firmly between her lips, Joe could still hear her scream when he chewed off her nipple and swallowed it.

Chapter Nine

Alicia bit down on the ball gag and tried her best to kick out at her attacker as she felt his teeth clamp down on her left nipple. Her legs were securely fastened to the pole wedged between her ankles, keeping them spread wide and making her feel even more vulnerable. She screamed her voice raw when she felt his teeth bite harder and harder, the tug as he began tearing into her breast and ripping her areola free from her body. Her stomach rolled with nausea as she watched the nipple disengage from her breast between his clenched teeth, staring in horror as he chewed it, his eyes fluttering as if in the grips of the most profound rapture, then finally swallowing it and licking the blood from his lips with a satisfied grin. Her breast throbbed, pulsing in agony where her flesh had been. It had taken a heroic effort to keep from regurgitating with the gag in her mouth and drowning on her own vomit.

The big college boy turned his head toward her one remaining nipple. Alicia tried her best to move away from his mouth but the chains held her firm. His mouth groped for her breast and then seized her nipple between his teeth. Alicia bucked and thrashed as she felt his teeth begin to saw through her right nipple.

The pain was somehow both intense and erotic. Recalling all the pleasure he'd just given her and marrying that to the pain she'd just experienced at his hands as well as the horror of seeing him devour her nipple. It created a confusion of emotions and sensations within her. She hoped that eating her nipples was perhaps the worst he would do. Perhaps just a fetish that, though painful and revolting, did not mean he was a serial killer. She didn't want to die. She'd heard about the things that perverts did to women. She didn't want to be tortured and mutilated. The thought of a slow painful death made her begin to sob uncontrollably.

Why had she come alone to the house of a man she'd met at a swinger's club?

Because you're a sex addict, her mind answered back.

Why had she allowed this stranger to chain her up like this?

Because you're a sex addict, it replied again, *and now you are going to be tortured and murdered and probably mutilated and cannibalized.*

Alicia wept openly as she watched the big cannibal gnaw away her other nipple. A vicious and uncharacteristic hatred swept over her. This man had tricked her. He had been kind and loving to her just so that he could lure her here and hurt her. She wanted to kill him. She wanted to rip his eyes out, to castrate him, to make him scream the way he'd made her scream. But she could do nothing and soon her burning rage turned back to the more familiar fear and sadness. Once again she had fucked up and this time it would more than likely lead to her death. Still, there was a part of her that hoped he was not a killer, not just because she was afraid of dying.

Alicia was ashamed at her body's reaction to the cannibal's assault. How could she still be attracted to that monster? She closed her eyes to avoid looking at him as he tugged and pulled at her nipple with his teeth. He had his thick venous dick in hand, stroking it furiously. Watching him was turning her on even more, even as the hatred and revulsion came boiling back up inside her. She bit down on the ball gag and concentrated on the pain to try to combat her own traitorous body's unwelcome arousal, yet she knew that the problem wasn't in her body but in her mind. She was all fucked up and she'd known it long before tonight. If she were normal she wouldn't have even been in that club to begin with.

Joe's teeth sawed through her nipple and she started to scream into the gag again as he tore it from her and gobbled it up with that bizarre look of ecstasy on his face. He was still masturbating and he stood up so that he towered over her with his cock hovering directly above her head. He swallowed and his whole body went rigid and then began to quiver as an orgasm whipped through him. He aimed his turgid meat at her face. The monster erupted with a roar, once again baptizing her face in his seed. She wanted to bite his cock right off of him and spit it back in his face but the gag in her mouth prevented her.

"You evil motherfucking pervert! You sick bastard! You twisted crazy fuck!" she screamed in rage at him, but the gag in her mouth prevented any of the words from leaving her mouth as anything but incoherent shrieks. She was sure he had gotten the picture, though. His eyes softened with emotion when he looked at her as if her words had wounded him. Ridiculously she almost felt sorry for him, sorry for hurting him. She knew it was the victim in her talking. The sick creature that believed she deserved all of this. That she'd deserved every hateful thing a man had ever done to her.

Alicia fought hard to keep her hatred burning, but even with the big cannibal hovering above her, she found it hard to hate him. He was just doing what men do: hurt women. Women like her always got hurt. It was the way her life had always been. And when Joe eventually killed her it would just complete the cycle of violence that had begun with her very first sexual experience, consensual sex turned gang rape in the basement of the local gang leader.

Men had never been kind to her. Why should she have expected her life to end any differently than this? Watching him cum while chewing up her nipples had convinced her that she was going to die. Still, she did not find the thought as terrifying as she should have. A part of her had always known that she would end up this way. Ever since the day her father caught her in the garage giving blowjobs to twelve guys from the neighborhood street gang and she'd gone down on him too to keep him from kicking her ass, she knew that she was no good. Alicia's father had looked at her with hurt and disgust on his face after he'd ejaculated down her throat. She'd giggled as she saw the defeated look on his face. She licked her lips thinking about how things would change around the house now, how she'd replace her mother as the woman of the house.

No way he could tell her what to do or keep her

from doing whatever she wanted now that she'd sucked his cock. Alicia would always wield the power to not only get him thrown in jail, but ostracized from family and friends, and excommunicated from the church. He'd been tempted into sin by his own adolescent daughter. Alicia had hurled her laughter like daggers at his back as he fled the garage. Later that night he'd blown his head off with a shotgun. Alicia had run into the garage to find him sitting at his workbench with the shotgun still clenched between his teeth, the top of his skull and all the contents of his brain pan sliding down the bare Sheetrock in a gruesome collage of blood and gray matter. She had screamed loud and long. She'd never stopped screaming. Every time she came she screamed out for her dead father.

At the funeral everyone had asked the normal question: "Why did he do it? He had so much to live for." Only Alicia had known why. He killed himself because he'd had sex with his own daughter and because he'd enjoyed it and he'd have done it again. Alicia ran away from home after the funeral. She couldn't face her mother knowing what she'd done. She didn't even have the luxury of one of those tragic stories that most runaways had. She hadn't been raped or molested by her old man, she'd molested him, seduced him to avoid punishment. Yeah, he could have resisted, but she knew he wouldn't. At age twelve she already knew all about what made men weak.

She'd saved her little brother from being forced into joining the Puerto Rican gang that ran the neighborhood by sucking off the whole crew. She hadn't done it just for him, but because she'd always wanted to feel a man's cock in her mouth, ever since she'd discovered those videos under her father's bed. So she'd done it and she'd liked it, and she liked the fact that the toughest guys in the neighborhood now treated her like a woman and not like just another dumb kid. So she did it again and again until she got caught.

After she ran away, she'd gone to live with some of the guys from the gang, getting gang raped almost daily until she was able to afford her own place. Alicia had known then, as she lay on that sweaty mattress in the basement of a gang member named Big Monk, that her life story would be a tragedy.

Fuck that! I don't deserve this! I don't deserve to die like this! She tried to struggle free of her bonds but the straps did not yield. Her eyes shot daggers at her captor as he wiped her blood from his lips. He turned away from her enraged stare with a look of shame and stood up from the bed.

"Fuck you! *You* should be ashamed. Now let me go! Let me go!" she screamed at his back, but once again the ball gag smothered her words.

She watched as Joe staggered out of the bedroom, and she was afraid that he would leave her there alone. As much as she feared the things he might do to her, being left chained up in this dark apartment terrified her even more. She tried to scream for him to come back but her strained cries just barely squeaked out around the rubber ball shoved firmly between her teeth.

Chapter Ten

Joe walked out of the bedroom in a daze. He plopped down on the couch and stared at the ancient black-and-white television as if awaiting revelation, but he'd received his revelation back there in the bedroom. The disease was progressing. He'd now mutilated a woman. More than that, he'd eaten some of her flesh and ejaculated while doing it. He had crossed the line. A deep depression settled over him as he considered himself, who he was, and who and what he was becoming. The possibility of killing was now more than just a sweaty fantasy haunting his wet dreams. It was very real and very imminent. He had to figure out what to do with her now.

There was no way Joe could release her after mutilating her breasts; not without going to jail. He would face charges of kidnapping, rape, assault, and of course cannibalism. He'd spend a minimum of twenty years behind bars unless he got an early parole for good behavior or pleaded insanity. He considered checking himself in to an insane asylum. He could go right to the hospital and tell them about the girl chained up in the apartment, about how he'd chewed off her nipples and would probably eat the rest of her if nobody stopped him. He'd tell them about how he couldn't look at anyone without wondering how their flesh would taste, which appendages would be the most tender, which organs would melt on his tongue like an extravagant confection.

Perhaps they would give him a nice padded cell, drug him, and give him group therapy sessions with other cannibals and murderers. Maybe they would give him private sessions with a psychiatrist who would listen to tales about his childhood. About how he'd creep down the hall at night to watch his mother and father fuck through the keyhole in the door. How his father would strangle her until her face turned blue just before he came, growling like a wolf. How he'd once seen his father cut a stray dog to pieces or how he'd been kidnapped and molested by a young child killer when he was eight. Maybe they would cure him. Maybe they would give him shock treatments or chemical castration or a lobotomy. Maybe they would declare him legally sane and he would go to prison after all and get raped or murdered himself by some big angry convicts.

Joe shuddered. He did not want to risk turning himself in. He did not relish the prospect of ending his days wrapped in a straitjacket and locked in a padded room, drooling on himself in a near catatonic stupor from a cocktail of antipsychotics. Besides that, he didn't want to release Alicia. He wanted to taste more of her succulent flesh.

Joe curled up on the couch and tried to ignore the whimpering cries coming from the next room. He didn't know what he would do with her, but whatever it was, it wouldn't be tonight. It was already nearly sunrise and he had a class at 10:00 A.M. That left him barely four hours of sleep. He didn't want to be late for class. Joe was convinced that somewhere there was a cure for his illness and that with the help of the professor he would find it. First he had to convince the man that he wasn't a lunatic with some ridiculous implausible theory by finding the proof himself. That meant a trip back to the library.

Joe knew that he was getting close. Finding the link between the werewolf and vampire mythology and the serial killer phenomenon might lead directly to a cure. If he was right, those old myths not only held the answer to how the disease was transmitted but also how it could be stopped. He wasn't willing to drive a stake through his own heart and nail himself inside a coffin or chop off his head and fill his mouth with garlic. Those were the last-ditch remedies for those monsters who had progressed to the point where they could no longer be saved. There had to be a less dramatic solution to the cloying hunger that raked at his mind and spirit, beyond all the hype and superstition. He had to find the cure soon. Before he killed Alicia.

Sunlight ripped the curtain of night, bleeding morning into the sky just as Joe finally succumbed to sleep. He tossed and turned fitfully on his couch and dreamt of the day he'd been kidnapped from the playground by a budding child murderer named Damon Trent, who'd no doubt intended to make him his first victim. He could still hear the fat teenager's tittering, high-pitched voice, like an overexcited young girl's, as he dragged him into his minivan and sped off down the street with Joe kicking and screaming for his life in the front seat. Joe still had the faded bite marks and knife wounds on his ass, chest, neck, arms, and thighs from where the man had abused him.

No one knew why the kid had released him the next morning instead of torturing him to death, as he would with his later victims. Perhaps he had thought Joe was near death anyway and would die of exposure before anyone found him. Perhaps he'd had mercy. He certainly hadn't shown mercy to his next three victims. He'd torn them apart. Joe could still remember the feel of the knife plunging into his rectum as the man stabbed him repeatedly, and how he'd screamed like the world was ending, convinced that he was dead.

When Joe woke up, drenched in his own sweat and screaming at the top of his lungs, the sun was already high in the sky and his alarm clock was blaring. It was time for class.

Joe dressed and showered before going back into the bedroom to confront his captive. She looked awful, with blood caked on her breasts and stomach. She'd urinated on herself sometime during the night, unable to ask to use the bathroom with the gag in her mouth or perhaps hoping that she'd make herself too disgusting to rape. Joe removed the ball gag then lifted her up and carried her into the bathroom where he scrubbed off all the blood and washed her tenderly, lovingly, fighting to keep his mind on getting to school on time. He led her to the toilet and watched as she relieved herself, glaring at him murderously the entire time. He did his best to avoid her gaze. He knew he deserved her hatred. When she was done using the toilet he washed her again.

Joe carried Alicia over to the bed and affixed another chain to a loop in the ceiling, which he then connected to her wrist restraints. The chain was slack enough to allow her to move about the bed but if she tried to get off the bed she would wind up dangling in the air 'til he got home. He explained all of this to her and her eyes began to tear up again.

"I'm sorry," Joe said to her as he kissed her on the cheek. "I just can't help myself. I really don't want to hurt you. I just don't know how to stop."

He turned to walk out of the door.

"You are beautiful, though. So beautiful."

Then he left, locking the bedroom door behind him. Alicia heard the front door slam and the dead bolt click into place. Then she was alone. Alone in a madman's apartment with no way to escape.

Chapter Eleven

Alicia sat in silence for a long moment listening to the sound of her own breathing, trying to steady her pulse and keep herself from going crazy and perhaps going into shock. She began to catalogue her injuries. Aside from the nauseating ache in her bruised and bitten breasts where her nipples had been torn off, she had no major injuries. She had a few other bruises from where the college boy had smacked her buttocks and pulled her hair as he grunted, growled, and thrusted deep into her. Nothing she wasn't used to.

Her wrists were scraped raw from trying to wriggle out of the leather restraints last night after she'd been left alone. Joe had cleaned them as best he could with hydrogen peroxide but still the skin ripped and bled as she tried again to squeeze out of the leather cuffs. Again, nothing she wasn't accustomed to.

Joe had left a bucket by the side of the bed in case she had to use the restroom before he returned. On the nightstand he left a bowl of water. Alicia would have to kneel on all fours and lap it up like a kitten in order to drink from it with her arms still bound be-

hind her. She didn't want to think of what she'd have
to do in order to use the bucket.

Her shoulders were killing her. No matter how she
turned on the bed her weight rested on them unless
she turned over onto her face, which aggravated the
throbbing pain where her nipples had been, or sat
completely upright, which felt uncomfortable with
the bar wedged between her legs keeping them
apart. Even when she set upright, Alicia's shoulders
still felt under pressure from being forced backward
with her arms locked behind her.

Alicia tried to scream again. She thrashed, kicking
and bucking on the bed, hoping someone would
come to her rescue, but she didn't hear a single
sound coming from any of the other apartments. Either the walls were soundproof or there were no
other neighbors. She thought about what the rest of
the building had looked like, the smell of garbage
and urine, the cracked drywall and deteriorating
paint, the fact that she had not seen any evidence of
anyone else on her way to his apartment.

The lobby had been dark when she'd come stumbling in late last night and there had been no sounds
of televisions or radios or children crying, lovers
quarrelling. It had seemed completely empty to her,
but she'd paid no attention to it, attributing it to the
lateness of the hour. She'd been too busy concentrating on getting some of that young gorgeous college
athlete's cock to think about how shitty his apartment building was. Now that she knew that her gorgeous athlete was a kidnapper and a cannibal, she
wondered if perhaps she'd been lured into an abandoned building. The gang she used to hang out with
had once converted an entire vacant department

store into one big crack house and shooting gallery. Maybe she was in a condemned apartment building that he was just squatting in?

Giving up on screaming, Alicia began once again trying to work her way free of the restraints. The pain in her wrists competed with the pain she imagined if the cannibal returned to finish his meal. She began to jerk and pull furiously at the cuffs, only succeeding in cutting the leather deeper into her already abraded skin.

"Oh God! I'm going to die here!" She began to cry again and forced herself to stop. That wasn't going to help anything. It would only get in the way of her thinking. She had to come up with a plan.

Maybe she could talk him into releasing her from the cuffs when he returned? He did seem to be remorseful. He even seemed to really like her. Maybe he wouldn't kill her after all? Then she remembered the look on his face when he bit into her breast. He hadn't looked himself. He hadn't looked human at all. The thing that she'd seen gnawing into her nipples had been all appetite and lust. Maybe he had two personalities? One that was caring and gentle, the one who'd washed her wounds and cleaned her up this morning and apologized for hurting her before leaving, and one that was vicious and dangerous, the one who'd lost control. Somehow she had to talk one of them into letting her go.

Chapter Twelve

Joe walked to the campus in a daze. He imagined that the fog rolling through the street was emanating from him. He felt protected by it. As long as the fog remained to cloak his thoughts he didn't have to face what he'd become in the last twenty-four hours. He didn't have to think about the pain in that Spanish girl's beautiful eyes when he'd bitten into her breast. It wasn't just the physical pain that had caused that wounded look. It was the pain of betrayal. She'd thought she'd found the perfect man in him.

He'd seen the look before. Even before he'd started having the uncontrollable urge to eat human flesh there had been his maniacal sex drive. Women would be amazed at his stamina when he would make love to them all night and then further amazed when he would call them the next night for a repeat perform-ance. It would go on for weeks with him seeing them every minute of every day for marathon sex ses-sions. Then, he'd suddenly lose interest and disap-pear without a word. Usually after meeting another woman. Or when his collection of women grew too vast for him to keep track of and he would simply

forget about some of them as he met new ones. None
of them would ever suspect that there were others.

No way he can make love to me for three or four
hours straight and still have anything left for anyone
else, they would think.

But Joe was a sex addict. His bedroom was like a
revolving door. He knew exactly how long each
woman was good for, when they needed to leave for
work, or pick their kids up from day care, or would
just be too exhausted or chafed for another round.
When he wasn't having sex he was hunting for new
sex partners. Then he'd started having the urges and
everything began to change.

He'd experimented with S&M before, even extreme bondage and blood play. It was more pleasure
than he'd expected to derive from whipping a man's
naked ass with a cat-o'-nine-tails or sticking needles
through a woman's labia or burning a woman's nipples with a candle flame or the powerful orgasm he'd
had when he'd strangled unconscious a kid he'd met
on campus while fucking him in the ass with a dildo.
The kid dropped out of school the next day and had
never returned.

Joe's enjoyment of these things had been completely unexpected. The fact that he'd wanted to
take it further was even more unexpected.

He'd been circumcising a man at an S&M sex
club. The man had approached him with this huge
uncircumcised cock in hand. He had big blue puppy-
dog eyes that looked wounded but trusting. His body
was lithe and delicate like a young girl's, in stark con-
trast to the hardened flesh straining between his
thighs. He had a castration fantasy. So Joe had
agreed to circumcise him. He had just sliced off half

his foreskin when he'd suddenly had the urge to bite the man's penis off. He imagined chewing it up and swallowing it, what the tender flesh would taste like going down his throat. He plopped the man's foreskin into his mouth and began to chew it. The man's eyes had widened in amazement and a tremor of excitement had gone through the crowd of onlookers, many of whom were masturbating as they watched them play.

The rush of pleasure that went through Joe's body all the way down to his manhood was overwhelming as he consumed the morsel. Then he'd lowered his head down between the man's thighs, baring his teeth, preparing to devour that luscious nine inches of rigid flesh, to bite the man's penis clean off. Joe could sense the man's excitement and terror rising as they combined into a rapture that vibrated through him like a bass drum. Joe's mouth enveloped his cock and the man moaned as the pain from where the razor had done its work mingled with the pleasure of that rough slippery tongue probing the wound.

As the man watched his throbbing hard cock disappear between Joe's lips and push its way down his throat, he let out a sigh of soul deep ecstasy. Joe's teeth bit into the base of his cock and the man shuddered on the edge of orgasm. He began to convulse with a screaming climax as he felt Joe's teeth bite deeper and begin to tug, trying to tear his cock right off of him. He ejaculated down Joe's throat and Joe released him, gagging and coughing. The man smiled at him with a look on his face of utter satisfaction.

"That was incredible, man! Do you want me to do you now?"

Joe ran out of the club, horrified by both what he

had done and what he'd been about to do. Now he had done far worse.

Joe awoke from his reverie standing in the campus courtyard, not knowing how he had gotten there. There were three minutes before his class started. He sprinted across campus, arriving at the lecture hall just as the professor was preparing to begin his lesson.

"We were just talking about you, Joseph. Thanks for joining us. Take a seat please. As I was saying . . . cannibalism is at the end of the continuum of a sadistic murderer's evolution, the ultimate expression of dominance and control, predation at its base essence, the devouring of human blood and flesh to satisfy sexual fantasies. This actually ties in with your theory of a progressive disease, Joseph. If we assume that serial murderers are like drug addicts in that they develop a tolerance for normal 'lesser' forms of pleasure then they would eventually develop a tolerance for the run-of-the-mill rape-and-murder scenarios requiring more extreme stimulation, multiple victims, an increase in the frequency of their attacks, and an increase in the level of violence.

"Trophy taking begins to go beyond jewelry and photographs into the harvesting of body parts for later use in necrophiliac activities, to relive the murders. In some cases these trophies become the very reason for the murders as in the case of Jeffrey Dahmer, part of his compulsion to own his victims. Some murderers find secluded places where they can not only murder their victims but also store their bodies, to maintain control over their victims even after death. This degenerative cycle leads to the most extreme psychosexual behaviors. Cannibalism is at the pinnacle of this arc. To consume their victims is the ultimate expression of control. Once they devour them they own them forever. They will always be a part of them."

The professor seemed to be staring directly into Joe's eyes as he spoke, as if each statement was for his sole benefit. As if he knew. Joe shifted nervously in his chair and wrung his sweaty hands. The professor's words bore down on him like accusations and Joe had the sudden feeling of being on trial. This is what it would feel like when they caught him. He stared intensely at Professor Locke as the polished old gentleman described the inner workings of his mind as clearly as if he had read his thoughts, saw each lurid fantasy and felt each shivering sensation, giving voice to the demons in his soul in front of a crowd of strangers.

Joe wanted to scream and run out of the room. Instead he forced a smile onto his face and endured the onslaught of words until he couldn't take it any longer.

"But what if it isn't just about control?" Joe suddenly blurted out.

The entire room turned to look at him and he felt suddenly vulnerable and exposed.

"What else would it be about, Joseph? A man murders, rapes, and devours a stranger. What else would it be about other than to prove his dominance and power? To sublimate another human being to his will? These men are sadists!"

"No!" Again everyone turned to stare at him. Joe nervously stood and took a deep breath to steady his voice. "I mean . . . maybe not all of them. Not all of them torture their victims. Some kill them quickly before they do anything to them. Maybe not all of them mean to cause pain."

"Then why do they do it, Joseph?"

"Maybe it's love." A roar of laughter rose up and Joe looked from face to face while the blood rushed to his cheeks.

"Love?"

"Yes. What is love but the desire to unite with the love object? That's why people get married, to make two souls into one. But of course that's merely symbolic, imperfect. Marriage is an illusion of a true union. Cannibalism is the real deal. It could be the ultimate expression of love."

Professor Locke stared at Joe with concern clearly visible on his face. The entire hall was staring at him, speechless. Some of them had smirks on their faces and others wore scowls of disgust. All of them clearly thought Joe was crazy. Joe stood there with his hands held out before him as if beseeching the professor to understand him.

"I-I'm sorry, Professor." Joe plopped down into his chair.

"Nothing at all to be ashamed of. I respect your passion and your . . . uh . . . interesting perspective. You may be closer to understanding these monsters than you think. You are absolutely right. That's exactly how some of these monsters would justify their actions. Jeffrey Dahmer, for instance, said he just wanted a friend who would never leave him. But when it comes down to it, those are all just rationalizations. These monsters do it because it gets them off. Because they enjoy hurting and humiliating people. They enjoy the power. They enjoy the control."

He was staring directly into Joe's eyes again as he spoke. Joe's mouth creaked open as if to say something but he had no words left within him. His mind was reeling as if he'd been struck.

I'm a monster, he thought and then looked around to make sure he hadn't spoken aloud. He snapped his mouth shut and leaned back in his chair.

Professor Locke smiled and turned his back to the class to erase the blackboard, shaking his head as if laughing at some private joke.

Joe gathered up his books and sprinted from the room, nearly knocking over several classmates as he dashed out into the sunlight struggling to catch his breath. The world seemed to be closing in on him. It was as if they all knew. They could sense the monster in their ranks. The sun shone down upon him like a spotlight in an interrogation chamber, revealing all his secrets. He knew now why vampires shunned the light.

It took a long time before Joe pulled himself together enough to go to his next class, a sociology class based on the writings of Joseph Campbell called "Man and Myth." He'd taken the class hoping they'd get more into vampires and werewolves and other cross-cultural demons. The professor kept promising to get to those topics but so far all he seemed to talk about were dragons and fairies and the Christlike resurrected savior myths that seemed to pop up in culture after culture all over the globe.

He squeezed into a desk chair and tried to make himself as inconspicuous as possible. Still, he felt as if every eye was upon him. A few of the students from this class were the same students from his psychology class and he could hear them whispering about him behind his back. His own roommate was among them.

Joe spent so little time at the dorm that he barely knew the kid. All he knew was that his dad was some kind of computer whiz who made twice what Joe's parents made and spoiled the hell out of their effete, socially inept little son. He was an absolute cliché of nerddom. The kid was always on the damned computer. His entire life revolved around it.

Joe could count on his fingers how many actual conversations he'd had with the guy. But then, Joe was never home anyway. Most of his time these days was spent at his apartment in the abandoned tenement building south of Market Street or at the library. Now, with Alicia tied up in that old building, he'd be spending even more time there.

"He gives me the creeps, man. And I have to live with the guy!"

Joe caught a few random snippets of conversation and bristled with a silent rage. His rich, computer-role-playing-game-geek roommate was adding more flame to the rumors and innuendos.

"I hardly ever see him. He leaves right after classes and sometimes he doesn't come back to the dorm at all, sometimes not for days. I saw him in the library one night reading about serial killers. I came back the next day and he was still there, in the same clothes, reading the same book, as if he'd never left. The guy is weird."

"Yeah, he's weird, and fucking huge! He could probably snap your neck with one hand," a slender black kid from the track team interjected just as the professor began to scribble on the blackboard.

Joe looked at what Professor Douglas was scribbling and got excited. At last the man had gotten off dragons and saints and onto something Joe was interested in.

"Shape-shifters. Werebeasts. The loup-garou, the Wendigo, the poor cursed soul that turns into a wolfman by the light of the full moon. We've all heard of werewolves but there are other werecreatures in myths and legends from almost every corner of the globe. They appear in the folklore and mythology of almost every culture. The Inuit tribespeople have a legend about the Adlet, a race of dog people that were the result of a mating between an Inuit tribeswoman and a great red dog. These weredogs are said to still haunt northern Iceland in search of human flesh. You'll see this theme of human animal couplings resulting in monsters repeated over and over across cultures.

"These could have evolved as a way to warn against what would have been seen as aberrant sex acts involving animals. The Slavic people have a legend that beautiful women who misuse their physical gifts to seduce men and cause mischief may return from the grave as sultry shape-shifters called rusalki who, like the legends of mermaids and sirens, lure men out to sea to watery graves. It's easy to see the warning here. Most legends are based on fear and the fear of the power of a woman's sexuality is very powerful even to this day.

"Then there are people who are said to have become monsters by making pacts with Satan. The Portuguese have the legend of the Bruxsa, a woman who turns into a gigantic birdlike harpy and sucks the blood of her own children. Germans have the boxenwolf, which is more like our traditional were-wolf and is likewise believed to be a person who has made a pact with Satan for the power of the wolf. The warning there is again quite obvious: Stay in the church. Don't stray from the religion of your culture.

"The term ghoul comes from a mythical shape-shifting creature from the Arabian desert that transforms endlessly from an ox to a camel to a horse and has a voracious appetite for human flesh. In Ghana there's a demon called the dodo that often appears as a snake and is rumored to be another ravenous devourer of humans. In Japan there's a fox demon called the kitsune that is said to possess humans and deplete the energy of its victims, draining them dry. Some of them are humans that have turned into werecreatures and others are demons that can simply appear as humans."

"How do they turn themselves back?" Joseph didn't care what the other students thought of him now. He had questions to which he desperately needed answers.

Professor Douglas turned toward Joe with obvious annoyance at having his lecture interrupted.

"Yes, Joseph? You had a question?"

"The werewolves that are just humans who have turned into monsters. How do they turn themselves back into humans? How do they get rid of the curse?"

The professor scratched his ratty overgrown goatee and pondered Joseph a moment, perhaps trying to decide if the boy was genuinely curious or just trying to make some kind of joke. He'd had Joseph in the previous semester and knew that the serious young man was not genuinely the comedic type.

"Well, let's see. There are many different theories on how to rid yourself of the curse, according to various legends, though none of them seem to have a very high success rate. Generally, once you invite these demonic animal spirits inside they are nearly impossible to get rid of."

"But—"

Joe wiped the sweat from his brow and tried to steady his voice. He could feel himself growing more and more agitated, his desperation evident in the way he fidgeted in his chair and rang out his hands constantly.

"But you said there were many theories about different cures. What are the theories? What's the cure?"

"Well, we'll get to that, Joseph. I don't want to get off track. First I want to discuss the different myths themselves and their similarities," the professor said, trying to keep from losing control of the discussion.

"But you know, right?" Joe rose from his chair. He was sweating again and he had a look of desperation in his eyes.

"Uh-oh. Here we go again," one of the other students mumbled. Joe was pretty sure it was his roommate. He ignored him.

"I mean, you know what the cure is? Right?"

"Joseph. These are just myths. Now take your seat, please."

Joe looked around and, realizing that he was once again making a fool of himself, slipped back into his chair.

"I-I'm sorry, Professor."

Professor Douglas peered curiously at Joe over his glasses.

"That's quite all right, Joseph, and I promise we

will get to your question. It's just difficult to really understand the cure without understanding the disease."

"You mean how they became werewolves in the first place?"

"Yes, the theories on that vary from culture to culture and even within cultures. There are a number of different ways to evoke the animal spirits. The most common way as in the shamanic 'skin walkers,' the French loup-garou, and the vicious leopard men of West Africa, is to don the skin of a wolf. Some don full skins and some, as in the loup-garou or the berserkers, wear only a belt or a vest fashioned from the hide of the animal they wish to become in order to invoke the transformation. Others rub their skin in salves and ointments made of animal fat or even human fat. The leopard men drank a magical concoction brewed from the intestines of their human victims, which they believed gave them their lycanthropic abilities. Some believe you need only drink water from a werewolf's tracks in order to become one yourself.

"There are magical texts, which prescribe complex rituals for the invoking of the werewolf spirit. One recommends removing all of your clothing and rubbing your skin in a magical ointment made from the fat of a wolf and mixed with anise, camphor, and opium, then donning a wolf pelt and drinking beer mixed with wolf's blood. You can see how such a complex ritual, particularly with the imbibing of alcohol and opium, coupled with the person's desire to become a wolf could easily lead one to believe he had indeed transformed.

"There are likewise many cults and sects that have

wild drunken orgies in which live animals and even humans are consumed and animal hides are worn. During these rituals many of these initiates believe that they have become animals. The Maenads, who worshipped the wine god Dionysus and the horned god of the forest Pan, had wild drunken bacchanals in which they consumed live animals and humans and let wolf pups suckle at their breasts. The Issawiya, a shape-shifting cult from northern and western Africa, likewise engaged in these wild organized rituals in order to gain their powers. During their ceremonies they would dress a calf or a bull in human clothing and then rip it to shreds and devour its flesh raw."

"But that's for people who *wanted* to become werewolves. What about those who were cursed, who became monsters against their will?"

A round of snickers circled the classroom. Joe turned around to glare at them and the room fell silent. He turned back to the professor.

"Well . . . there's usually only a few causes for that and that's either by being scratched or bitten by someone who is already a werewolf or by involuntarily drinking their blood, or by being cursed by a witch or sorcerer."

Joe paused for a moment in deep thought.

"So, let's say someone is bitten and gets infected with this virus. How do they cure themselves?"

"You mean for those who have become lycanthropes involuntarily, I assume? There are some who believe that if you sever the lineage at its source, the original shape-shifter that spawned that particular line, then you will release all those wolves he created from the curse. That original werewolf would be the one who acquired his abilities voluntarily. He may still don a wolf's skin when he hunts and he'd probably be envious of his offspring who manage the transformation without any trinkets or rituals. But most agree that the only surefire way is a silver bullet through the heart, severing of the head, or burning them alive."

Joe shuddered and fell silent. If what he suspected was correct then the man who'd abducted him over a decade ago, stabbed, mutilated, and nearly killed him, was the werewolf he needed to kill in order to be free. Joe stared at the professor in shock, not hearing another word the man said.

He was thinking about confronting Damon Trent again.

Chapter Thirteen

Joe went to his art class and was surprised to see the model from the afternoon before waiting for him at the door.

"Here! I wanted to pay you for that painting."

She stepped forward and thrust a check into his hands for one hundred dollars.

"You don't have to do that. I can't take this."

"Are you saying you don't need it? You mean you aren't a starving student like the rest of us? What's your secret?"

"No, I'm not saying I don't need it. I definitely need it. I'm starving more than you could ever imagine."

"Then take the money."

Joe slipped the check into his pocket.

"You can use it to take me out to dinner if you'd like."

"Uh . . . I'm kind of involved with someone at the moment."

"In love?"

"Maybe. I'm not sure."

"But you don't cheat on her?"

"She satisfies me."

"Well, that's good then. Keep the check, though.

And if you ever need . . . more, then you give me a call, okay?"

"But I don't know your number."

"It's on the check."

Joe pulled out the check and saw that it did indeed have her name, address, and phone number printed on it. The model winked at him then walked into the art studio and dropped her robe. She smiled as Joe stumbled into the room, staring at her in that desperate way he had about him.

You're going to be mine, big boy, she thought.

Joe sat down and immediately attacked the canvas. In minutes he had run out of red paint. His canvas looked like a massacre.

The model wasn't his type but something about her set him afire. She was such a willing victim, like Frank but a female. There was no way he could have sex with her, though. Not after what had happened with Alicia. He was afraid of what he'd do to her. Besides, it would have felt like cheating.

"I need more paint."

The teacher walked over and stared at his gruesome canvas. She gasped audibly.

"I ran out of red."

"Uh . . . yes . . . I'll go get you some more." She scurried away from Joe, nearly tripping over the easel in back of him.

Joe could smell her pheromones and those of the model comingling in the air. It was like having a ménage à trois through his nostrils. The model's nipples were erect and pointing right at him. Her eyes zeroed in on the bulge in his crotch. She licked her lips when she saw him looking at her. Joe turned away.

"Don't tempt me," he growled under his breath.

The teacher came back with the red paint and Joe once again took his frustrations out on the canvas. It was bloodied and bruised when he finally left the room for his next class. He left it sitting on the easel and felt some pride when he saw the model and the teacher staring at it and whispering.

Let them fuck each other. It's a hell of a lot safer than what I'd do to them, Joe thought as he hurried off to math class.

If anything could douse the fire in him it was sitting in a classroom balancing equations for an hour and a half.

Joe sat through over an hour of math, trying his best not to think about the scrumptious meat chained up in his bedroom. The numbers on the page kept jumbling up in his head and at the end of the class his paper was still blank. He balled it up and tossed it in the trash on his way out the door. He'd much rather get an incomplete than a zero.

Joe left the mathematics lab and walked back across campus to the library. The sun was beginning to set and the fog was already rolling slowly across the manicured lawn toward him. A cool breeze slipped through the trees and across the grass, whispering beneath his clothes and across his skin. Joe sighed and shivered. After having his face glued to a page full of senseless mathematical equations for over an hour, the cool moist evening air was refreshing, soothing. It calmed the beast inside him.

Joe felt relaxed and sedate as the fog caught up to him and sucked him in. Still, he could not stop thinking about Alicia. He didn't want to hurt her again. He had to find a cure for himself.

He tensed as he remembered what Professor Locke had said:

Sever the bloodline. Kill the original werewolf.

Hopefully, there was another way. Joe hadn't thought about Damon Trent in years. Not until the hunger had started to come upon him and he'd looked into the bathroom mirror to see the same pitiless lust-clouded eyes of his long-ago victimizer staring back at him. He should have known then that the man had passed something evil on to him.

The librarian looked up and smiled nervously as Joe entered the building and stalked past her desk. Joe rolled his massive shoulders and smiled back at her with a leering smile as he dragged his eyes over her thick curves. Her smile faltered and fell from her face, landing in a hard trembling line. She lowered her eyes and turned away. Joseph smiled wider.

Joe struggled to maintain control over the beast raging within him but the smell of her perfumed skin was driving him mad. He walked past her and into the rows of bookshelves, reeling like a drunken man. He stopped in front of a book in the mythology section called *Vampires in Fact and Fiction*. He pulled it off the shelf and walked with it back to the huge oak table in the center of the room. He opened it and turned to the section on ways to become a vampire. There was some nonsense about being born on Christmas Day or being excommunicated from the church that Joe immediately discounted as superstition, then there came the part about being bitten by a vampire or drinking the blood of the undead.

Joe quickly turned to the section on destroying vampires and read about nailing them into their coffins by driving a wooden stake through their hearts or through their skulls so that they could not rise to feed. There was a prescription that called for decapitating and burning the corpses of vampires or dragging them out into the sun. Filling their mouths with garlic or placing host wafers in their coffins so that they could not lie there. Joe turned more pages until he came to a section that reiterated Professor Douglas's own remedy for the werewolf curse. Curing a vampire of the curse likewise called for finding and killing the original bloodsucker. Joe slammed the book shut and sat there thinking, first about Damon Trent the child murderer and then about Alicia, whom he would surely murder and consume if he did not cure himself. He got up and walked over to the computer to do a search on Damon Trent.

Chapter Fourteen

Alicia was fast asleep when the door slammed, waking her from her dreams and plunging her back into the nightmare of reality. Joe stalked into the room looking excited and agitated.

"I don't know what to do! I don't want to hurt you, but I can't see him again. I just can't face him again!"

He strode back and forth, gesticulating madly, whipping himself into a frenzy. He stopped abruptly and plopped down next to Alicia, startling her and causing her to shrink away.

He rubbed a hand lovingly over her voluptuous ass as she quivered in fear and began to sob.

"Talk to me. Tell me what to do," he said, staring deeply into her terrified eyes.

"Let me go. You should let me go right away before you do something you'll regret."

"If I let you go I'll just find another woman."

"Then turn yourself in. They have people who can help you."

"Doctors? Psychiatrists? They'll just lock me up with this hunger still gnawing at me each and every day. That would be torture. No, I need to find a cure, another cure, a different cure."

"Joe. Listen to me. You have to let me go, Joe. You can't keep me here. They'll catch you."

"You're right. I can't keep you here forever. I'm going to have to go after him. But I'm taking you with me."

Alicia had no idea what the man was talking about, but it didn't sound good.

"You have to go after who?"

"Damon Trent. He's the one who made me what I am. I have to find him. Destroy him. In order to destroy the curse."

Joe sat down and told Alicia everything and she listened, not just in order to gain his confidence and trust, but because she was legitimately curious. The story he was telling was unbelievable, but by the time he was done he almost had her convinced.

"So you believe that this Damon Trent guy passed on some type of virus to you when he molested you and that's what's causing you to change?"

"It's changing me into a killer! And if I don't find him then you're going to wind up being my first victim."

As much as it chilled the blood in Alicia's veins to hear that he was thinking about killing her, she was encouraged by the fact that he hadn't murdered her yet and also by the fact that he didn't want to. He didn't want to hurt her. It was that virus inside him making him crazy. It sounded ridiculous when she repeated it to herself now, but when he'd told her about the correlation he'd found between the werewolf and vampire legends and the evolution of the serial killer it almost made sense to her. If he could just find and kill that fucker that infected him then he'd be cured and he'd let her go and maybe they could even go out again sometime once he was normal.

Alicia knew that she was being a fool. Why would she want to go out with the guy who chained her up and bit her nipples off and was more than likely going to murder her?

Because you're a sex-addict, her subconscious answered back.

The likelihood of him curing himself by plunging a stake through the heart of a serial child murderer was so remote it was crazy. Still, it was the only thing she had to hang her hopes on.

"I'll help you."

"What?"

"I'll help you find him . . . and kill him."

Joe stared into Alicia's eyes for a long moment. He saw an honesty and a trust there that was almost childlike. There was loneliness there too, and a need—the need for love. He reached out and stroked her long curly black hair and leaned in to kiss her.

As Joe's lips touched hers Alicia screamed at herself: *Bite his lips off! Bite off his fucking tongue! Kill Him! Kill Him!!!*

Instead, she returned his kiss. Their tongues dueled and danced and Joe lovingly caressed her beautiful body, careful to avoid her savaged nipples, which were still raw and tender. He kissed her throat and sucked the sweat from the hollows of her collarbones. He licked the salt of her tears from her cheeks and brushed his lips against her eyelids. He sucked her bruised lips and kissed the tip of her chin. Then he laid her down and removed the leg spreader from between her ankles, slipping off her restraints and kissing the chafed and torn flesh beneath, shivering at the meaty metallic taste of her blood.

Joe stroked her buttery caramel thighs and Alicia moaned in appreciation. She tried to tell herself to fight him, to kick him off and run for her life, but he was so big, so strong. She doubted she'd have had a chance of overcoming him even for a second and she was enjoying his touch, enjoying the emotion in his eyes, in his soulful moans, and delicate caresses. As much as she hated to admit it, she was falling for him. She gasped as he lowered his weight on top of her and parted her thighs, entering her with cautious probing thrusts.

He lowered his head to the nape of her neck and she stiffened, momentarily certain that he would bite her again, tear out her throat like a vampire. But when he raised his head there were tears in his eyes.

"I love you, Alicia. You have to help me."

"I will. I promise."

That night they made love, gently, softly, sweetly. They gave and took, exchanging pain for pleasure, solitude for solace, and when they were done they held each other and wept for both their lives.

Chapter Fifteen

Damon was towering above him as eight-year-old Joey rounded the corner on his BMX bike. The overweight high school dropout stood in the middle of the sidewalk in his Windy City Deep Dish Pizza delivery uniform, his van idling at the curb, and the passenger door swung wide. He leered coyly at little Joey with a lecherous scowl on his face and a cruel gleam in his eyes. His smile was even more threatening. It was the predatorial rictus of a hyena approaching weakened prey.

Joe tried to steer around him but the fat teenager stepped right into his path, causing Joe to slam on his brakes and skid out, nearly flipping over the handlebars. He was just about to cuss the chubby loser out when he felt the boy's fat fingers close around his throat and lift him from the bike. Joe tried to call out, but he could get no air in or out of his lungs. He pinwheeled his arms and legs in the air as if he were trying to swim away from an onrushing shark as the boy carried him across the sidewalk and into the idling van. The fat kid smelled like pepperoni and ammonia. That's the last thing Joe remembered thinking before the van doors slammed shut, sealing out the midday August sun and the joyful cries of the kids playing just yards away in the park.

Joe woke up with his fist clenched tight around Alicia's throat. Her eyes were bulging out of their sockets, her tongue lolled stupidly from her mouth, and her complexion was turning the prettiest turquoise blue. He jerked his hands away from her neck and jumped back, scooting to the other side of the bed, startled by what he had done. Alicia was gasping and choking as she sucked air back into her depleted lungs. Joe was breathing hard with sweat bulleting down his face.

"I'm sorry. I'm sorry. I-I was having a bad dream. I didn't mean to—I mean, I didn't know what I was doing."

"You almost killed me! You're crazy! Oh my God! You're fucking crazy! Heeelp! Heeeelp!!!"

Joe shook his head in exasperation and reached down to pick up the restraints from where he'd tossed them on the floor. He seized one of Alicia's legs and slipped the leather cuff around her ankle. This time she did try to kick, to fight back. She aimed a kick at his face and her heel caught him in the jaw as he reached out for her feet, causing his head to spin and his lip to split open and run red. Joe barely seemed to notice. He grabbed both of her ankles and flipped her over onto her stomach.

Joe's breath caught in his throat as that perfect ass rolled into view, wobbling temptingly in the moonlight. The hunger came rushing upon him urgent and insistent. He sat on Alicia's back as she continued to scream and struggle, seizing her ankles and placing the leather cuffs and leg spreader back between her ankles. Then he turned and cuffed and chained her wrists again as well.

"Noooo! Nooo! Don't do this!"

"I said I wouldn't hurt you and I won't—not if I can find the cure."

Joe trussed her up, reinserted the ball gag into her mouth and reattached her to the chain hanging from the ceiling before he hurried out of the room.

Chapter Sixteen

Emma Purcell was reading a dog-eared copy of *Tropic of Cancer* and waiting for the two law students on the computers and the four medical students half asleep on the couches and lounge chairs to finally realize that nothing they did in the next four hours was going to help them pass a test they hadn't prepared for earlier. She was startled when the massively muscled psychology student suddenly appeared at her desk.

"Uh, c-can I help you?"

"I need to find someone."

"I'm not sure I understand."

"There's a man I need to find. I was hoping you could show me how to search for him on the computer."

"Oh, sure. There're several searches you can run to track someone on the computer. Here, I'll show you." Emma rose from behind the desk and immediately felt the large creepy student's eyes lunge for her, charging over her curves and invading her most intimate areas. She felt simultaneously frightened, annoyed, and aroused, sensations she was used to experiencing in his presence. Her nipples hardened and stabbed the sheer fabric of her blouse. Joe stared at her heaving bosom with unselfconscious lust. Emma's face colored. She turned her back to him and sat down at the computer.

Emma had to admit that the boy was extremely good-looking. He exuded a savage sexuality that was nearly oppressive. She could feel his hot breath on the back of her neck as she tapped the keyboard and logged on to the Web.

"Uh . . . so who are we looking for?"

"His name is Damon Trent. He would be almost thirty by now."

"Do you have any idea where he might be? A city? A state?"

"He would still be in Seattle; either in prison or a mental institution."

Emma's fingers hovered suspended over the keys. This was more of his bizarre research.

"What exactly did he do?"

"He raped and mutilated a couple young boys about twelve years ago."

"That's sick! I'm not going to be a part of this! What is this twisted morbid fascination you have with these monsters? Look, you're online now. I'm sure you'll have no problem locating your murderous pedophile. I've got work to do back at my desk." The librarian stood and turned to leave.

Joe placed a hand on her shoulder and gently eased her back into her seat.

"Please. You have to help me."

"Why? Why should I help you with this obsession? A child murderer? Why would you want to know anything about a man like that?"

Joe's voice lowered and tightened to a deep self-conscious mumble. The librarian could feel the boy's body tense as he spoke.

"Because I was one of the boys this particular monster assaulted."

The librarian's eyes widened then softened and moistened with emotion. Her mouth fell open and her body slumped back into the chair, as if physically struck by the student's unexpected confession. She placed her hand atop his and turned to look him in his eyes. Her bottom lip trembled and her voice lowered to a soft, maternal whisper.

"Oh my God! I-I'm sorry. I didn't know. No wonder you're so obsessed with finding out what makes them tick."

"Will you help me?"

"Of course."

It took no time at all to locate their killer.

"He's not in Seattle anymore. He's in Tacoma, at the state mental hospital in a special unit they have for violent sex offenders."

Joe scrolled down the screen, reading about the hospital where Damon Trent had been kept since he'd openly confessed to drinking the blood of young boys and was declared unfit to stand trial a dozen years ago. Trent believed that he could absorb the souls of his victims by imbibing their body fluids. The article, written two years after his incarceration, said that Trent claimed the doctors at the state hospital were deliberately trying to drive him insane by depriving him of human blood to drink.

Joe wrote down the address and phone number of the hospital and turned his attention back to the thick meaty librarian. He'd wanted her for a long time and though he had needed to locate Trent, he'd really come down here for her, using his search for the child rapist as a way to get close to her.

"Would you have a cup of coffee with me?"

"I don't know. I've got a lot of work to do. Besides, I'm old enough to be your mother. Why are you so interested in me?"

"Because you're beautiful and I need a friend right now."

It was the right thing to say. Joe had been rehearsing it from the first day he'd seen her. Her need was so obvious you didn't have to be a con man or a predator to spot it. Emma needed to be needed. There was a deep loneliness and sorrow within her, like one of those chimpanzee mothers who cradle their miscarriages in their arms for weeks, refusing to accept their death. Joe played on those maternal instincts lying dormant within her, starving for a purpose.

"I know I frighten you. We can take separate cars and go to the café down the street where there will be lots of people."

"That sounds awful. I'm sorry. It's not that I think you'd hurt me. It's just that . . . those books you read . . ."

"I'm a psychology student and I'm trying to understand what turns normal human beings into these vicious predators. One day, I hope I can find a cure for their madness."

"I think that's admirable, but I hope you won't be offended if I take my own car and meet you there?"

Joe smiled wide.

"Thank you."

They talked late into the night. Emma told him about her two failed marriages. Her first husband beat her and her second left her for her sister. She had a daughter who ran away from home five years ago, only two months after her sixteenth birthday.

"Do you ever hear from her?"

"She calls every once in a while. When she's in trouble or needs money or just needs someone to listen to her. I'm a good listener. I don't know where she is now, though. She hasn't called in months."

"It must be hard, not hearing from your daughter in so long."

"I cope."

Joe nodded and looked down at the scrap of paper with the name Damon Trent written on it, followed by the phone number and address to the State Hospital for the Criminally Insane. He rolled the slip of paper over and over in his hands as dark shadows slithered through his mind.

"What did he do to you?"

"You don't want to know."

"Maybe not, but you need to tell it. I can see that you're hurting. It might help to talk."

Joe didn't want to talk to her anymore. He didn't want to get too close because he was still planning on murdering her, but maybe talking about these horrors would be just the distraction he needed. Perhaps it would calm him down until he could get her alone.

"I was riding my bike when he attacked me. I turned the corner and he was just standing there, grinning at me. I tried to turn the bike around and run. I could tell that he was going to hurt me. Of course, I had no idea how bad. I thought he was going to beat me up and steal my bike or something. Then he grabbed me by the throat. He squeezed so hard that I couldn't even scream. I couldn't breathe. I felt like I was going to pass out. Then he threw me in the back of his pizza van."

Joe took a deep breath and rubbed his bare arms to warm himself as chills raced the length of his spine.

"It's okay. You don't have to continue if it bothers you."

"When we got back to his place, he undressed me. He started punching me. Then he started stabbing me. He stabbed me dozens of times, raped and sodomized me. I remember him licking my wounds, lapping up the blood like a kitten licking milk. His eyes were all glassy and vacant. He kept me down in that basement for days, feeding on me. Somewhere along the way I passed out. Then he put me back in the van and dumped me back in the park. I was the lucky one. I was his first victim. He got much more violent with the next ones before they caught him. Those he kept. They never got to see the sunlight again. They died down in his basement."

The librarian was crying when Joe looked up. Joe reached out and brushed a strand of hair from the librarian's face, cupping her cheek in his hand and leaning in to peer into her sad eyes. He wiped away her tears with his thumbs. Something about her sorrow was reawakening the monster, turning him on. He could feel the drive roiling like a furnace, burning at the root of him, hard and insistent.

Joe thought about Alicia, still chained up back at the apartment. He thought about her magnificent ass. The soft sumptuous mound of tender fat and all the things he wanted to do to it, to her. All the things he would do if he didn't curb his appetite with something else. Something like this librarian.

"I want to kiss you."

The librarian jerked away, shocked by Joe's forwardness. It was Joe's firm belief that when most women ran it was because they wanted to be chased. He seized her face in his hands again and pulled her toward him. Greedily he sucked and bit at her lower lip as he kissed her aggressively. She never struggled or made any attempt to resist him. Rather, her body melted to his touch as if it had been locked stiff with tension released the moment their lips touched. She responded to his kiss with her own, the desperate hungry embrace of a woman starved for affection, in need of a man's love.

She was out of breath when Joe leaned back in his chair and picked up his coffee. He stared at her with those same rapacious eyes that had long intimidated her as he sipped the scalding brown liquid. Emma trembled with want. Embarrassed, she reached for her own coffee, lifting it up and then placing it back on its coaster. She looked back into Joe's terrible, wantonly sexual eyes and felt another wall crumble. She closed her eyes and let out a long sigh.

"What do you want, Joseph? What do you want from me?"

The air between them became hot and thick with a palpable lust. Joe licked his lips. He was recalling the taste of Alicia's nipples when he'd eaten them and imagining what it must be like to consume a woman's entire breast.

"I want to make love to you."

"You just want to fuck me," she sighed, looking

down into her lap. Then she looked back up and her eyes were furious with lust. "But that's okay. I think I want to fuck you too."

She leaned forward and took his hand. Together they rose from the table and walked out into the parking lot.

"You'll be gentle with me, won't you? I haven't been with anyone since my husband and I divorced five years ago. You'll take it slow, won't you?"

They were almost to her car. She pulled out her keys and opened the car door.

"Promise me you'll be gentle with me."

"No," Joe said.

His huge powerful hands clenched tight around her throat and jerked the librarian up onto her tiptoes. As he closed his fingers tight around her windpipe she kicked and scratched, dragging her manicured nails through the skin on his forearms and punching at his face. She raked his throat with her fingernails, breaking off the plastic tips in his flesh before she blacked out. Joe stuffed her into the car and drove her across town to the apartment building on Folsom Street.

Chapter Seventeen

Alicia lay on the semen- and sweat-stained bed contemplating her fate, entangled in a confusion of emotions. A few hours ago she had been confident that she would survive this. She had felt like she was connecting with her captor, like she understood him a little and that perhaps he understood her as well. Then she'd woken up with his hands locked around her throat and his eyes vacant and sad, looking through her at some tragedy from his past. Yet he was still strangling the life from her. She'd struck him repeatedly but he hadn't seemed to notice. She had nearly passed out before he finally snapped out of it as if awakening from a dream.

As she gasped for air, Joe had looked at her with a mixture of confusion and embarrassment. Then he'd turned away and when he turned back he had the restraints in his hands. The look on his face had been one of defeat and resignation. She was now afraid that he would give up on trying to cure himself and would decide that he was too far gone to be saved. If that was the case, then she was a dead woman. She had to get him to try. At the very least, she'd have more opportunity to escape once they were traveling on the road than she had locked in this little room.

The front door opened and Alicia heard a sound like something heavy being dragged. Joe stalked into the room looking excited and agitated. He was not alone. Alicia looked down and saw a frightened woman, naked and trussed up in duct tape, at his feet. She was big and fleshy, zaftig like Alicia herself, only older and white, pale as a newborn. The woman looked up at Alicia, at the chains around her wrists and ankles, the ball gag, the dried blood caked on her mutilated breasts, and she began to scream against the duct tape secured over her mouth.

Joe turned toward Alicia with a wild expression on his face and an erection pressed urgently against the fabric of his pants. He was panting heavily and his pupils were dilated so wide that very little of his irises were visible. He looked like a speed freak wired out of his skull.

"This is for you, Alicia!" The handsome young man knelt down and peered into the Spanish girl's horrified eyes. He wiped her curly raven black hair out of her face and stared at her for a long moment in that peculiar way he had that made her feel like something on a dessert tray.

"The hunger is just so strong. I was afraid I'd kill you tonight if I didn't do something. So I'm going to use her to get me by until we can find the cure together."

Alicia didn't want to know what he meant by "using her" but she could guess. And what she guessed brought tears to her eyes and made her stomach flip. She wanted to try to talk him out of it but he hadn't removed the gag from her mouth and she suspected that was deliberate. He undid the chain that secured her to the wall and dragged her into the bathroom.

"I don't think you want to see this," he said as he closed the bathroom door.

The door latch didn't catch and the door creaked open just a crack. Alicia wished that it hadn't because she couldn't prevent herself from looking, no matter how terrified she was.

She watched as Joe removed all of his clothing. Once again she marveled at how finely sculpted his body was. He walked out of the room and came back with a long skinny knife, a filleting knife. The woman began to squirm as Joe knelt down over her with the blade.

He cut the tape from around the librarian's ankles and knelt down between her thighs. Alicia felt a twinge of jealousy as she watched him lick and suck at the woman's fat pussy. The woman ceased her struggles. Her legs spread wider and her hips thrust forward to meet his tongue. Suddenly, her body began to buck and convulse with what could only have been an orgasm. Then her flesh began to run red.

Alicia could hear the savage snarls and the hideous sounds of ripping flesh as Joe tore at her delicate flower, tearing into her labia with his teeth and devouring huge chunks of the tender flesh. He seized both her thighs, one in each arm, as she began to kick and struggle. The tape fell away from her face and her screams came pealing through the room.

Joe lifted his head for a moment and Alicia could see the rapturous expression on his gore-streaked face as he chewed the bits of vagina he'd torn from the librarian. The woman was still screaming when Joe crawled up her body and began biting at her breasts. He was not nearly as tender with her as he had been with Alicia. He bit deep into the meat of her breasts, tearing off her nipples and devouring the tremendous mammaries in huge gulps of sweet sallow fat streaked with red. He used the knife, sawing away her breasts to get more of the woman's tender flesh off her chest and into his gullet. The woman's anguished cries were more terrible than anything Alicia had ever heard.

Alicia turned away when she saw Joe amputate the woman's entire left breast, exposing the gleaming white bone of her rib cage. He brought the quivering mound of flesh up to his lips and voraciously consumed it. Blood washed over his fingers and down his arm, pouring from his mouth with each bite and dripping off his chin and down his neck. He licked the blood from his lips between bites like sweet nectar, like he was eating a mango or a papaya and not human flesh.

The woman's screams were subsiding, becoming moans and whimpers. She was in shock and dying from the massive loss of blood and the traumatic damage done to her. Alicia turned back to look as Joe turned the woman over.

Where her vagina had been was now just a ragged hole ringed in torn and lacerated bits of flesh. Her breasts were completely gone down to the ribs. Bits of meat lay puddled on the floor amongst the pools of blood. The woman landed on her belly with a wet sticky *swap!* that caused her rotund ass to jiggle. Alicia knew what was about to happen next.

Joe took more time and care here. This most luscious piece of meat, the most prized delicacy, he would not squander. This was to be savored. He began slicing the thick fatty meat of her ass in thin cuts and sliding the tender slivers of meat into his mouth. This lasted for nearly five minutes before he could no longer restrain himself and dove headfirst into her ass, ripping into it just as he had done her breasts. To Alicia it seemed to go on all night.

When the sun rose, Joe lay in a pool of coagulating blood draped across the vandalized corpse of Emma Purcell like a bloated tick, fat off her blood and flesh. He'd completely consumed her breasts, most of her ass, chewed away her vagina and even cut her open and eaten her ovaries, liver, and kidneys. His crowning act of barbarity had been to saw through her sternum, crack open her rib cage, and cannibalize her heart. Drunk off blood and heavy with half-digested meat, he rose drowsily from the floor and turned toward the locked bathroom door. Only it wasn't locked.

In the two-inch gap between door and door frame, Joe spotted two almond eyes wide with shock. He started toward the door and heard Alicia scurry away toward the back of the bathroom. She was terrified.

Joe passed his reflection in the mirror and saw the ghastly, loathsome thing that stood naked in his bedroom, a ghoulish grotesquerie caked in dried blood and gore from head to toe. He smiled and the hideous abomination smiled back at him with teeth blackened with old blood and raw flesh. No wonder Alicia was afraid of him. He no longer bore any semblance to a human. He had transformed the previous night, become whatever detestable monster the virus within him was morphing him into. But what had he become? A vampire? He looked at the blood that covered half the room and drenched his own skin and doubted a vampire would have been so wasteful. Joe stared down at the remains of the librarian. He'd never heard of a vampire doing that to its victim. Serial killers do that . . . and werewolves.

Joe walked into the next room and into the kitchen. He used dish detergent and a sponge to wash the blood from his face, hair, and body. When he was done he mopped the already splintered and warped hardwood floor. He emptied the contents of the bucket and refilled it with more water and Pine-Sol, added some bleach, then dragged the bucket into the bedroom. He thought it would be wise to clean up a little before trying to drag Alicia out of the bathroom. He didn't know how much she had seen through that little crack in the door, but he could at least spare her the further trauma of seeing the aftermath of his passions.

Emma Purcell's mauled and masticated remains disappeared into a plastic bedsheet and a cheap area rug. She was then dragged into the next apartment where her corpse would sit and decompose until Joe could figure out what to do with it. All evidence of her death in that dingy little bedroom was scrubbed with ammonia and washed down the sink. When Joseph turned toward the master bath door, the room looked even cleaner than it had before he killed Emma. The acrid pungency of ammonia and bleach had completely masked the smell of fetid blood.

The beautiful Spanish girl with the full red lips, the caramel skin, the luxurious mane of curly black hair, thick meaty hips and thighs, full breasts, and fat perfectly rounded ass, sat in the bathtub shivering. She rocked back and forth moaning quietly.

"Alicia?"

At the sound of his voice she began to scramble like a trapped animal, trying to claw her way through the shower tiles. Her wrists were still bound but somehow she had gotten her arms from behind her back to the front. Her shoulders were turning blue and Joe suspected that she had dislocated them. Cautiously he approached his traumatized victim. He reached out and carefully removed the ball gag from her mouth.

"Alicia . . . I'm sorry that you saw that. I didn't mean for you to—"

"You ate her! You ate that woman! She was screaming and you just kept biting her!" She began to tremble convulsively as the image of this gorgeous man that she'd once been so excited about sleeping with, cracking open that woman's rib cage and ripping her heart out as if he were shucking an oyster from its shell flashed through her mind. She recalled his face, covered in an oily red mask of blood and tissue, his eyes wild with an unfathomable bloodlust. This man who she'd almost forgiven for chaining her up and biting off her nipples, who she'd begun to fantasize about curing of his psychotic dementia and living happily ever after with.

"Alicia, I'm trying so hard not to hurt you. I don't *want* to hurt you, but the hunger was getting so strong. I-I was afraid I wouldn't be able to control myself. I had to do something!"

Alicia curled up into the fetal position at the bottom of the tub and began to cry.

Joe reached in and lifted her from the tub. He brought her back over to the bed and chained her up again.

Joe scrambled some eggs and made bacon and toast but Alicia would not eat it so he left it by the side of the bed along with fresh water. He emptied the bucket that sat alongside the bed and replaced it, just in case she needed to use it while he was gone.

"I have to go. I'll be back later."

It was far too early for class so Joe walked across campus to the gym, getting there just as the wrestling team was finishing up their weight training and the football players were starting to pile in. Joe was bigger and stronger than most of the players on the team. He knew they thought he was crazy for not playing, but he had more important things to do than run up and down a field chasing a weather-beaten pigskin.

Ignoring the loud laughing and joking from the players, Joe began stacking weight onto the bar. He loaded 225 pounds onto the weight bench to begin his warmup and then proceeded to do two sets of fifteen reps with it. He ended by bench-pressing 405 pounds, doing nearly five hundred on the decline press and 365 on the incline. He then did some curls with 180 pounds and finished with five hundred stomach crunches.

With every grueling set of exercises Joe's mind went inexorably back to Trent. He couldn't get that damned pedophile out of his mind. He had to find him and kill him and that meant he needed to get a car, preferably a van so that he could transport Alicia without having to lock her in a trunk. He had the librarian's wedding and engagement rings and about forty dollars from her purse. The engagement ring was a huge solitaire, at least three carats. Her last husband had probably purchased it for four or five grand. Joe thought he might be able to get seven or eight hundred for it at a pawnshop but more than likely he'd have to settle for five or six hundred, an eighth of its value. That meant some very cheap transportation. If he went to a used car lot it would probably be enough for a down payment.

Joe grabbed a forty-five-pound weight and placed it on his chest as he groaned and strained his way through another fifty crunches. When he stood, his abdominal muscles were wound up tight and starting to cramp. He stretched backward as far as he could to loosen them up before he went to hit the showers. By the time he had undressed and stepped into the shower it was empty. Everyone had hurried to finish washing before he stepped in. He made them nervous. Joe knew that as soon as someone found the librarian's body he'd be the first suspect.

He doubted that anyone had seen him going in and out of the abandoned apartment building. The building was located in a commercial area that closed up at night and he never went there during the day. There were nothing but derelicts and drug addicts down there at night after all the businesses closed and they would not be inclined to speak to the police. That's why he had chosen it. He didn't have to worry about nosy neighbors. Still, everyone knew he stayed at the library late almost every night and he was sure Emma had told others about the type of stuff he read. Besides that, he just hadn't done a very good job at concealing his sexual peculiarities.

No one knew for sure just what his malfunction was, but the general consensus was that the huge psychology student definitely wasn't quite right. His sexual deviancy shone like a beacon whenever he stepped into a room. In many cases it had worked for him, attracting women looking for a new thrill, but now he was sure it would work against him once they found Emma's half-eaten corpse in the apartment next door to the one he was squatting in. Everyone would point the finger at him. Before he left for his trip, he would meticulously wipe down everything in the little apartment and then burn the whole thing to the ground. Everything would be okay. By the time the cops sifted enough evidence from the ashes to connect him to the crime he would be long gone.

Joe started to whistle as he made his way across campus to his psychology class.

Chapter Eighteen

Everyone turned to look at him as Joe walked into the room. The cops had been there. He could tell. They had been asking questions about the librarian and his name had come up. That meant they would be back.

Joe slipped down into his seat and stared defiantly at the professor, waiting for him to begin his lecture. They had nothing on him, not yet anyway, so he still had every right to be there. The professor stared back at him with an expression that was full of questions and suspicion. His hand shook as he raised it to scrawl on the blackboard.

The eyes of his fellow students crawled over Joe's flesh. He imagined he could feel each of their curious stares like a legion of worms trying to wriggle their way into his mind to harvest his thoughts. It made him itch. He scratched the back of his neck as if to rake their stares from his skin. The professor kept looking back over his shoulder at him as he wrote on the chalkboard. Joe knew he had burned that bridge. It was obvious that everyone, including Professor Locke, suspected him of having done something to the librarian. Professor Locke had spent most of his

career profiling and apprehending serial killers. If
anyone could spot the monster in their midst it
would be him. There was no way the professor
would help him now.

"There have been many theories that have tried to
link the compulsion to kill to brain abnormalities.
There was once a theory that murderers possessed
an extra Y chromosome. This was, of course, dis-
proven. There have been theories that have sought
to link early head trauma to violent criminal behavior. Neurologists have even presented CAT scans
that actually showed increased brain activity in the
limbic region of violent sexual offenders and de-
creased activity in other areas of the brain. They
have found that most signature sex murderers were
themselves victims of physical or sexual abuse or at
the very least mentally abused, but then there were
others, like Ted Bundy, who had very normal and
happy upbringings. And then there are, of course,
people who have been abused, who have had brain
traumas, and who have active limbic systems that
don't grow up to murder strangers. So what makes
them do it?"

The professor turned to look directly at Joe.

"Are they just evil?" the professor asked.

Joe raised his hand and he felt the students on either
side of him flinch. Professor Locke stared at Joe's rising arm then looked around the room as if seeking the
class's approval before calling on him.

"Yes, Joseph?"

"Is it possible that it is an evolutionary mutation?"

"A what?"

"An evolutionary mutation, part of natural selection. Man is the only creature on the earth without a

natural predator, except other men. Perhaps as our population explodes Mother Nature has felt the need to select certain individuals to act as population control. Perhaps giving them drives and instincts that other humans don't have, which genetically predisposes them to mass murder—to cull the herd, so to speak. In the wild the weak and the helpless would have died off, killed by other animals, other predators, but civilization and our technological advancements have made for the possibility of even the weakest human beings surviving and flourishing. As a result, a world that was adequate to support small tribes is now populated by nations of millions, smothering the earth and draining it of all its resources; killing it like a cancer. Just three hundred years ago there weren't even a billion people on the planet and now there are six billion. There are more people alive right now than have ever lived. Perhaps nature is just seeking a remedy for the plague. Isn't it possible that murderers are the natural antivirus?"

Joe didn't care about the stares and the whispers. After today he would have to get out of town. This would probably be his last opportunity to pick the professor's brain before the cops came knocking on his door.

"Well, Joe, if what you suggest is true and signature killers are just men who are higher up the food chain than us, not a glitch but an advancement in the natural selection process, then there would be no hope to cure these individuals. There would be no need for the psychiatrist, only the policeman and the executioner."

"Perhaps that's why no one has ever cured one," Joe replied.

"I think I liked your virus idea better. At least that one contained a little hope."

"Yeah, I liked it better too."

The class ended and Joe left the lecture hall and walked quickly to his sociology class. He scoured the campus for signs of police. They had no evidence that the woman was even dead, just that she was missing. Someone probably called when she hadn't shown up for work and they couldn't get an answer at her apartment. He'd parked her car down in the projects at Hunter's Point and caught the bus back home. By the time they found it the car would probably be completely stripped and they would assume she'd been the victim of a carjacking. Except that half the fucking campus was probably telling the cops that Joe hung out at the library every night and he was sure a few of them had seen them at the coffee shop. If they somehow found his apartment they'd find the body. But by then he'd be in Seattle— killing Damon Trent.

Chapter Nineteen

Joe's sociology class seemed to be exploring darker and darker subjects. His constant questions were certainly a major impetus behind the trend but he could not take sole responsibility for it. They'd begun by talking about Indian folklore and the subject of the Wendigo had come up.

"Both the Chippewa and Ojibwa tribes tell a similar story of a fierce warrior who would cut off a piece of his enemy's flesh after defeating him in battle and eat it to gain strength. This warrior soon developed a taste for human flesh and began to prey on his own tribe. He ceased to hunt animals and sustained himself solely on other humans. So the Master Of Life, the Great Spirit, decreed that if he chose to live as a savage beast then he would forever appear as a monster and transformed him into the Wendigo. Now he is said to prowl the forests and frozen wastelands of North America, starving for human flesh.

"They say that anyone who commits the sin of cannibalism will likewise be cursed with the spirit of the Wendigo, becoming a monster that must now eat other humans to survive."

The students were silent as kids sitting around a

campfire listening to a really good ghost story. They seemed to be waiting for the traditional shock ending. Most of them were looking at Joe as if expecting him to suddenly grow hair and fangs.

"Once you become one of these monsters, how do you reverse it? Does it say how they're cured?" Joe asked.

The professor shook his head in exasperation and sighed deeply.

"They aren't cured, Joseph. Once they cross that line and become cannibals, they remain monsters forever."

"But that can't be! There has to be a cure!"

"Settle down. It's only mythology. No need to get yourself all worked up."

Prudence was not one of Joe's strong points and he had once again drawn the snickers and stares of his peers. He lowered his head and crossed his arms over his chest as he settled back into his chair.

The professor continued. "Well, then. Normally in Native American folklore, the ability to take on the shape of animals was used for purposes of spiritual enlightenment, healing, and personal growth. Even evil shape-shifters didn't generally attack and eat humans. This horrific trait was solely that of the Wendigo, and the legend of this creature appears to have been used to warn against the practice of cannibalism."

"Was there any truth to the legends? I mean, did anyone claim to have actually seen one?"

The professor closed his eyes and cupped his forehead in his hands, trying to maintain his composure.

"It's an old legend. And though I'm sure there were a great many who believed in it a century or two ago,

I'd be surprised if anyone gives it much credibility nowadays."

"Well, maybe they should," Joe replied.

He fell silent, his eyes daring the professor to inquire further. The professor stared back with the unasked question lying flat on his tongue.

Did you kill that woman?

Suddenly Joe felt claustrophobic in the little classroom. He stood quickly, nearly flipping his chair over as he snatched up his backpack and made for the door. The professor flinched when the huge sophomore stormed past.

"That's a very disturbed kid," he whispered as Joe left the room and the door shut slowly behind him.

Chapter Twenty

Alicia trembled as she lay on Joe's filthy sheets, which still smelled of blood, sweat, cum, and urine. Her legs were spread wide and bound along with her wrists. She had never been more terrified. The room still stank of death even beneath the overpowering chemical smell of Pine-Sol and bleach. In her mind she could still see the body of the heavyset woman her captor had devoured where it had lain on the floor. The wood where her blood had pooled and co-agulated was now bleached lighter than the rest of the floor. Alicia's ears still rang with the woman's screams, sending shivers up and down her spine. That woman had died in unimaginable pain.

Alicia knew she was going to die next. No matter how kind the big college kid had been to her before he'd left this morning. No matter how he'd tried to reassure her that he would never hurt her that way. The Band-Aids on her nipples said otherwise. She was dead.

Even if he was right about the serial killer virus, that it was something like the vampire or werewolf curse, Alicia was still not convinced they could re-verse its effects. Especially not after last night.

Joe had consumed both blood and human flesh. If he had not been damned before he was certainly damned now and that meant Alicia was fucked right along with him. Still, as long as he believed he could cure himself there was hope for her to escape.

Her wrists were getting infected where her skin had abraded from her daily attempts to wrestle free of the restraints. They would have time to heal now, though. Alicia had given up on trying to break free. She laid her head down on the pillow and dreamt about her father.

In her dreams he came to her, wiped the blood from her stomach, undid her restraints and told her he loved her and forgave her. He looked younger now, though, stronger, as if death had restored his youth. He wiped the tears from her face and kissed her forehead. Then he began to comb her hair. She couldn't remember her father ever being this gentle and nurturing in life. He looked so different now. He looked . . . just like Superman.

Chapter Twenty-one

After leasing the Ford cargo van for their trip, Joe had gone back to the apartment to get Alicia ready to travel. He'd found her in a deep sleep, mumbling to herself. She'd woken up just as he'd started to dress her.

"Joe! I thought . . . I had a dream that my dad was here."

"You looked so happy."

"I was."

Joe knew what she meant. She had been happy until she'd woken up to find herself still locked in an apartment with a murderer.

"We're going on a trip."

"We're going after that child killer, aren't we?"

"Yes. We're going to Washington."

Chapter Twenty-two

The big muscular college kid hadn't been to an SAA meeting in almost a week. And Frank hadn't seen SuperPredator online lately either. His ass still hadn't healed from his last encounter with the gorgeous cannibal. Still, all he could think about was another private moment with the clean-cut muscle-bound man with the hard blue eyes that scurried over every inch of you as he spoke as if sizing you for the kill, eyes that seemed to rip their way inside and invade every inch of you. He wanted him again, but he feared what another session with the SuperPredator might do to him.

He'd had a hard time explaining his wounds at the emergency ward. Luckily he was such a regular that they had barely listened to a word he said. They just called for a psychiatrist to visit with him while they bandaged up his mutilated ass. Once he'd managed to convince the bored psychiatrist that he wasn't suicidal or delusional, he'd been released with a prescription for painkillers and a recommendation to seek professional help. Frank had smiled warmly and left. He'd masturbated to the memory of the pain as he drove himself home, nearly crossing the yellow line into oncoming traffic when he recalled Joe's reaction as he slurped down the sliver of flesh sawed from Frank's buttocks.

It had shocked him to see the man ejaculate by merely tasting a small morsel of his flesh. He'd never felt so loved as he had seeing the pleasure his meat had brought to the big carnivore. The hunger that sprang into the man's eyes after the orgasm subsided had been terrifying but extremely erotic. He wanted to give more of himself to Joe, to see the predator's eyes roll up in his head and his body shudder as the ecstasy of blood and meat erupted from him. It had been obvious that the man had wanted more of Frank . . . much more, perhaps more than Frank could survive. Still, Frank was willing to risk it. He hadn't been able to think of anything else since he'd run in terror from Joe's run-down apartment building.

Reading the cannibal fantasies on the Long Pig site had almost convinced him it was worth losing his life for the experience of being consumed by such a powerful predator, to bind his flesh forever with that beautiful man. Finally, Frank couldn't resist any longer and decided to go visit his SuperPredator again.

He'd had more than a few whiskey sours when he walked brazenly up to the front door of the run-down building and rang the bell to the apartment where Joe was supposed to live. He couldn't imagine that anyone really lived in such a place though, especially not the beautiful well-groomed Clark Kent look-alike. But this was where he'd met him for their little rendezvous just a few nights before. He rang the doorbell a few more times without an answer.

Then he pushed on the front door and it swung open easily, revealing the same dusty old lobby where he and Joe had exchanged flesh and blood for sweat and semen. It was empty and looked like it had been that way since before Frank was born.

"Hello?" Frank called out softly and heard only his voice echoing through the dank stagnant air. The place smelled like a damp moldy basement.

Frank crept cautiously inside and closed the door behind him. The oppressive darkness that swooped in on him, choking all light from the room, panicked him. Without the glare of the streetlights outside it was total blackness. A chill of dread scurried over Frank's flesh, raising goose bumps, as the old building seemed to swallow him in one great gulp. Frank quickly swung the front door open again to let a little light in. Even with the faint light creeping in from the street, Frank had a difficult time navigating his way to the stairs. There was no way he was going to risk climbing into the building's rickety old elevator and getting stuck inside. From the way this place looked it would be decades before anyone found him.

He remembered what apartment Joe had told him to ring and began making his way up the stairs toward it. The alcohol coursing through his bloodstream had made him a little braver than normal, along with the fact that he was as much addicted to the adrenaline rush of fear and pain as he was to that of orgasm. Still, he jumped at every sound as he crept his way up the darkened stairway toward the apartment on the fifth floor.

"Joe! Joe, are you up there?"

He was calling out mostly for the reassurance of

hearing his own voice echo back at him, the one familiar sound in this tomb of squeaking stairs and rats. When he reached the fifth floor he stuck his head out and was assaulted by the odor of urine, fecal matter, and decay. Again he wondered if anyone but a few stray cats, some rats, and perhaps a dog or two, lived in this place. He could see some of the hippies who wandered up and down Haight Street begging for change and reeking of marijuana and patchouli oil living in a place like this, but Joe would have been horribly out of place. Perhaps this was just the place where he took his lovers (To murder and eat? What was that sickening smell?) to fuck.

Frank nearly ran down the hall to room 510. He skidded to a stop just outside the room in which his dream lover was supposed to reside, surprised to find the door open.

"Joe? Are you in there?"

There was no response except for a loud thump from somewhere deeper inside the dingy sparsely-furnished apartment. Frank crept in and surveyed the apartment. It looked like a jail cell. There was only one lamp, a small eighteen-inch television and VCR atop a milk crate, two folding chairs, a table, and the paintings.

The walls were lined with acrylic paintings of figures bathed in red. Frank moved closer to them and realized that the figures in the paintings were not just bathed in red. They were bleeding. Slowly his eyes began to make sense of the chaos on the canvases. The pink and tans represented human flesh. Meat opened up so that the muscle and sinews showed through the skin. The white was bone. And the red was obviously blood. The paintings looked like people turned inside out. And there were pieces missing from them. Some were missing legs or arms. Some were obviously women without breasts. Some had no heads. Some had heads with no faces. Many were of men or women with their sex organs removed. In the place of each anatomical omission was a ragged hole, bleeding down the canvas.

Frank heard the loud bump again. It was coming from the bedroom.

"Joe? Are you okay in there? It's me. Frank."

Frank pushed open the door, saw the woman who was now handcuffed by her wrists and ankles with duct tape wrapped around her mouth. He looked down at her breasts and could see the Band-Aids over her nipples. Whatever had happened, the panic in the woman's eyes told him that it had not been consensual.

There was a slight trickle of blood from a small cut on her forehead, presumably from where she had fallen off the bed. Her ankle cuffs were still attached to a chain in the ceiling that would have made it impossible for her to move more than a few feet from the bed. She was flopping around, trying to get to her feet, and when she noticed the diminutive little man standing there her eyes began pleading with him for help. She held her wrists out and shook them at him, imploring him to remove the handcuffs, but he had no key and was beginning to fear for his own safety. The best thing for him to do, he reasoned, would be to get the hell out of there and call the cops.

He started to back out of the room and the woman's pleas became more insistent. She shook her hands violently at him and pounded her feet on the floor. Her eyes began to tear up with frustration as Frank scuttled backward out of the bedroom. The more panicked she became the greater Frank's resolve grew that he was definitely in the wrong place and in danger of getting far worse than he had bargained for if he didn't leave now.

Frank's eyes darted from the woman to a painting that sat on the floor outside the bedroom. This one was larger than the rest and it was of a voluptuous woman chained up on a bed like this one. Only the woman in the picture had no breasts at all and her chest was opened up like a rose in bloom.

This was the only painting where the face was rendered clearly. It was almost ultrarealistic, like a snapshot. And it was obviously the woman on the bed. The same wounded eyes. The same dimpled cheeks. Only the woman in the painting was screaming in some twisted marriage of pain, terror, and ecstasy. It was a powerful image. Frank wondered if the woman had seen it. It was what her future would be if Frank didn't come back with help. The smell of death and decay was now omnipresent and seemed to rise like a warning siren, singeing the hair on his nostrils and telling him to get out.

"I'll get help. I'll be back. I promise," Frank said, speaking both to the woman on the bed and the one in the painting. The present and the probable future.

His eyes drifted away from hers, trying to avoid her silent pleas, and as they swept the rest of the apartment he suddenly recognized himself in one of the paintings. This one was even worse than the rest. It was painted in mostly whites and reds. Bones and blood. Almost all the flesh had been completely removed. Only the face remained, the eyes staring heavenward as if in rapture, the mouth slack as if in the aftermath of orgasm. Frank's legs trembled and threatened to buckle.

Chapter Twenty-three

Joe had just left to get gas in the van when he spotted Frank in his rearview mirror, crossing Folsom Street, heading for the front door of his apartment building. He was instantly enraged by the intrusion. He had given the little man a chance to walk away from this yet here he had come, sticking his nose back into Joe's business, begging to be murdered. He had heard of deer that would bare their throats to the wolf when they became old or sick, seeming to long for the predator's jaws at their jugular to end the misery of their lives. Long pigs apparently had the same fatal instincts.

Circling the block rather than risking a dangerous U-turn in the middle of Folsom Street, Joe felt his adrenaline pulse and his heart rate quicken. The monster was awakening. By the time he made it back to the front of his building Frank was nowhere to be found and the front door was wide open. Joe punched the dashboard so hard that it cracked.

"Shit!" he roared as he pulled the van to a halt and dashed out onto the sidewalk and into the building.

The lobby was empty. Frank must have taken the stairs up to the top floor, looking for him. Joe punched the button for the elevator and waited impatiently for it to descend. His mind went over different scenarios for Frank's destruction and disposal. Joe smiled when he noticed that he had gotten an erection. Perhaps this would be just what he needed to tide him over for the long trip to Seattle. Another fresh kill to snack on. He stepped into the elevator and rode it to the top floor, pacing impatiently, anxious for the kill. The doors whooshed open and Joe stepped out into the hallway, in time to see Frank backing slowly out of his apartment with a trembling hand clutching his mouth and the other thrust out in front of him as if to ward off an attack. Yet the one thing in that building in any condition to attack him wasn't in the apartment but in the hallway behind him.

Joe charged him, sprinting down the hall at full speed with his head low and his arms outstretched as if preparing for a football tackle. The last thought Frank had before impact was just how much the big college kid really did look like Superman, especially when he was flying like that.

Joe leapt forward and struck the little man in the solar plexus with his shoulder, knocking the wind out of him and driving him straight through the door across the hall, which turned to kindling under the tremendous impact. As soon as Frank felt the squishy wetness beneath him, he knew what that horrible putrid smell had been. It hadn't been a dog or a cat after all, rather what the cats and dogs had been feeding on.

Frank screamed as he looked down to see his arm sunk up to the elbow in the flayed and ruptured chest of a female corpse. Her eyes stared at him, frozen wide in terror. Her lips and much of her cheeks had been eaten away, as had most of the flesh on her torso, arms, and thighs. The scant flesh that remained was mottled with purple and blue spots and bloated where it had not been torn open. Frank looked from the feral felines and diseased vermin scurrying away in the dark to the handsome and enraged giant storming through the open door toward him. He was unsure which of the animals had eaten the most of the dead woman's corpse. Fortunately, he had little time to consider it before a fist collided with his jaw and he slipped into darkness.

Joe looked down at the little man who lay draped unconscious over his most recent meal and tried to consider what to do with him. He was still fat off Emma's flesh and though he was powerfully aroused by the thought of fresh meat, he knew that his hunger would be tenfold by the time he reached Seattle. Perhaps if he could somehow keep Frank's body fresh he'd have something to snack on along the way to give Alicia a better chance of surviving the trip. Joe considered for a moment how much easier it was becoming to make these kinds of decisions. He was rapidly becoming a monster, a calculating killer. Still, he reasoned, as long as he kept Alicia alive, as long as he could resist the temptation to devour her luscious body, then the transformation was not yet complete. He was still human, at least partially.

He already had one hostage so it made no difference to him if he had to increase that number to two. If he kept Frank alive then he wouldn't have to worry about his meat spoiling and the rats and other scavengers getting to him the way they'd gotten to the librarian. Most of her meat had been wasted. He'd managed to save a little of her buttocks and organs in his little hotel-sized refrigerator before the rest of her had become cat food. Still, he'd found Emma's cold flesh unsatisfying. He hadn't yet progressed to the point where he could get the same joy out of carrion. He preferred his meat alive and kicking. He'd try to preserve Frank, eating only small rations of his flesh for as long as he could keep him alive.

He dragged the small man's body across the hall, removed all of Frank's clothes, and began wrapping him in duct tape. It disturbed him to see Alicia staring at him as he trussed up the little man so he picked her up and placed her back on the bed face-down. Then he dragged Frank's limp body into the bathroom and slammed the door shut behind him.

Frank didn't awaken until Joe dumped him into the shower and turned the water on full blast. The little man's eyes darted in every direction, seeking a point of reference and an avenue of retreat. He gagged as water rushed into his nose and squeezed his eyes shut as it flooded them. When he felt the hand slide between his legs and lather up his genitals he opened them again.

The huge man was leaning over him and washing him as if he were an invalid. Frank started to protest but then realized that there was a gag over his mouth. Next he noticed the silver tape cinching his ankles and wrists together. His cock sprang to life as the huge hands stroked it with a fistful of suds even as his asshole clenched tight in fear. When he saw the hunger that leapt into SuperPredator's eyes, he tried unsuccessfully to will his throbbing organ to wilt.

Joe began to stroke the man's cock more aggressively. He held it under the shower and washed all

the soap away as the little man's thick penis swelled
to an impressive length and girth. It was beautiful.
Joe wanted to taste it right now. To grind it up with
his blunt little teeth and swallow it. He was mesmerized, watching the impressive organ swell even larger
as the little man struggled in vain to free himself, obviously aware of the purpose for which he was now
being prepared.

Frank felt a bizarre combination of fear, elation,
and deep sexual enjoyment as he considered his
predicament. Naked, bound and gagged, being jacked
off by a gorgeous muscular young man who was apparently a cannibal and murderer who had already
tasted of his flesh and enjoyed it. The giant was staring at Frank's cock with undisguised hunger and
Frank tried hard not to think about what it would
feel like when he inevitably bit it off. Then the cannibal lowered his head between Frank's legs and Frank
felt the man's tongue slide the length of his cock.
Frank felt the orgasm rip through him as the big man
licked and sucked on his cock as if he were tasting
him rather than trying to bring pleasure. Frank's semen doused the big man's handsome face.

The powerfully built cannibal paused to look up
at Frank with cum dribbling down his nose onto his
lips. He licked the man's seed from his lips and
smiled in a way that seemed to be more a baring of
teeth than an expression of joy, then knelt back
down between the little man's thighs.

At the last second Joe changed his mind about biting off the man's cock and instead knelt down and
took a soft, wrinkled, hairy testicle into his mouth
and bit through his scrotum. The little man
screamed as Joe sawed through his nut sack with his

teeth, ripping away the skin and sucking the small round testicle into his mouth, severing it from his body with one bite. Frank was unconscious when Joe dragged him back into the bedroom chewing on one of his rubbery testes, which tasted to him like calamari. Joe was disappointed to see Alicia crying when he entered the room with the little man in tow. Her eyes zeroed in on Frank's hideously wounded, bleeding crotch.

"Don't worry. He's still alive." Joe wiped semen and blood from his chin then sucked the cocktail from his fingertips. Alicia felt her stomach turn.

Joe swallowed hard. He smiled and Alicia watched the big predator's tongue probe his bloodstained teeth for bits of flesh as his grin widened. She started to retch and Joe leaned over and removed the gag from her mouth just before she regurgitated into the bucket on the side of the bed.

Part II

Chapter Twenty-four

Detectives Montgomery and Volario stared down at the smoldering skeleton the firefighters had dragged out of the inferno and tossed on the sidewalk. There was little flesh left on the carbonized bones and half of what remained had been charred to a cinder. They were both grimacing as the smell of burnt hair and barbecued meat roared in their nostrils.

"Do you think this was a homicide?"

One of the firemen who'd recovered the body from the ashes was leaning over Montgomery's shoulder, peering down at the sizzling corpse. He didn't look so good. Shock had leeched all the color from his face and his pupils were wide as bullet holes. Montgomery was afraid the man would vomit all over him. He wouldn't have blamed him. The smell alone was stomach-churning. The detective moved over just in case.

"I'm pretty sure the fire didn't do this," Detective Montgomery said, turning to his partner and pointing down at one of the corpse's legs, which seemed to have survived the fire relatively intact except for the absence of meat on the thigh where something had cut away at it. There were long scrapes on the femur where someone had obviously shaved the meat off of it with a sharp blade.

"Are those teeth marks?" the wide-eyed young fireman asked. There were circular bruises on the calf, with indentations that had broken through the skin where something appeared to have bitten down hard. It looked like a human bite mark.

"Yeah. It kinda looks like it, doesn't it? I think this one was dead long before the fire started."

The young fireman began to weave back and forth, like he was going to faint. With his curly red hair, explosion of blotchy freckles, and dimpled cheeks, he looked more like a choirboy than a fireman. His innocence added a surreal quality to the horror they were slowly piecing together.

"It almost smells sweet, doesn't it? Like barbecued pork," Montgomery said. Then the fireman did turn and drop to his knees, regurgitating.

"It looks like quite a bit of it is missing. There's hardly any meat on it at all."

Even with much of the flesh burnt away it was obvious that something else had been at work on the body. Its chest cavity appeared to have been broken open and gutted. All of the internal organs were missing and all the flesh had been cut away from the chest and pelvis, making it impossible to identify the sex of the body without an autopsy. Volario held a handkerchief over his nose in a vain attempt to stifle the stench of both the burnt corpse and the young fireman's vomit.

Two more firemen came out of the still smoldering building, carrying a half-melted, misshapen, white box: a small apartment-sized refrigerator.

"Uh . . . detectives? I think you should see this," one said.

They opened the little refrigerator; it was stuffed with meat that had cooked inside it during the blaze. It took a second for Montgomery to notice what it was that had the two firemen so spooked. Then he saw it.

"It looks like we've found the rest of the corpse," Volario said as he peered inside. Montgomery just stared without saying a word.

"Who-who would do this? I mean . . . why would someone, why would anyone do something like this?" The fireman looked to be in his midforties, though he obviously spent a lot of time in the gym and could have passed for a much younger man if not for the worry lines in his face. He'd probably seen a lot out here during his many years with the SFFD, maybe even as many bodies as the detectives had, but this was completely beyond his experience. He looked from one detective to the other, waiting for them to offer some explanation. They stared back at him, equally perplexed.

Inside the little refrigerator was a liver and kidney, part of what appeared to be a loop of intestines, thick pieces of meat that could have come from the victim's back and thighs . . . and half of a human face that had been neatly cut away and removed in one piece.

Chapter Twenty-five

The night was completely black except for the occasional headlights from passing cars or the glare of the overhead streetlights tossing eerie shadows across the walls. Frank's limp body bounced and rolled beside her as Alicia lay in the back of the van headed up the California coastline, taking the 101 North toward Tacoma, Washington. She was thirsty, hungry, and scared. Joe was getting worse. He had come back twice in the last couple of hours to take pieces of flesh from Frank's buttocks, which he greedily stuffed into his mouth without waiting until he was at least in the front seat and out of her sight.

Again she'd watched as he masturbated himself to orgasm while chewing on the thick chunks of human flesh. The little man that he was feasting on ejaculated as well and Alicia thought she would scream. This was completely insane.

The last time the van stopped Joe crawled back into the van with them again and cut off the wounded little man's remaining testicle, which she assumed he later consumed as well, though gratefully he'd done so out of her sight. Her fellow captive had not lost his erection during the entire procedure and Alicia was certain that he would have ejaculated again had he still had his testes. His screams of pain were horrific, even more so for their similarity to ecstasy.

Frank was still leaking blood from his many wounds despite Joe's attempt to cauterize the deep cuts with a Bic lighter. The flesh had curdled and blackened and Frank had yelled his vocal chords raw while Joe held the flame to the masochist's ransacked scrotum. The screams had loosened the tape that Joe had clamped over his mouth and Joe had not replaced it before climbing back into the driver's seat and starting the engine. The slender little man drifted in and out of consciousness, mumbling to himself as they drove along the freeway. Alicia kept reminding herself that eventually they would have to stop for gas and then she would have her chance to escape, though the restraints still presented a problem.

The van turned sharply and began to bounce along what was apparently an unpaved road. Alicia was sure that they were on some type of dirt trail. She and Frank accumulated more bumps and bruises as they were tossed around in the back of the van. Frank began to mumble to himself again, delirious with pain. Alicia listened for a moment to his incoherent ramblings. At first it just seemed to be random words thrown out in no discernable order. Then she began to make sense of what he was saying.

". . . Cut cleanly and swiftly. Remove from the chest as quickly as . . . For the best taste it should still be beating . . . when seasoning is added . . . Bay leaves, three garlic cloves, one whole onion . . . one beef bullion cube, cook on a low . . . twenty minutes . . ."

Alicia scampered away from him when she realized that he was reciting a recipe; a recipe for a soup made from a human heart. She hummed to herself to drown out the sound of Frank's ranting and tried to keep track of how long they had been driving off-road. When the van finally rolled to a halt there were no sounds from other cars. No gas pump noises or sounds of pedestrian foot traffic like you would expect to hear at a rest stop. There was only the sound of crickets chirping to their mates in the distance.

Alicia heard the van shut off and the driver's-side door slam. Joe was coming back again.

The van door opened and Joe reached in and scooped Frank up like a sack of dirty laundry. The terrified little man was mumbling about roasted thighs in garlic butter when Joe tossed him over his shoulder and reached a hand out for Alicia. Alicia wanted to tell Frank to shut up, not to give their captor any ideas. She'd seen that glazed look in Joe's eyes often enough to know that it preceded violence. She looked beyond the big man and saw that they were parked in a dark, heavily wooded area. The full moon shone overhead like an omen. A werewolf's moon. There was not another human being in sight. No one to hear them scream.

Alicia shook her head defiantly when Joe motioned for her to take his hand. Then she began to cry.

Something in Joe's eyes softened as he watched the terrified woman sobbing in the dark. She was so beautiful. Something innocent remained untouched within her. Something that her long procession of lovers had not despoiled. Something that even Joe could not corrupt. It humbled him. It was like looking at the face of an angel. He felt like a vicious savage ripping and tearing through the Garden of Eden in pursuit of Eve.

Joe's own face cracked with sorrow and confusion. He withdrew his hand and ran it over his forehead and through his hair. He didn't know exactly what he was about to do, but the monster was roaring and snarling within him, and he was certain that at least one of his captives would not survive a trip into the woods with him. His eyes darted around as he tried to make up his mind what to do. His eyelids shut and Joe let out a long slow breath, composing himself. When he opened them he looked right into Alicia's watery eyes. The monster was quiet now. Now it was just Joseph Miles, looking at the pain and fear of another human being. He tossed Frank back into the van and slammed the door shut.

Chapter Twenty-six

The van stopped again and Alicia could hear Joe step out of the driver's-side door and shut it behind him. She listened to his shoes crunch the dirt as he walked toward the back of the van. She could still hear the sounds of traffic and when he opened it she could see that they were parked in the breakdown lane along the freeway. Joe climbed into the van and she and Frank both tried to wriggle away from him. Joe's forehead wrinkled and his eyebrows knitted together. He looked as if it hurt him that they were frightened of him.

"I know how you feel. I didn't realize it before, but this looks just like the van that Trent stuffed me into when he kidnapped me. Even in midday it was dark back there. I can only imagine what it must be like at night." He could barely look at her. He reached out and removed the gag from Alicia's mouth. "I'm sorry about all this."

"Joe, you have to stop this. You need help. Look at what you've done to this poor man—and that woman. That woman that you . . . you ate!" Alicia shuddered.

"I'm trying to get help. You have to believe me. If I had a choice I wouldn't be doing any of this but I have this curse, this disease! It's driving me crazy! I just don't know what to do!" His eyes searched hers as if he would find the answers within them.

"So you're just going to give in to it? You're going to eat him too—and then what about me? Joe, what if there is no miracle cure out there? What if you kill this Damon Trent guy and the hunger doesn't get any less?"

"I can't think about that."

"You need to think about it! You need to learn to fight it or you'll just keep killing until they catch you and lock you away or kill you!"

Joe leaned back against one wall of the van, deep in thought. He reached out and stroked Alicia's face.

"You are the most beautiful woman I've ever seen. You know that?"

"I don't believe you and I don't think it matters."

Joe reeled back with his eyes wide, visibly stricken by Alicia's harsh words.

"Well, if you weren't so beautiful I would have eaten you already. Believe *that!*"

Now it was Alicia's turn to recoil. She stared at the huge man with the superhero face and was surprised to see him grin back at her and wink. Suddenly she began to laugh. The absurdity of a serial killer who'd just eaten one woman and partially cannibalized the man she'd been riding with for the last few hours, joking about her own probable murder, was the most ridiculous thing she could imagine. Even as she laughed the tears flowed without relent. Joe reached out and wiped the tears from Alicia's eyes as he continued to stare at her like an object of worship. Alicia smiled back even as fresh tears ran down her face.

"I hope I'm more than just a pretty face to you? That's not enough to sustain a relationship you know. I mean . . . you hardly know me," she said. Her voice still shook with fear, but she was trying to remain in control.

"I know that you've been hurt too," Joe said. "I could see it in your eyes from the moment I met you. You're one of the walking wounded just like me. But you've overcome it. You're a fighter. Even in this situation you're holding up pretty well. That alone tells me that you've been through a lot of pain in your life."

"Nothing like this," she said.

"Then like what?"

Alicia went silent.

"Tell me." He took her hands in his and raised them to his lips where he kissed them softly. She began to cry harder now. Her body shook with the force of it. Joe gathered her into his arms and held her. "Tell me."

"I seduced my father and . . . he—he killed himself. He shot himself in the head and it was my fault! I'm a fucking whore just like he said I was! I killed my own father!"

Joe didn't try to pretend to know what she was feeling now or what had motivated her to have sex with her father. He knew that he could never understand what had made her do such a thing any more than she could understand what made him hunger for human meat. Instead he continued to hug and rock her in his arms.

"I forgive you," he said as he cradled her against his chest. "I forgive you."

Joe cried with her as he held her tight against him.

Women were so beautiful when they were sad. Her tears glistened on her cheeks like a string of diamonds as the moonlight beamed through the windshield onto her face. It broke Joe's heart. He leaned down and kissed her dampened skin, licking the salty tears from her eyelashes.

She pulled away from him and wiped her eyes with the back of her hand. She looked up at her captor expecting to see that homicidal lust she'd come to know all too well, but instead she saw a shocking paternal tenderness. His eyes reflected her own sadness back at her as if her pain had wounded him. It was a depth of compassion she would have never expected in such a beautiful monster.

"I forgive you too," she said and surprised herself by meaning it. She knew what Stockholm syndrome was. She'd heard of victims who'd begun to identify with their kidnappers, even falling in love with them, and knew that this was exactly what she was doing, but she didn't care. She was falling in love with a cannibal, a kidnapper, and a killer and it was the most loved she'd ever felt. Whether the look in his eyes was love, lust, or just hunger, no one had ever looked at her that way before, with such passion and desire. No one had ever needed her like that. She leaned forward and kissed him and once again they made love as Frank lay in the back of the van moaning in agony.

"I'll try to fight it. I'll try for you," Joe whispered in Alicia's ear as he lay atop her, inside her, with his erection slowly diminishing after their combined orgasm. He crawled back up into the front seat and drove off without putting her gag back on, though he did handcuff her again.

They talked all the way to Seattle as if they were little more than a couple out for a drive in the country.

"Do you still think this is just some kind of disease you have? You still think that you can cure yourself by killing this guy?"

"I'm actually getting more and more convinced by the moment."

He pointed up at the sky, at the big luminescent face of the full moon hovering just at the end of the road.

"Ever since that moon rose, the hunger has been almost unbearable, just like the werewolf legends. I can feel changes inside me. My canines seem to be getting sharper and longer."

He looked up into the rearview mirror and bared his teeth. Alicia looked at his teeth in the reflection and shrugged her shoulders.

"You may not notice it, but I can feel them growing."

He turned to her and stuck out his tongue. There was a small red gash on the tip.

"I cut my tongue on my own teeth. They don't fit the same in my mouth as they did just last night. And look at my jaw. It's like the muscles are getting bigger, stronger. I feel like I could crush bones with my mouth now. Like soon I won't even need a knife. I'll be able to rip a person apart with my teeth alone."

"You're starting to scare me again, Joe."

"Nothing's changed between us. I promise not to hurt you again."

"But what about him? Are you going to kill him?"

"I don't know if I can stop myself. It's a long drive to Seattle and I don't even have the desire for regular food anymore. I can smell his blood. It's so rich. I wish you could experience it the way I do. The taste. The smell. It's like I can experience his entire life through his flesh. I can absorb it all. All his joys and agonies, his passions and sorrows. It's all there in that smell. It's maddening. I feel like I can smell his thoughts. You know, when I ate that librarian, it was like I absorbed her. Like she became a part of me. Everything she was assimilated with my flesh. I can still feel her inside, in my blood. That's how I know that killing Damon Trent will cure me."

"Why? I don't understand."

"Because I know that he can feel me inside of him too. Because I can still feel him inside of me."

Frank stirred in the back of the van. He was regaining consciousness again.

"Eating Frank is different," Joe said, glancing back at him. Half of the man's buttocks were gone, as were most of his genitalia. The rest of him was mostly skin and bones and hard muscle. None of the tender meat that Joe hungered for. There wasn't a whole lot on him left to eat. He looked back over at Alicia and tried not to think about how wonderful she would taste.

"There's no fear in him. I mean, his fear is different, more sensual. He enjoys it. He can feel the communion, us joining together as one. He wants it. I can feel it. He wants to become a part of me. I wish you could feel it too. The way he does. I wish you could see how beautiful it could be." His eyes crawled over Alicia's voluptuous hips and thighs and lingered on her big heavy breasts. The monster stiffened in his pants and Joe's eyes glazed over, sparkling with hunger as his jaw creaked open and he instinctively licked the tips of his canines before dragging his tongue across his lips. Alicia shuddered and turned away from his ravenous gaze.

"Joe, when you talk like that it doesn't sound like you *want* to be cured."

Chapter Twenty-seven

Damon Trent stared out the barred window and tried to tune out the pandemonium of the other patients as they fought over the TV remote. The television flipped back and forth between Tyra Banks and *Sesame Street*. He tried to quiet the cacophony in his mind as his own lusts spoke to him, seducing him with images of blood and flesh. Damon's mind swirled as the cocktail of antipsychotics and antidepressents in his bloodstream mired his thoughts. He could barely feel the lives he'd consumed over the narcotics. Their whispering echoes were indecipherable to him now. They had faded like yellowed photographs worn away by time. He barely noticed them anymore and with the drugs he could no longer feel their warmth.

At times he imagined that they had never been there at all, that he'd never slaughtered and bled them dry, never drank their blood until it sloshed in his distended stomach, pregnant with life force. At times he imagined that that their blood and souls had finally worked their way through his system and passed through his bowels.

But he knew they were still there. Their blood was

forever bound to his. He felt like Renfield, Dracula's little acolyte, only the souls that Damon had devoured were not those of spiders and flies or even rats and birds. He was in many ways much more like Dracula himself than Renfield. Damon had fed on human lives. Uncorrupted innocent lives, too young to have been sullied by the world, too young to have acquired the taint of lust and hatred. Years ago he had gorged himself on them, on their water-pure essences, until his own blood had burned like molten lava in his veins, searing with their memories and emotions. He had felt like a force of nature then, like a walking, breathing world, like a god. But that was long ago.

They were old lives now, withered and decayed. They no longer burned in his blood like electricity as they had when he'd first drunk their souls through the holes he'd cut and gouged in their flesh. They were dead now. Ghosts. They fluttered listlessly in his empty stomach like butterflies, or rather the protoplasmic phantoms of dead butterflies. Their voices were a tepid draft that raised goose bumps on the back of his neck.

Only one life still warmed him as it traveled his circulatory system. It was only a tiny spark, yet compared to the ghosts it was as radiant as a star and growing stronger. It was from the one he'd only taken a tiny piece of. The one he hadn't killed. The one who was still out there becoming just like him, acquiring lives just as Damon had done himself before they had locked him up and chemically castrated him. He could feel his last living victim drawing closer like a minnow lured by the glow of a luminescent lure right into the jaws of an anglerfish. Only this was no minnow. It was another predator and it wanted to consume him. He knew. But he would consume it first. He needed it to warm his stale blood.

He stuck out his tongue and tasted the air.

"So close," he whispered. He could sense the man drawing nearer, dragging other souls with him. More souls to warm Damon's blood.

Chapter Twenty-eight

They had been on the road for more than ten hours, driving all day and well into the night along Interstate 5. They still had at least another five hours of driving ahead. It was pitch-black now but morning was fast approaching.

Frank was delirious with shock. He lay in the back of the van, slipping in and out of consciousness, ranting incessantly about past lovers and injuries and, most disturbing to Alicia, he kept quoting recipes for the consumption of human flesh. Everything from testicles ceviché to fingers in lemon butter. It was making her nauseous and it seemed to be turning Joe on. Frank regained consciousness for a moment. His eyes cleared and his mind swam through the miasma of pain and fever to reach the surface for a moment. What he had to say was even worse than his ranting.

"Joe? Joe? I know you can't take me to Seattle with you . . . not like this. My wounds are infected and I'm still bleeding. I'd stick out like a sore thumb. I know you're gonna have to kill me before you get there. Please, just do me one favor and let me go the way I want to go, the way I've always dreamed of dying."

"And how is that?" Joe asked. Alicia couldn't believe she was hearing this conversation.

"I want you to roast me alive on a spit, and then I want you to devour every piece of me. Don't leave a single scrap. Promise me that if you do this you won't leave until you've eaten all of me. I don't want the worms and coyotes picking at my remains. I want to become a part of you. I want all of me inside you."

Joe had read long pig fantasies on the Internet for months, and being roasted on a spit was the number one fantasy. For all their talk and all their teases and come-ons, he'd always doubted that any of the message board masochists had the nerve to go through with it. It was hard to imagine that even such a severe masochist as Frank would really want to undergo something so brutal and painful. Joe had read all the sweaty dialogues between long pigs and eager chefs with skepticism. Who would seriously offer their flesh up to be consumed by a stranger they met on a message board? And to be roasted alive at that? Yet here was one of them—and he was absolutely serious. Joe was positive of the man's sincerity and he was certainly willing to give the little man his fantasy and fulfill his own in the process.

"I promise."

"No, no, no! You can't do this!" Alicia said. "You can't be serious! You can still get him to a hospital. He can live. You don't have to do this. This is crazy!"

"It's already done. He's right. I'd have to kill him anyway."

"How the hell are you going to cure yourself if you keep giving in to the curse and killing people?

Every time you eat somebody it'll only get stronger and harder to quit."

"This isn't a twelve-step program. Every time my stomach growls or my dick gets hard you're both in danger. And the more I fight it, the more the hunger grows, the more I'll need to eat to calm the hunger when it eventually overcomes me. Like I said before, it's either him or you. And in a few hours I'll be hungry again. I'll be very hungry. I've been fighting it for hours already. A decision has to be made soon."

"Oh my God. Oh my God. Oh my God." Alicia rocked back and forth with her knees drawn up to her chest and her handcuffed wrists tucked tight between neck and shoulder, staring at Frank, who seemed to have slipped back into dreamland and was grinning stupidly as he once again began quoting recipes. She imagined him with a skewer going through his ass and out his mouth, twisting on a rotisserie, and her stomach heaved.

In Portland, Oregon, they pulled off I-5 onto Patton Road. Joe drove along the dark road for a mile before he noticed a gas station under construction and leapt out to search the solemn structure for supplies. He came back with a piece of rebar six feet long and tossed it into the back of the van. They stopped again at a little store that sold camping supplies and Joe bought two bags of charcoal, some lighter fluid, and some hickory chips. The hickory chips bothered Alicia more than anything. They had obviously been purchased to add flavor.

They entered Forest Park and the darkness redoubled, swallowing them in a stygian gloom. Joe drove another half hour into the park before he stopped the van.

The back of the van was now tacky with Frank's blood, urine, and excrement as his body evacuated its contents. Joe wrinkled his nose as he hefted the little man onto his shoulders and charged off into the woods. Before he'd left the van, he'd once again bound Alicia's ankles and switched her handcuffs to behind her back so that she wouldn't be able to escape. She sat in the dark praying for Frank.

Joe carried his half-conscious meal deep into the park before dropping him to the ground in an area that was obviously used for cookouts. There were small metal barbecues bolted to concrete slabs next to picnic tables. They were far too small, however, for what Joe had in mind. Then he spotted the hole just on the edge of the picnic grounds. It was about five feet wide and four feet deep and filled with ashes from a charcoal fire.

Someone had themselves a luau, Joe thought as he considered his good fortune. He'd have to make it a little bigger, but it would work. All that remained was to prepare Frank.

Joe returned to the man lying in the grass and knelt to pick up the rebar. He then walked over to the picnic tables and began sharpening one end of the steel reinforcement bar on the edge of the concrete slab. It took him nearly ten minutes before it was sharp enough for his purposes. Frank was wide-awake when the huge predator walked back over to him.

"There's some Ruffies in my back pocket. Rufinol. It will dull the pain and slow my heart rate so that I don't bleed to death too quickly. It's in my pocket."

Joe reached into Frank's pocket and pulled out a small box that looked like cold medicine but was covered with Spanish writings.

"You sure you don't want me to kill you first? You really want to be alive for this?"

"I want to watch you consume me. I want to see the pleasure on your face when I become a part of you."

Frank swallowed a fistful of Rufinol and in minutes he was drowsy and sluggish. Joe shrugged his shoulders and rolled him over on all fours. He spit on a finger and then slid it into the man's anus to lubricate it as best he could.

"This is going to hurt," he said as he slowly began threading the sharpened steel bar up through the man's rectum. Frank began to scream, thrash, and convulse against his restraints as the bar forced its way into his anus, tearing the soft tissue and ripping deep into his rectum, puncturing his small intestines and leaking septic fluid into his bloodstream, throwing him into anaphylactic shock. Blood and fecal matter began to spray out of his vandalized asshole like a faucet, drenching Joe's arms and chest in a chunky brown and red deluge. Ignoring the explosion of excrement and gore, Joe shoved harder and the rod pierced Frank's stomach as it plowed through him.

Frank was hyperventilating. His blood pressure rose quickly and then began to plummet as bile and stomach acid poured into his thoracic cavity and began eating away at his liver and lungs. He tried to curl up into the fetal position but the rigidity of the steel bar would not allow him to bend.

"I can angle it toward your heart and kill you quick."

"No! Don't!" Frank said as he began to shiver. His pulse rate dropped further. He was dying from shock. His eyes were now fixed and dilated as the gut-wrenching agony assailed his nervous system in response to the gouging, puncturing, and tearing of his vital organs. Then the Ruffies went into full effect, dulling the pain only marginally but enough to stabilize his blood pressure and heart rate. He was slowly coming out of shock though he was now completely paralyzed, unable to offer even the slightest resistance even if he'd been inclined to do so. It was a good thing too. The next part would be the worst.

Joe angled the bar to the right and slightly up and shoved with all his might. The steel rod slid along the inside of Frank's rib cage, narrowly missing the heart and lungs before exploding out of the top of his shoulder. Frank's eyes went wild in lieu of the scream his paralyzed vocal chords were unable to form.

It was nearly half an hour before Joe returned to the van. His arms and chest were covered in gore. But not his face. He hadn't eaten yet. He reached in and grabbed Alicia, lifting her onto his shoulders. That's when she smelled the smoke permeating his clothing. Hickory smoke, like a barbecue.

Joe carried her almost a mile into the park before she spotted the fire. The big carnivore had dug a pit and filled it with charcoal as if he were roasting a Khalua pig. Frank lay across the open pit with the piece of rebar going straight through him. His eyes were glazed in horror but he was still alive and in agony. His skin baked and sizzled as the flames licked at his flesh. The hickory smoke wafted from the open pit. Alicia began to cry, then her stomach growled in hunger, reacting to the delicious smell of roasted pork, and she regurgitated in revulsion.

"Oh my God! You're cooking him alive! He's in so much pain! Don't let him die in pain!" Alicia sputtered out as vomit and bile burned its way up her throat and out onto the cool grass. She began to fight against her handcuffs, trying desperately to reach the agonized man burning on the flaming pit. She wept uncontrollably and screamed out to the night. Joe stalked over to her and grabbed her by her jaw. His piercing blue eyes burrowed into her skull as he turned her head to face him.

"Look at him, Alicia! He's already dead! This is how he wanted to die. You can't save him. He's already been saved."

"Then kill him quickly! Don't just let him suffer!"

"He'll be dead soon enough. But first he'll get his wish. I promised him, Alicia. I owe him this much. Let him have his fantasy."

"*His* fantasy? This isn't about *him*. All of this is about you! It's *your* fantasy! You're the one killing him. You're the one who's going to eat him! And what about me? What about me, Joe? Is this what you're going to do to me? Truss me up like some pig and roast me on a spit?"

"Alicia—"

"You're evil! You're just fucking evil! You don't want to be cured. You just want to stay a monster! You're enjoying this! How could I have possibly thought I loved you? After all that you've put me through. How could I have possibly thought that you wouldn't hurt me? That maybe you loved me too? You're going to kill me just like all the rest!"

"I-I—" Joe let her go and turned to look at Frank. The man was suffering. His entire body convulsed as the flames boiled the blood in his veins. But all Joe could think about was how delicious the man looked. How good he would taste. Joe knew then that his humanity was almost gone. The only person he still felt anything for other than hunger and lust was Alicia.

Alicia curled up on the cold wet grass and began to sob. Joe felt her pain reach out to him and he crushed it before it could lodge in his heart. He knew that his increasing attachment to Alicia was becoming a hindrance. His massive muscles tensed beneath the fabric of his shirt as he stared down at the helpless woman weeping at his feet and pulled the knife out of his ankle strap.

She looked so beautiful in the dark, her black hair shimmering in the campfire and starlight. So innocent and vulnerable. The predator in him howled. His monster leapt to life. He imagined fucking Alicia hard in the grass and his stomach roared in response. Quickly the fantasy changed to one of him sawing off her calves and quadriceps and greedily cramming them into his mouth. There was now no difference between the two appetites.

Frank's eyes were glazed in shock and rapturous anguish. He was far away, barely alive. Joe leaned in to saw off a piece of his hamstring with the serrated diver's knife.

Joe stared into the dying masochist's eyes as he consumed his blackened meat in great gulps and thought he saw a contented smile cross the man's face before he shivered one last time and expired. Joe shivered as well as he felt the man's essence slide down into his belly. That familiar ecstasy washed over him, as he felt all that the man had been merge with his flesh. Joe cut again, tore off large hunks of Frank's flesh with his bare hands, barely even chewing before swallowing them, singeing his fingers in the broiling flesh, eager to consume every ounce of the man's dwindling life force. Instantly he felt an entire lifetime of Frank's joys and sorrows, including the voluptuous agony of his death charge through him like a lightning bolt. It was overwhelming. Joe fell to the ground, writhing with an orgasm that threatened to break him apart as waves of excruciating pleasure ignited his nervous system.

From where Alicia lay in the grass she watched Joe's orgiastic convulsions with awe and confusion. Human flesh was so much more to him than mere sustenance. He seemed to be possessed. He was in the throes of a passion that defied description as he ripped poor Frank to shreds. A part of Alicia longed to know such intensity of pleasure herself. Her mouth watered and a moistness spread between her thighs. Another part of her longed to inspire it, once again jealous that another person had given such ecstasy to the beautiful cannibal she was beginning to think of as her own.

With her arms and legs still bound she began to inch her way closer to the campfire, inhaling the mouthwatering aroma of hickory-smoked human flesh. Joe now had his pants down around his thighs and his enormous erection in hand, furiously masturbating as he continued stuffing steaming handfuls of broiled flesh into his slavering mouth. He looked down and spotted Alicia, who was now almost at his feet. Instantly he recognized the hunger and lust in her eyes.

After shedding the rest of his clothing he dropped beside her and offered Alicia a piece of Frank's blackened calf muscle.

Stockholm syndrome, Alicia thought, even as she opened her mouth wide to receive the gift.

Without chewing she slurped down the hot flesh and felt a chill vibrate through her as the horror of what she had just done gripped her. This was soon followed by a tingle of arousal at having done it in full view of her lover and captor. Joe began ripping off more of the flesh and feeding it into Alicia's mouth as he kissed and caressed her neck and breasts, building her passion. Boiling-hot blood dribbled down her neck and cleavage as she consumed more and more of Frank's corpse. Joe lapped the stream of liquid life from her skin and used his knife to cut the duct tape from around her wrists, then her ankles, allowing him to kiss his way up her thighs to her moistening sex.

Lost in rippling waves of ecstasy, Alicia blindly reached out and ripped off another piece of Frank's flesh. Even without looking at it she knew what she had grabbed as soon as her hands closed around it. Still she tugged hard until it tore free. Joe rose up from between her legs and slid himself inside of her as she brought Frank's severed penis to her lips. She clenched the charred organ between her teeth and Joe bit down on the other end as he thrust his own hardened flesh deep between her thighs. They reached a mutual screaming, snarling release almost immediately as they shared the exotic delicacy. Alicia collapsed into the arms of her captor and together they lay in the glow of the campfire, watching Frank's remains sizzle, crackle, and burn to a charcoal cinder.

Twenty-nine

The two detectives had been waiting all day for the autopsy report from the body they'd found in that old apartment building south of Market Street. They both had a bad feeling about it.

"You think that could be our librarian?" Volario asked.

"No reason to assume that yet," Montgomery said. "That building was pretty far from the campus."

"Yeah, but did you see her shoes? Kenneth Cole. Not Prada, but not exactly Payless either. Pretty nice for a homeless woman or a streetwalker."

"Which still leaves a whole host of other possibilities. A lot of people get killed in this town besides prostitutes and derelicts."

"Yeah, but anybody with shoes like that has to have a job and that means somebody would miss her if she was gone. And the only recent missing person we have matching someone of that height and body type is the librarian."

"Height and body type? We don't even know if that was a woman yet. And how could you tell if she was big or small with half her flesh missing?"

"The leg. Some slim model type wouldn't have a

leg that thick. And she was still wearing those Kenneth Cole pumps, which would lead me to believe it was probably a woman."

"You know as well as I do that that's no safe assumption in this town."

The phone rang and they both reached for it at the same time. Montgomery got to it first.

"Detective Montgomery here. Yeah? Finally! What did you find? And did you get a match? Damn. Okay. I'll be by to pick up the report later. Thanks for the call."

"What? Was that the lab? What did they say?"

"They matched the librarian's dental records to the corpse."

"I knew it!"

"And they also confirmed the presence of saliva in some of her wounds. Those were human teeth marks. In case there was any doubt, we've definitely got a serial killer on our hands."

"Not a serial killer. Not according to the FBI. He won't be classified as a serial killer until he kills three more people. Right now all we have is a homicidal sexual predator with one victim."

"You got any doubt that there are more victims out there or that there will be?"

Montgomery sighed. "Nope. You're right."

"I guess we need to take a trip back to the college?"

"We need to talk to that kid they were all talking about. That Joseph Miles. Everyone we spoke to said he'd probably killed her and that was before we even knew she was dead."

"That's just because they think the kid's weird. He's probably just one of those death metal gothic freaks that like to act dangerous and mysterious to impress girls."

"Yeah, that could be. But that's probably what the cops in Columbine thought about those Trench Coat Mafia kids before they went on their murder spree. For some of those kids it's more than just a fashion. Some of them really are disturbed."

Thirty

Professor John Locke had spent all morning answering questions from the police about his student, Joseph Miles.

"You say he was obsessed with serial killers? How could you tell? I mean, this *is* a course about serial killers. One could say the same thing about you or anyone else who attends your class."

Detective Montgomery was a large, athletic-looking black man with a short Afro and sideburns. He wore a midlength leather coat and dark sunglasses that he had a habit of tilting down to the tip of his nose when he spoke so he could look over the top of them directly into your eyes. He looked like something from a seventies blaxploitation film, a poor man's Shaft. His eyes were deadly serious, though, and he spoke in clear, crisp tones like a newscaster or a politician and not the slang drawl you would have expected looking at his haircut.

His partner was a middle-aged Spanish-looking guy who wore a pin-striped suit that looked like someone had fried a hamburger on it. What hair remained on his balding cranium was pulled back into a ponytail barely the length of a thumb. He looked more like a mafioso than a cop. He didn't shake hands or introduce himself when they walked in but immediately walked over to the bookcases on the wall and began scanning the titles.

Professor Locke followed the greasy-looking detective with his eyes while he answered Detective Montgomery's questions.

"So what made this kid any different from the rest of you?" the detective continued.

"Joseph took it all very personal. Whenever you suggested that these people were just crazy or evil he became very defensive, even hostile. He had a theory that there was a virus that creates signature sex murderers."

"And what did you think of that?"

"It's ridiculous. But I didn't want to discourage the boy so I told him to continue researching it and if he could find proof of his theory I'd give him an A for the year."

"Perhaps he was doing research when he killed that librarian?" Detective Volario asked, seeming to take interest in the conversation for the first time.

The professor glared at him and shook his head in annoyance as if he were speaking to an ignorant and petulant child.

"That's a rather extreme supposition. People don't kill to get good grades. They kill because of severe psychological problems."

"You mean he's crazy?"

"Not legally, no. At least, there's no way I could know that without testing him. But even if he's innocent, and please remember that he very well may be, I still wouldn't turn my back on him. He's got a lot of problems."

"You act like we're planning on lynching him or something," Detective Volario said with a sneer. He was holding a large volume titled *A Criminal History of Mankind*. "You read all these books, Professor?"

"No other reason to have them," Professor Locke replied.

"I guess it's no wonder that you attracted one of these monsters to you then."

The professor ignored him. "Do you have any other questions, Detectives?"

"Just one more. Did you do any experiments to test out his theory, that he had some kind of serial killer virus?"

"No. If he had come to me with a more apodictic theory I would have given it more credibility, but what he was proposing was just plain ludicrous."

"Apodictic? What does that mean? I dropped out of college, Professor. You're going to have to speak a little more simplistic for me."

Professor Locke crossed his arms over his chest and smiled.

"It means demonstrably true."

"Yet he claimed to be the living proof of the theory?"

"But at the time I didn't know he was talking about himself. I assumed it was just general speculation."

Detective Montgomery stepped closer to the professor until his breath was in the man's face.

"That's funny, Professor, because all the students we spoke to said it was quite clear that he was referring to himself when he spoke about this virus theory. Even you said he took it all very personal. So you didn't bother to do any research at all to see if maybe he was suffering from some curable illness?

You didn't bother to contact the police or even a psychiatrist or a virologist? I mean, you're a prominent criminologist, a psychologist, a former FBI profiler who's worked on dozens of cases. If you had called us up and told us you had a student in your class that you suspected might be a killer we would have taken it seriously."

"But how the hell could I have known for sure?"

"It was your job to know. That's how you made your living when you were with the FBI, right? Telling all us ignorant locals how to spot killers? Yet, you let one sit right in front of you every day without saying a peep to anyone and without trying to get him any help. You just let him get sicker and sicker until he eventually murdered someone?"

"You don't know that it was him."

"But you do. Don't you? I can see it all over your face. You know it was him. You know you fucked up. And right now you're probably thinking of how this fuckup is going to affect your reputation and your career."

Detective Volario stepped up beside his partner. "My partner's right. You fucked up big time. If I was you, I'd do everything I could to help us catch this guy and restore your reputation before this gets out. 'Killer Student of Noted FBI Profiler.' That's a headline you don't want."

"I've got an apodictic theory, Professor. I believe this student of yours is going to kill a lot more people."

Detective Volario picked up a book from the shelves. The title on the spine was the same as the title of the course, *Abnormal Psychiatry: Serial Killers and Why They Do It.*

"Is this your book? It has your name on it. You wrote this, right?"

"Yes, I wrote it."

"Wow. I bet this is really going to fuck up your sales."

The professor opened his mouth to reply but nothing came out but a helpless squeak. The detectives scowled contemptuously and shook their heads in disgust before turning their backs on him and walking out the door, dropping their cards on his desk as they exited.

The detectives had just left when the phone rang. Professor Locke didn't recognize the voice immediately.

"Professor Locke?"

"Yes, and who am I speaking to?"

"It's true! My theory is true!"

"Who is this, please?"

"It's me, Joseph. Joseph Miles. Your student? Remember I had a theory that serial killers suffer from a transmittable disease like lycanthropy?"

"Do you realize that you are the prime suspect in a murder, Joseph? The police are looking for you in connection with the death of the campus librarian. They found her body in an apartment building downtown after it burned to the ground. There are witnesses who say that you lived there. The cops have been all over campus interviewing students who say you were obsessed with vampirism and cannibalism. Apparently the victim was mutilated or disfigured in some way that further links her to you. Your picture has been in the newspaper. They're convinced that you did it."

"I know, I know. But listen, I think we're really onto something here!"

"We? I want no part of this. I'm calling the police as soon as you hang up!"

"You don't understand, Professor. I'm sick! I contracted this disease when I was a kid. I was kidnapped by a child killer and I survived. Only, he passed his curse to me. Now I've passed it on to someone else!" His rambling sounded almost delighted.

"What are you talking about, Joseph? Where are you? You need to turn yourself in."

"I can't. Don't you see? If I'm right and the disease is transmittable then there's a cure and I think I've found it!"

"Joseph, you are sick."

"Professor, you have to listen to me. There's this girl that I bit—"

"You bit someone! Oh my God, Joseph!"

"Yeah, but I didn't kill her. Anyway, last night *she* took a bite of human flesh and loved it! She has the hunger now just like me! I passed on the virus. That proves my theory! Which means that all I have to do is track it back to the original host, the carrier, and I can put an end to it for good. I can cure us both and probably others that he's infected."

"Listen, Joseph, the fact that your girlfriend took a bite out of someone and got off on it is not proof of a virus but only proof that you've passed your fantasy to someone else and probably screwed this girl's head up pretty badly. She identifies with you so she's sharing your delusion. It's a common occurrence in killers. Many of them work in pairs, from Leopold and Loeb to the Hillside Stranglers and even

Bonnie and Clyde. There've been many cases of serial killers using their wives or girlfriends to lure prey. They feel helpless and trapped and so they begin to side with their abuser, to identify with them, even going so far as becoming their accomplices in future murders. It's a defense mechanism, nothing more. Gary Heidnick used a girl to lure other girls to his basement to be tortured, raped, and murdered. Without him she'd have never harmed anyone and once he was locked up she never hurt anyone again. Joseph? Joseph, are you still there?"

The solemn whine of the dial tone abraded his eardrums. He slowly lowered the phone back into its cradle, then picked it up again and dialed the Centers for Disease Control. He had some research to do.

Thirty-one

After spending nearly an hour in traffic trying to cross the Bay Bridge during rush hour, Detectives Montgomery and Volario pulled up in front of the modest upper-middle-class home of Lionel and Virginia Miles, Joseph Miles's parents. The elder Miles had worked as a construction superintendent for one of the largest homebuilders in America for the last twenty-five years until his recent retirement, and his home had been built by the same company. It was two stories high with a dash stucco finish painted a solemn gray, with decorative stone around the doorway and on the courtyard walls. An ornate iron gate hung at the entrance. The door was a sturdy hand-carved oak that must have cost well over two thousand dollars, but he'd likely purchased it at a sizeable company discount.

Detective Volario put on his most endearing smile and knocked on the front door. His warm, friendly smile hit a brick wall. Lionel Miles opened the door and stared down at him as if he were a particularly annoying parasite in need of a good swatting.

It was readily apparent where Joseph Miles had acquired his height. His father towered over the two detectives. Even with his potbelly and graying hair he looked as if he could give the two of them more than they could handle. His arms were thick with muscles hardened by years of hard labor and his chest was broad. He looked like a professional wrestler or an old-time blacksmith. His face was like a piece of worn leather.

"What the hell do you want?"

"Sir, my name is Detective Volario and this is Detective Montgomery. We need to ask you a few questions about your son."

A scowl creased his face. "Well, I haven't heard from the boy since he went off to college." He began to close the door.

Montgomery placed a hand on the door and held it open. The old man pushed against it but the detective held it firm.

"We still need to talk with you. It'll only take a moment. Do you mind if we come in?" Montgomery stuck a foot in the doorway but the old man moved to block him from entering.

The large black detective and the even larger old man stared eye to eye for a long, tense moment. The air bristled with hostility. Lionel Miles had to have been in his midfifties but he was no less formidable for his years. Veins stood out in his neck and forearms as his body tensed. His eyes bore down on the detective, sizing him up, then suddenly the old man wilted. He turned and stalked back into the house, leaving the front door open.

"So, what do you want to know about my boy?"

The detectives looked at each other and let out a deep sigh of relief. For a moment there they were sure they were going to wind up going toe-to-toe with the big guy, and they weren't exactly confident how such a battle would have turned out.

"Your son may be a material witness in a murder and we need to locate him."

The old man's eyes narrowed in suspicion. "You mean he's a suspect, don't you?"

"Why do you say that?"

"Why else would two detectives show up on my doorstep willing to take me down to find out if the kid is hiding in here or something?"

"We weren't going to—"

"Save it. We both know you were."

"All right, so *is* the kid here?"

"I told you before. I haven't heard from him since he left for college. We ain't real close."

"Then you won't mind if we search the house?" Volario asked, turning to look around the room.

The living room was sparsely furnished but clean. There was a fifty-two-inch flat-screen TV tucked into a built-in wall unit, along with a surround-sound stereo system and DVD player. Across from that was a leather couch and a plush leather recliner. There were few pictures in the room. No family portraits. Not a single picture of their son. Not so much as a wedding photo. Knives adorned the walls, though. A samurai sword, a British saber, a Scottish broadsword, an Indian Ghurka. Montgomery took it all in without a word.

"Now if you want to search the place, you'd better get a warrant. Either that or you're going to have to knock me down."

"Relax, big fella. Just a few more questions and we're on our way."

"You've got my attention. So go ahead and ask."

"You don't seem very surprised that we're here. Any reason you think your son might be involved in something like this?"

"Something like what? You haven't told me what you think he's done yet."

"We found a librarian from his school murdered. Mutilated and sexually assaulted. He was the last person seen with her before she disappeared."

The detectives were shocked by the expression that burst onto the old man's face. His chest swelled up and it was obvious that he was struggling to suppress a smile. At first Montgomery was perplexed. Then he realized what he was seeing on the man's face. It was pride.

"No, Officers. There's no reason I would think my boy would be capable of something like that. Joe's soft. He used to wet the bed when he was a kid. He ain't no killer. Don't let all those muscles fool you. His momma spoiled that kid rotten. I'm surprised he ain't turn out to be one of them faggots you see runnin' all over town, kissin' and holdin' hands. Now if you excuse me, the missus'll be home from the market anytime now and she's not real fond of visitors."

"Well, thanks for your cooperation," Volario replied with a look of disappointment.

The detectives walked out of the house and were not surprised when the door slammed shut behind them.

"Man, that guy was creepy as hell. Maybe we should be looking at *him* for this? Did you see all the knives and shit on his walls?" Volario's eyes were wide and he was breathing hard. His hands shook as he raised a cigarette to his lips and groped in his pockets for his lighter. He looked as if he'd just been in a gunfight.

"If Joseph Miles is our guy, then I can certainly see where he got it from," Montgomery added, looking over his shoulder.

Thirty-two

The Tacoma skyline filled the windshield as Joe rolled into town with Alicia curled up in the front seat, looking well fed and content just as the first nine-to-fivers were beginning to scramble from the nest to catch the early worm. Joe stopped the van at a gas station and ran in to get directions to the psychiatric hospital.

"You visiting someone or checking in?" asked the long-haired, flannel-shirted, grunge-rock reject who worked the cash register. He had beautiful greenish blue eyes like seawater. Joe wondered how those vibrant orbs would taste and imagined sucking them out of his skull like boiled oysters. The boy waited for a response to his little witticism and seemed to grow nervous when Joe merely continued to stare into his eyes.

"Uh, okay, yeah. The hospital's down past the airport heading toward the center of town. You can't miss it."

Joe smiled, turned, and walked back out to his van.

Joe drove the five miles into the center of town and had no trouble finding the hospital. He drove past and continued farther into the city. He needed to find a place to hide Alicia.

Alicia snuggled up beside him. She was still bound but Joe had allowed her into the front seat. He trusted her more now. Even as her heart filled with an affection that she assumed was love for the monstrous predator beside her, shame colored her cheeks. She had eaten a man and enjoyed it.

She didn't know if Joe was right. Perhaps he *had* somehow passed his sickness on to her when he had bitten her. But she doubted it. She had eaten Frank only to be closer to Joe. She wasn't exactly hungering to bite into anyone else. There wasn't that all-consuming appetite working within her the way it had worked inside Joe, twisting his guts as if he were starving. She couldn't have reached orgasm just from tasting poor Frank's flame-broiled cock the way Joe had, not without Joe's organ pounding in and out of her. She wouldn't have tasted Frank's flesh at all if she had not wanted to get closer to Joe, to understand the passions that drove him and perhaps to share them, if he hadn't made it look so sensuous. If he hadn't looked so powerful and sexual as he stroked his huge cock and crammed pieces of Frank into his mouth. If she hadn't been such a slut to have lusted after and now possibly to have fallen in love with the murderous psychopath, there was no way she would have eaten poor Frank.

Why do I let myself do these things? she wondered, and was shocked when Joe answered as if he had been in her head listening to her doubt herself.

"You know why you get off on being with me? Because you're a slut. But that's why I love you. I'm a slut too. We're both whores and so what? We are what we are. Fucking makes you happy so why shouldn't you fuck? Why should you feel guilty about it? Is there anything that makes you feel more alive than having a fat cock between your thighs? No. Nothing except maybe having one in each hole. And what's wrong with that? You've let society make you hate yourself for your appetites. You hate yourself for enjoying life. That's stupid. Be a slut and be happy," Joe said, waving his hand at her dismissively.

Alicia was shocked. Part of her wanted to listen to him and to know the type of freedom he was talking about. The other part was appalled and wanted to slap the shit out of him.

"I'm not a slut!" she hissed, eyes glistening with outraged tears.

"Yes you are, Alicia," Joe replied without taking his eyes off the road. "And I love you for it. We could never be together if you weren't."

"Bullshit! This fuck-society crap is just another way for you to justify giving in to your own appetites. Eating people, people that you know and claim to love!" Her eyes raged over his face as if seeking a way into his head. Joe held his eyes fixed on the road as if afraid to face his accuser. "You're just saying all this shit because you don't really want to change! You're starting to like it. You're addicted and you're afraid of how boring life would be without the high you get from eating other human beings. I know. It's the same way with me and sex. It's the only thing that makes life worth a damn to me and I can't imagine living one night without it. And you're afraid. Now that you're here you're scared to death of confronting that crazy man again."

Joe's face darkened and his jaw tightened. The muscles flexed as if he were biting down on something too hard to penetrate. Now that she was really looking at him, his jaw really did look like it had gotten bigger.

Thirty-three

Professor Locke had been on the telephone for hours and was amazed at what he was hearing. "You mean it's possible?"

"Theoretically? Yes. But there's simply no proof. And you say a college kid came up with this theory?"

"He claims to suffer from it."

"Fascinating."

"They think he may have killed someone. Ate them alive."

"My God!"

Doctor Wilfred Dougherty worked in the Neurology department at the Centers for Disease Control in Atlanta. Locke's call had been transferred to him after the professor had been laughed at or hung up on by nearly everyone else.

"You know, there was a police forensic psychologist who put forth a theory that brain trauma in the early developmental years could be found in as many as 73 percent of all serial killers. You could see increased activity in the limbic system of the brain. It even showed up on CAT scans."

"So what happened with that?"

"There were an equal percentage of normal, nonhomicidal people in the community who showed the same brain abnormalities. Almost every kid falls off a swing or gets hit in the head with a baseball at some point. But they don't all grow up to be serial killers. But this is the first time I can recall hearing a theory of a bloodborne pathogen that affects the limbic system so severely that it stimulates the human prey-drive, basically creating a human predator. It's like something from a horror novel."

"But you say it's possible?"

"Well, the area of the brain that we call the limbic system, actually the limbic basal-ganglia thalamo-cortical circuit or visceral brain, controls our flight-or-fight emotions as well as our sex drives. It's involved in storing memories and creating emotions and is thought to play a central role in processing all impulse-related information. A disease that could affect the limbic system and increase serotonin levels in the amygdala, the rage center, could lead to severe rage-impulse related disorders perhaps severe enough to account for ninety-nine percent of all serial killers. Add to that the trauma of having been assaulted by a serial killer in the first place, with the virus that his body fluids passed on to you affecting the hippocampus where that memory is stored, and you could easily have a situation in which one serial killer creates another simply by biting him. But all that hinges on the existence of a disease that could affect the amygdala in this way. So far there's no proof that such a thing exists."

"Shit." It was all the professor could think to say. "Could it be cured? I mean, if it existed?"

"The brain is a tricky place. Brain cells are the only cells in your body that don't reproduce. Once they're dead they're gone for good. This fragility tends to make any changes to the neurological system rather permanent."

"You said that an increase in serotonin levels might be responsible for the violent sexual behavior? It's an impulse-control disorder, in fact an obsessive-compulsive disorder. Only in this case it's the compulsion to kill. They use serotonin inhibitors to treat other addictive compulsive behaviors, drug abuse, alcoholism, even compulsive gambling. This is basically another addiction we're speaking of, an addiction to sadistic sexual homicide. Why couldn't it be treated the same way as other addictions?"

"I thought of that, and theoretically it would work. If the rest of the theory held up, then the administering of serotonin reuptake inhibitors should do the trick. Unfortunately, the success rate at treating addictions with psychotropic drugs has not been encouraging. Like all recovery techniques, we found that it only works if the subject wants it to. But like all addictions there's a reward attached to it. Drug abuse, alcoholism, sexual addiction, compulsive shopping or gambling, and serial homicide. In the addictive personality, these behaviors give them a high that's almost irreplaceable. They do it because it feels good. In many cases it's the only thing in their lives that feels good to them. We would in effect be asking them to give up that feeling of euphoria for a life of relative boredom. They may not want to do that, no matter how many drugs you pump them full of."

Professor Locke thanked the doctor and hung up. He sat in the dark for hours wondering what to do. Then he sat down at the computer and began trying to find out all he could about Joseph Miles.

He began by logging on to the university database and searching through his school records. He wasn't sure exactly what he was looking for, but if Joseph believed that he was afflicted with this disease then it followed that there must have been a point at which he would have contracted it, meaning he himself must have been victimized by a serial killer.

It didn't take the professor long to locate the anomaly he was searching for. It was in his elementary school records. Back in fifth grade, Joseph Miles had been excused from school for three months due to ". . . severe medical and emotional trauma . . ." The professor then went to the website for the local newspaper, the *Seattle Ledger*, to check for any articles that might coincide with that date. He found the connection in a sensational headline that electrified the hairs on his neck.

TEN YEAR OLD BOY SURVIVES CHILD MURDERER!

Last month, a ten-year-old boy, whose identity is being protected due to his age, was discovered bleeding badly from several stab wounds, apparently the victim of a violent sexual assault. Police now have a man in custody that they say matches the description the young boy gave to the police.

Seventeen-year-old Damon Trent was arrested yesterday on suspicion of the rape and murder of six other young boys in the Seattle, Washington area. When the police entered Trent's home to execute a search warrant the remains of three of the missing boys were found in his basement in what witnesses described as "vats of blood." Further investigation uncovered several containers filled with blood as well as a bottle in which blood had been combined with red wine apparently to improve the taste.

It is now believed that the boy who was attacked last month may be the only surviving victim of this vicious child killer. In a press conference following the arrest of Damon Trent, Detective Wayne Williams stated that the ten-year-old boy was ". . . most likely the killer's first victim. His savagery increased with each subsequent attack." When asked about reports that Trent claimed to be a vampire who gained power by drinking his victim's souls through their blood the detective declined to comment.

The professor inhaled deeply as he read further reports of Damon Trent's arraignment and trial and finally his sentence to a hospital for the criminally insane in Tacoma, Washington. If Joseph really believed that there was some correlation between this attack and his own dementia, then he might be going back to Washington to confront Trent.

"They got to you too, huh?" Professor Douglas interrupted, standing in the doorway and smoking his pipe in a deliberately professorial pose. Locke winced as if struck and jerked back in his chair.

"Jesus, man! You scared the shit out of me!"

"Sorry. Those detectives visited you too, I see."

"Yeah."

"They're pretty good at laying the guilt on." Douglas swaggered into the room, still puffing on his pipe. "So what did you find?"

"It looks like Joseph survived an attack by a serial

killer. You know about his theory that serial killers are the result of a transmittable disease?"

"Yeah. He was asking me about how vampires and werewolves transmit their curse and how to cure it. Oh my God! I told him the only way to cure the vampire's curse was to kill the head vampire."

"That's about what I figured he was up to." Locke turned his computer screen toward Professor Douglas as a new headline flashed on the screen:

Vampire Killer Found Not Guilty by Reason Of Insanity

"He's going to kill the head vampire."

Thirty-four

Joseph rented a room in an extended-stay motel that had monthly and weekly rates, three miles from the state hospital. Alicia waited in the van, chained to the steering wheel as he walked into the office to pay the deposit and get the keys. They had scouted the neighborhood for the perfect place. Joseph parked across the street and watched the flow of traffic in and out of the motel before picking a secluded room on the first floor of the dilapidated two-story structure for its privacy and isolation. It was far from the office at the end of the parking lot near the trash Dumpsters. A row of overgrown shrubs covered the front, blocking the view from the street. It was perfect.

"Yeah, it's not the Four Seasons but you'll have all the privacy you could want. None of your neighbors are terribly interested in having the cops come in here, and neither am I. Just don't be cookin' meth or makin' any other kind of drugs in there and don't bring any kids in your room. We don't need that kind of trouble. The hookers are bad enough."

Joe gave the desk clerk his last three hundred dollars to rent the room for the week; then he went back to the van to secure Alicia in her new home.

"We're here."

Alicia looked back at him with wide eyes filled with that familiar confusion of lust and fear. Her long curly tresses lay limp and damp with perspiration and road grime, pasted to her scalp like a bad toupee. She flinched when Joe reached over to lift her from the van.

"How can you still not trust me? After all we've shared together?"

He was right. There was no need to kill her now that she was an accomplice. Her teeth marks and saliva would be found on Frank's corpse along with Joseph's. In the eyes of the law she would be just as guilty as he. Still, that wouldn't stop him from killing her just to assuage his psychotic hunger.

She allowed him to toss a blanket over her and carry her to the door of the motel room, feeling deliciously vulnerable in his massive, sinuous arms. Part of her wanted to cry out for help but she was still confused about her own involvement in Frank's death and her feelings for the superpredator. Before she could make up her mind as to whether or not to raise the alarm, the door closed behind her with a resounding slam.

"Do you want me to bring you something to eat?" Joe asked as he tied her to the cheap motel bed.

"Nothing that screams and fights back."

"How about if I kill it first?"

Alicia blanched and shuddered, visibly appalled.

"That was just a joke."

"Was it?"

"Of course it was, but after the virus has worked deeper inside you, you won't find the prospect of live meat quite so distasteful."

"It's not *going* to work deeper because you're going to find the cure, right? You have to now. If there's a virus inside of me then I'll turn into a monster too. You don't want that, do you? I mean, if you continue like this, eventually you'll be caught. And no matter how good it feels to feed that hunger it'll feel a hundred times worse to be locked away where it's just going to gnaw at you forever with no way to feed it. That's what prison will be like when they catch you. Is that what you want? Is that want you want for me?" Her eyes were wide and sad.

Joe wilted beneath her gaze. His massive shoulders slumped forward and his head dropped toward his chest in surrender. "No, of course not. I love you and you're right. I've got to end this now."

Joe stood up and walked into the bathroom. He came back with a towel, which he wadded up and crammed into her mouth to gag her. She closed her eyes and tried not to think about the dingy rag as it was forced between her lips.

"I'm going to see Damon."

He turned and walked out of the room, leaving Alicia alone with her thoughts and fears.

Alicia fought back tears as she heard the door slam and Joe's footsteps strike the asphalt. She was alone again, chained to a bed in a strange room, in a strange town, with no one to count on but herself and the man who'd kidnapped her.

Her mind kept trying to go back to her youth, to the taste of her father's semen on her tongue. She fought the memory away only to have it replaced with the image of the librarian enjoying cunnilingus before being cannibalized by Joe and finally the smell of Frank's slow-roasted corpse and the succulent taste of his hickory-smoked genitals as they melted in her mouth and slid luxuriously down into her belly. She shook her head and screamed into the rag until the image fled and she was back in the room.

In order to keep her mind in the present, Alicia began investigating her surroundings as best she could while still tied to the bed. She listened to the sounds of life teeming all around her from the other grimy little apartments that adjoined her own tacky piss-colored prison.

Next door she heard a persistent knocking as someone tried desperately to awaken her sleeping neighbor.

Through the adjoining wall Alicia heard the door open, a few mumbled greetings, then silence. Minutes after the man had entered there began a chorus of grunts and moans and the bang and squeak of the overused bed. It was over almost as soon as it began.

Moments later the neighbor's door opened again and the same footsteps stalked off across the parking lot, followed soon by the sound of tears and curses. This would be repeated three more times before the day was fully born.

Trying to drown out the sounds from the room next door, Alicia stared up at the ceiling to watch a cockroach scamper across what must have been an immense distance for something so small, only to find itself ensnared in a dusty cobweb in the corner above her bed. Seconds later a miniscule spider, a third of the size of the cockroach, crawled out across the web and began to further entangle its larger prey in a silken cocoon. Soon the spider had latched onto the cockroach, sucking it dry. Life was rough all over. Alicia turned away.

She began counting the water and cigarette stains yellowing the antique white walls. She imagined she could see faces screaming out from the various blotches and streaks. Her stomach growled, reminding her of her last meal and almost causing her to regurgitate. She felt the bile scald her throat as she swallowed hard to keep Frank's remains down. She went back to staring at the walls, trying not to think.

This room was a wreck. It wore its history like a battered old soldier, each sin and vice leaving another scar on its aging façade. Alicia could see every poorly textured drywall patch where someone had shoved their fist or someone else's head through the Sheetrock. She could see where some disinterested handyman had made a cursory attempt at painting over blood splatter. The brownish red streaks had resurfaced through the paint as if something were buried within the wall and still bleeding. The bullet holes that were simply spackled and repainted.

As little care as had been taken in repairing the dump, even less had been taken in its original construction. She could count each and every stud in the wall where they were bowed or misaligned. The ceiling's lid line dove as much as two inches on one side making the room appear to be leaning. The caulking was uneven and the lead-based paint was peeling, curling up and flaking away like a bad sunburn.

Alicia closed her eyes and tried to sleep while the neighbor's bed renewed its squeak and bump, headboard gouging the drywall as it slammed repeatedly against the wall in rhythm with the sounds of ecstasy and despair. She heard someone cry out with a faked orgasm that sounded to her like a wail of torment. Then the door slammed again and Alicia drifted off, listening to her neighbor's anguished, wracking sobs.

Thirty-five

A dark blanket of clouds smothered the sky. Fat droplets of rain beat a steady pulse on the roof of the van as the heavens bled out into the city, drowning the citizenry like rats in a flooding basement. The rain was the second thing about his childhood Joe was able to recall with any clarity. It seemed that it had rained every day of his life right up until he'd left Washington. Now he'd brought the rain back with him.

Work boots, sneakers, patent leather wingtips, pumps, rubber boots, and myriad other shoes of every description splashed through the murky puddles as the last of the nine-to-fivers hurried off to work, now more than half an hour late. Everyone in this town seemed to belong here. There were no tourists. The people blended right in with the architecture, the food, and the drab, depressing weather. They were decorative accents added to give the place more flavor.

Joe navigated silently through the somber streets, his thoughts as chaotic as the weather as he looked from face to face, reading their stories in wrinkles and worry lines. Whenever their eyes landed on him he turned away, afraid that they would read the horror story etched into his own features.

Joe drove west on Bridgeport Way to Steilacoom Boulevard and turned left. Less than ten minutes later he pulled up at Fort Steilacoom, where the state mental hospital sat.

It was an impressive complex of red brick buildings, imposing edifices of concrete and steel, four stories high, with windows barred in wrought iron. It was a prison laid out on a sprawling campus dotted with tall evergreen trees and lush lawns. The buildings were old, though, and a hospital this size was bound to have major security leaks. Joe was already searching for them as he pulled up into the parking lot in front of the main building. The windows were all barred, however, and police cars came and went fairly regularly. Getting Trent out would be tricky.

As expected, Joe passed the clichéd drooling patients lounging on lawn furniture and sipping iced tea, their eyes fixed in a vacant stare. Nurses attended to them with pity and casual disdain, as if they were unaware of the crimes most of them had committed in order to be put there, and the danger they still represented. Even through their vacuous expressions, Joe could sense the hunger still burning inside them only slightly diminished by the antipsychotics and depressants the nurses were dutifully pumping into them. Still, armed prison guards stood close by, just in case one of the inmates had forgotten to take his meds and decided to get a little frisky. Joe continued across the lawn and up to the front of the main building.

Joe wasn't sure exactly what he was going to say in order to gain admittance into the hospital. He was hoping they wouldn't recognize his name as one of

Damon Trent's victims. He was also hoping that Trent's own perverse curiosity would make him eager enough to see his first victim all grown up to go along with whatever lie he came up with.

The withered old crone who sat behind the reception desk smiled up at Joe with a mouthful of pearl white dentures as he stepped cautiously into the lobby. Instinctively his eyes ravaged her, searching for an edible morsel on her hard-worn body, but the meat that sagged from her brittle skeleton had long ago withered and spoiled. She was in no danger of winding up on his menu. Not when there were so many more scrumptious delicacies wandering every street corner and darkened corridor.

"May I help you, young man?"

"I'm here to visit one of your patients."

"What ward is he in?"

"Uh, I'm not sure. He was pretty violent at one time. They might have him in isolation."

"If he's in isolation then they won't allow him to have visitors. What's his name?"

"Damon Trent."

"Trent? What's your name, sir?" The old crone's eyes narrowed in suspicion.

"My name is Joseph Miles."

"Are you on his visitors list?"

"I should be. I'm a relative. I'm his cousin. We grew up together." Joe smiled wide in an effort to reassure her, but her eyes remained hard and distrustful.

"Give me a second to check."

The octogenarian receptionist turned her profile to him and began tapping her spindly arthritic talons on the computer keyboard, calling up Trent's patient information. As she did so, she cast a glance at the two armed prison guards who stood chatting idly by the elevators. Instantly they stood at attention and began taking notice of the large well-groomed young man with the physique of a professional body-builder. Despite the smile he kept plastered to his face, they could sense danger from him.

"Oh, here it is. I'm so sorry, it seems your name *is* on his visitors list. It was added just two days ago. I'll still need to see some ID."

Joe fished into his pocket for his California driver's license and handed it to her.

"You say it was added just two days ago?"

"Yes. Mr. Trent requested the addition himself. Had his lawyer call the head nurse."

She handed him a visitor's pass and directed him through the metal detector and over to the elevators.

"Trent's room is downstairs. Wait a second and I'll have one of our orderlies escort you."

Joe was stunned. Two days ago he had first left San Francisco. Somehow Damon had known and was expecting him.

The two corrections officers continued to watch him as he shuffled nervously from foot to foot, waiting for an orderly to come and lead him downstairs. Joe kept his eyes straight ahead. He was used to being stared at, but the thick animal musk of testosterone wafting from the two guards was maddening. They were challenging him and his alpha-male instincts wanted to take up the challenge. He was already calculating the number of strikes it would take to bring them down before they could draw their weapons. The elevator doors slid open and a short, fat, black orderly stepped out and ushered him inside.

"You here to see Damon Trent, right? Step on in."

He held the elevator door open for Joe, smiling like an idiot. Joe smiled back at him, bristling inside.

Joe stepped inside, casting a furious glance back over his shoulder at the two officers. His lip curled into a snarl as his eyes locked with theirs. They started forward to confront him, unsure of why or what they would do. The doors closed, severing the fierce tension and leaving Joe to focus on the man waiting for him in the basement. He would have felt much better confronting Damon with a stomach full of meat from a fresh kill, warm blood drenching his skin like war paint. The two toy cops upstairs would have made the perfect prey. Their deaths would have made him feel stronger, better prepared for the coming madness. The orderly would have turned his stomach. He looked too greasy.

"So what do you want to see Trent for? You a fan or a relative?"

"I'm his cousin."

"Yeah. Uh-huh." The man continued to stare at Joe suspiciously. Joe wondered how many people snuck into this place to talk to the many serial killers housed here out of some perverse hero worship or to get interviews for newspapers. He wondered how many had come to see Damon Trent. Still, there was more behind the fat orderly's stare. The man acted as if he knew something. The doors slid open and they stepped out into a dimly lit hall.

"Here we are. He's right down this hallway."

A row of fluorescent lights flickered eerily in the empty hallway that led to Trent's room, casting swift shadows that chased each other across the institutional green walls. Joseph stepped out of the elevator and his nostrils flared with the aroma of insanity and disease, urine, feces, blood, sweat, and medication. Moans and screams, giggles and mad cackles seemed to come at him from all directions. He could hear someone shouting at the top of his lungs to tell Jesus he was here while someone else laughed uncontrollably in response and still another person hurled a foul stream of invectives at him. Joe felt his anxiety increasing, as the walls of the madhouse seemed to close in on him.

This is where I'll wind up if I don't cure this thing, he thought.

"So why did you decide to come visit yoooour . . . cousin after all this time?"

"None of your fucking business," Joe replied, tiring of the little man and his innuendoes. They stopped outside two large double doors that were locked with a keypad. A sign on the door read SEXUAL OFFENDER MAXIMUM SECURITY WARD. To the left of the doors an enormous black guard sat behind a desk reading a magazine.

"Yeah, fuck you too. Empty your pockets. We've got to make sure you ain't got no drugs or weapons on you."

The guard rose up from behind the desk and began patting Joe down without so much as an introduction.

The huge black corrections officer was even larger than Joe. He stood nearly six foot eight and had to be over three hundred pounds. Hard, blue-black muscle rippled beneath his uniform, which seemed to be struggling to contain his Herculean mass. His head was shaved as if to accentuate the scars on it, no doubt the result of street fights. Joe didn't want to imagine what it would take to bring down a man that size. Even without the Glock .40 on the guard's waist and the Monadnock PR24 baton dangling from his hip, he would have been a handful. He was an inmate's worst nightmare. The star of many a prison rape nightmare. His biceps looked like small hams. He had obviously made good use of the workout equipment the patients were probably too heavily medicated to appreciate. He slid his hands from Joe's shoulders down to his ankles and then up between his thighs, even grabbing at his crotch.

Joe passively submitted to the rough and invasive search before being allowed into the patient's ward. The guard turned all of Joe's pockets inside out, withdrew his wallet and keys, and placed them in a manila envelope. Then he sauntered back over to his desk and hit a button that unlocked the doors.

"You can pick up this stuff on the way out," he said, kicking his feet back up on the desk and going back to reading the sports magazine. The orderly pushed open the double doors and they entered the asylum. Joe could hear his own breaths and heartbeat as if amplified through a speaker.

The Sexual Offender Maximum Security Ward was nothing like the prison Joe had been expecting. All the doors stood open except a few where the patients had no doubt been confined for transgressions against whatever rules regulated life here. The rest wandered the halls gibbering to themselves or gleefully relaying their crimes to other inmates, comparing atrocities in breathless whispers, their lusts undisguised, eyes aflame with passion like old men reliving lost youth. Some sat hollow-eyed in chairs or on floors, perhaps staring backward at the childhood abuses that had first broken them and led them to destroy others.

"Most of these freaks here are child molesters and serial rapists. We don't get that many killers here. The state likes to see the killers go to death row. It makes the citizenry feel safer, you know what I'm sayin'? They don't like the idea that a killer might someday walk up out of this place because some fool doctor declares him sane, only to cut somebody else up. If they're locked up for life or taking that lethal injection then no one has to worry about that. Me, I'd worry more about the child molesters they're letting out of this place every day. There's no curing them. They all wind up right back here again and those are the guys that create the killers. Most every killer that's ever been in here was raped as a child."

Joe remained silent.

"Yeah, your cousin is kind of a celebrity around here. He's the most famous killer we've got."

Joe was relieved when they finally stopped in front of one locked door and the orderly pointed at it and grinned.

"Well, here he is."

Adrenaline spurted into his bloodstream and quickened his pulse as he approached the bulletproof window, and stared in at the pudgy little man sitting on the single bed in a dingy straitjacket.

The guard opened the door and ushered him inside. Joe hesitated, noticeably shaken.

"You've got fifteen minutes. I'll be right outside this door, watching. If you need help or want to leave early, just wave. Do not touch the patient. If you attempt to pass anything to the patient you will be removed and arrested."

"Thanks." Joe hadn't taken his eyes off Damon once. He shuffled inside the musty, claustrophobic little room and it was like stepping through a time machine. All the old emotions came flooding down upon him in one great avalanche that pounded the air from his lungs and weakened his knees. All the fear, the pain, the confusion, and then the murderous rage. The rage grew and grew until it obliterated all else and dragged the abused child this demon had violated back to the surface. Joe flexed his muscles and rolled his massive shoulders as if to remind himself that he was no longer a child. He was a man now . . . a very large and formidable man. A superpredator. The guard closed and locked the door behind him and Joe winced.

Damon Trent hadn't changed much since the last time Joe had seen him, grinning at him from across the courtroom at his murder trial more than a decade ago. Then, he had still seemed like some misguided delinquent. Everyone except Joe had found it difficult reconciling the awkward fat kid with the murders he was accused of, but the evidence had been irrefutable. Damon was found "not guilty by reason of mental defect" of six counts of first-degree murder after less than an hour of deliberation, then sentenced to this maximum security mental facility when state psychiatrists agreed that he suffered from psychotic delusions that impaired his ability to distinguish right from wrong.

The years spent locked in his six-foot-by-six-foot cell, staring at the antique white walls, baring his soul to a procession of disinterested shrinks, ingesting antipsychotics with his morning orange juice, didn't seem to have altered him much, but instead had settled and hardened his features. What was once baby fat was now elephantine rolls that smothered his neck and torso in layers of superfluous flesh.

His face was likewise round and pudgy and erupting with the same acne that had been there at the age of nineteen. His oily hair was still long and feathered back like the heavy-metal geek he'd been in high school. Nicotine-stained teeth gave his smile a monstrous gargoyle aspect. Still, he looked far too out of shape to be dangerous, like an oversized toddler. But Joe knew better. Shivers crawled under his skin as Damon's piggish little eyes gleamed out at him with a terrible cunning, following Joe as he entered the room and took a seat opposite him. The sadistic pederast's thick cheeks pulled back into a cherubic dimpled smile, hideous for its ironic resemblance to his chosen prey: young children. When he spoke, his voice squeaked as if he were still in the hormonal chaos of puberty.

"Welcome back."

"Fuck you, Damon."

"Okay. So if you aren't a fan then what brings you here?"

"You know who I am and you obviously know why I'm here."

"To kill me? How do you intend to do that with me locked up in here? That is, without trading places with me? I assure you, this is no place for a predator." Damon winked at him.

Joe's eyes widened.

"How do I know? How do I know what you've become? What you've done? The lives you've taken? How did I know that you were coming here? Because I'm inside of you, little Joseph . . ." He patted his stomach and licked his lips. ". . . and you are inside of me."

"And that's why I have to kill you."

"So kill me! The COs here are rather overzealous, though. Especially that big black son of a bitch. He nearly broke my arm once trying to wrestle me into a straitjacket. He doesn't know his own strength. If he didn't snap your neck like a twig, the other guards would shoot you dead the minute they saw your hands on my throat." Trent's dark beady eyes narrowed as his smile widened. He watched the veins in Joe's forearms protrude, his biceps bulge, wound with tension.

"My, you've grown! You're quite a big boy now. Not really my taste but I might be inclined to make an exception." Trent continued to tease, feeling safe with so many guards standing just beyond the next door.

"Are you kidding me? Are you seriously trying to intimidate me, you pathetic little worm! You attacked children because you were too weak and cowardly to go after real prey. I'm a true predator, not some simpering baby-fucker who couldn't get a real woman to look twice at him. Or a real man for that matter." Joseph began to laugh and he could see Trent visibly deflate.

"Shut up! Shut the fuck up! Stop laughing at me! You don't know what I am! You don't know the power I possess!" He looked even more like a spoiled child as he exploded into a tantrum. Tears squeaked out of the corners of his eyes and his bloated cheeks reddened with rage.

Joe rose from his chair and leaned forward until he towered over the fat little pederast whose hands were still cuffed in front of him, leaving him all but helpless. Joe's voice lowered seductively as his eyes locked in on Trent's.

"Your power has faded, Damon. You're just like them now. Weak. Helpless. *Prey.* How long has it been since you last fed? Let me get you out of here and we can feed together. Then you can show me how powerful you are."

Damon licked his lips salaciously at the thought of fresh meat, fresh blood.

"You're trying to trick me. I'm not going anywhere with you. So you can kill me? Rip me up into little pieces to rid yourself of the curse? Do you really want to be like those sheep that bad? What will your life be like without the hunger? Without the passion? Nothing can replace it, you know. Regular sex will feel like trying to masturbate in a full-body cast. Nothing will ever compare to what you've experienced. You'll miss it every day of your life until you eventually kill again. But with the curse gone, the killing won't be the same. It won't be as fulfilling. But you'll keep killing because it will be the closest you can ever come to what you can experience right now with just one bite. Only it won't be one bite. Without the curse it will take the consumption of several victims to even approximate the ecstasy the flesh gives you now and you'll gladly kill them all and more."

"It—it's true then? There *is* a cure? This is some kind of disease?"

"What do you think? Can't you feel the changes?"

"I think that you're going to stay in here for the rest of your life unless you let me help you."

"It's better than winding up on your dinner plate."

Damon sat back on his bed, grinning like a baby with a mouth full of his own feces.

Joe wanted to lunge across the room and crack open the pederast's rib cage. He wanted to tear out the man's heart and consume it. But Damon was right. Any violent actions in this place would quickly lead to his own death or incarceration. Still, he had to find a way to get the man alone so that he could end his pathetic little life and sever the bloodline that linked them both to the curse. He decided to call Trent's bluff. He stood up as if he was about to leave.

"I'll think of you the next time I feed. I'll imagine you slowly starving to death in here, eating meat loaf, creamed corn, and Jell-O."

Joe signaled for the guard.

"Wait! Wait a minute. What did you have in mind?"

Joe turned back around and waved the guard off as he took his seat again.

"Tell me what you know about this place. What's the best way to get you out of here?"

"Get me a gun and I can free myself."

"And then use it on me? Uh-uh, not gonna happen."

"Okay. Then how about a knife? I could probably take out that big bastard with a knife if I took him by surprise."

"Let me think about it."

"Nothing else to think about. There's no way they'd let you out of here with me."

"If you had to go to the hospital for an emergency, where would they take you?"

"Right here. This is a fully functioning medical hospital as well as an insane asylum."

"And what's security like in the medical wards?"

"Penetrable." Trent smiled. Joe wanted to peel his face off and leave him smiling forever.

Thirty-six

With the threat of death temporarily less imminent, Alicia had time to deconstruct herself. To tear herself apart piece by piece. She looked down at her body and began to catalogue her flaws, something she had not done since this ordeal began. From the moment she'd set foot into Joe's apartment, seemingly a lifetime ago, she had felt terrified, helpless, revolted, angry, aroused, ecstatic, and confused, but not for a moment had she felt unattractive. A man was ready to kill her because she was so sexy. What greater affirmation of her beauty did she need? It was her sex appeal that had first brought her to the notice of Joseph Miles and it was her sex appeal that was leading her to whatever fate awaited at the end of this journey.

Still, with the naked 100-watt bulb glaring down at her from the ceiling, the various bulges and blemishes seemed to glow as if lit by a spotlight. And with no one's eyes to see herself through but her own, her hypercritical nature rose to the fore and she began dismantling herself. Alicia wished Joe had been thoughtful enough to turn off the lights before he left. She'd gone more than seventy-two hours without once thinking that she was too fat, without worrying about the rolls at her hips or the stretch marks or cellulite. Now all she could see in herself were flaws.

She looked down at her oversized breasts, which had flattened out and fallen to either side of her rib cage, tucked beneath her armpits like pale, fleshy, water wings, and wondered why anyone would want to touch the hideous things. They were not round and perky like the silicone queens and faint stretch marks ran through them from the missing nipples nearly to her collarbone. They were so light and thin that no one else would have noticed them, but she did. She looked at the thick black mole beneath her left breast, wishing that Joe had had the empathy to bite that off instead of her nipples.

Sighing and scowling in disgust, she ran her judgment like a sharp scalpel over her belly; the lightning bolt–shaped stretch marks radiating up from her hairy pubic mound where her skin had yielded to the fat cells multiplying like cancer beneath it. Her bloated stomach jiggled with each sob as self-hate overcame her. She wanted Joe to hurry back. She needed him to tell her how beautiful she was. She needed him to look at her with those voracious eyes full of lust and appetite that seemed to gather her entire body into them and cradle her in their unwavering gaze. She wept herself to sleep praying for the return of her murderous kidnapper.

It was past dark when he returned. The door opened and slammed behind him. Alicia moaned softly in her sleep and tugged on her restraints before lying still once more. Joe slipped into the bathroom and clicked on the lights. Alicia winced and whimpered as the mortifying sound of metal on bone clawed its way into her deep, dreamless sleep, stirring up terrible butcher-shop fantasies.

Images of car crashes, autopsies, bondage, and blood play swirled through Alicia's mind in a kaleidoscopic orgy of meat and steel. She tried to resist the urge to look, not wanting to abandon the safety of sleep, not wanting to see any more horrors this day. But the scraping sound went on and on, slowly wrestling her up from her deep slumber to that hazy twilight just before waking. Here the sound inspired more dreams. Dreams of Frank being carved up and served to her. She saw herself taking a knife and sawing through his tibia, removing his foot and lifting it to her mouth. She bit into it and the taste was wonderful. Revolted, she forced herself fully awake.

Alicia opened her eyes and looked to her left where the scraping sound continued, echoing from the tiny bathroom. She looked inside and could see Joe's face reflected in the vanity mirror. He was deep in concentration. Intently filing his teeth into sharp points.

For a long moment Alicia just sat there, transfixed by his transformation. When she'd first met him at the sex club in San Francisco, Joseph Miles had looked clean-cut and conservative, the type of boy you took to family dinners and office parties to impress your friends and relatives. Now, just days later he looked like some type of psychotic modern primitive. Feral lust sparkled in his eyes like a drug addict fiending for that next hit. His face was unshaven. His pupils were dilated and his chest heaved with his quickening breaths. The hunger was obviously fully upon him. Now Alicia wished she had not talked him out of taking along some of Frank's meat for the rest of the trip as a snack. But the prospect had just seemed too horrible at the time, with her own guilt at participating in Frank's death still so fresh in her mind and the taste of his flesh still swimming on her tongue.

Alicia closed her eyes and prayed that she was not his next intended meal, while part of her longed to be consumed by him. She winced at his touch as he bent down to remove the gag from her mouth. Her eyes flew open and she nearly screamed as she found herself face-to-face with her cannibal lover. His eyes were intense, sparkling brilliantly with that danger-ous psychotic lust that both excited and mortified her.

"What are you doing?"

"I need to feed again."

He turned away from her and walked back into the bathroom, where he picked up the metal file again.

"But—but we just ate F-Frank?"

"It wasn't enough. Not enough to face Damon again. I need more food. More power."

"But who?"

Joe could see the fear in Alicia's eyes as he contin-ued to sharpen his canines, filing them into tiny arrowhead-shaped fangs.

"I want you, Alicia. I want you so badly." He stared at her large breasts and thick thighs and Alicia saw the erection swell in his pants as the monster awakened. She sucked in a quick breath as fear raised the hackles on her neck and arms and desire renewed the flow of moisture between her thighs.

She wanted to beg for her life. She wanted to scream and fight. But she was so weary. Alicia stared up at the big college boy as he grinned into the mirror with his remodeled smile. The jagged shards of ivory looked almost reptilian. Joe's gums were bleeding down his chin in long ropes of crimson saliva. There was very little humanity in the expression. Alicia shivered. Her entire body trembled with want. Her muscles locked in mortal terror.

Slowly Joseph turned toward her without bothering to wipe the bloody drool from the corners of his mouth. His hunger accompanied him like a separate entity that had taken up residence within his body and now shared it with the rest of his mind. A demon lurked behind his retinas, eager to unseat reason from its dominant position in his consciousness, leaving only a wanton bestial thing. She could see the monster within him now, mirrored in his flesh and in his ghastly smile. It was the same feral rictus she'd seen on his face after he'd consumed the librarian's breasts, the same snarling leer he'd displayed after biting through Frank's testicles. That smile was his hunger's true face and the sharpened canines gave it even more demonic ferocity. It was now the physical manifestation of his increasingly violent appetite and it was coming for her. Alicia cringed and tried to wriggle away as that horrible maw widened, obliterating everything else in the room, even the rest of Joe's features. It was only inches from her bedside where she lay bound helpless to the mattress. His face, his body, all that he was, swallowed up in that smile, drowned and washed away by that all-consuming hunger she could not understand.

When she felt his fingertips glide over her flesh it

was like an electric shock going through her nervous system. She had never known such exquisite, sensuous terror. Her body convulsed beneath his touch as if his very proximity could bring her to orgasm or death.

Joe's fingers slid down her stomach and between her thighs into the slippery wet warmth of her and soon she was quivering on the edge of climax. She watched the predator's mouth descend toward her chest and swooned as her flesh ruptured between his teeth. Joe bit down on her tremendous mammary and began to chew through it, sawing deep through the fatty tissue and into the muscle beneath. Alicia screamed even as she reached orgasm, watching her breast tear free from her chest.

Thirty-seven

The detectives showed up the next morning and sat in the back of the lecture hall during Professor Locke's lesson. Their presence unnerved him. He felt as if he were the one under investigation. The professor stumbled over his words and lost his train of thought in midsentence on more than one occasion. He knew that he probably looked guilty and wondered if that was why they were here. Had they shifted the focus of their investigation? Did they now think he was somehow involved? Maybe they thought he was hiding Joseph Miles somewhere or that he knew where the man was? In fact, he did know where Joseph was, or at least suspected. He was somewhere in Tacoma, Washington, preparing to break into a state mental hospital and murder a patient. He still wasn't sure that he wanted to tell the detectives, though.

They had been right about one thing. He had fucked up. He should have known how disturbed Joseph was. He should have known how dangerous he was. Joseph had come to him looking for help and he had failed him. He owed it to the boy to try to find a cure. He owed it to himself and his reputation as a criminal psychologist to stop him.

The lesson ended and Professor Locke turned his back on the class and began erasing the blackboard as they filed out of the room. He heard twin pairs of footsteps heading down the aisle and approaching him. There was no doubt in his mind who the footsteps belonged to.

"Professor?"

"Detectives. What can I do for you today?" Professor Locke kept his back turned as he continued erasing the words of Bertrand Russell from the board. He paused for a second to examine the last quote before scrubbing it away.

Science can teach us, and I think our own hearts can teach us, no longer to look around for imaginary supports, no longer to invent allies in the sky, but rather to look to our own efforts here below to make this world a fit place to live . . .

"Do you believe all that stuff, Doc?" Detective Volario asked. He was wearing the same suit he had on his last visit and it didn't look like he'd cleaned or pressed it.

"All what stuff?" The professor wiped the quote away and finally turned to the two detectives.

"All that stuff you said in your lecture about religion retarding progress and science rising up to replace it."

"If I didn't believe it, I'd be a theologist instead of a criminal psychologist. I minored in philosophy as well. To me it's just another way to study the human condition. When you ask what motivates a man to kill or rape or steal or, more importantly, what would keep a man from doing these things, it isn't very far from asking what it all means. What's the true meaning of life? What sense can be found in all this chaos?

You look into the minds of serial sexual predators day in and day out and you have to wonder."

"Why not hard science? Philosophy always struck me as a halfway point between science and mysticism for those who couldn't make up their minds whether to believe or not to believe," Detective Montgomery chimed in. Something about the large black detective's expression instantly put the professor on guard. The man was absolutely intimidating.

"All the sciences began as philosophy. Once a philosophical theory is proven it becomes the property of science. But without philosophical speculation, astronomy, psychology, biology, physics, and even quantum theory would never exist. Someday the search for the meaning of life will leave the realm of philosophy as well and become a science and when it does I'll go with it. Now I know you two didn't come all this way to discuss my atheism."

"I entered all the information I had on Joseph Miles and his unique killing signature into the national VI-CAP computer and I got a hit today. A young man from right here in the Bay Area was found in a park in Oregon, roasted on a spit and partially cannibalized. We went to his apartment on a hunch that he might somehow be connected with Miles and we found links on his computer to a cannibal-sex message board. We found the same link on the computer shared by Joseph Miles and his roommate. It's a pretty safe bet that Miles is the one who ate him. Your boy is out of control. Why do you think he'd be going to Oregon?"

Because it's on the way to Washington, where the man he believes passed this curse on to him lives.

He's going to kill that man in order to break the curse, Professor Locke thought.

"I have no idea," Locke said.

"Well, we have an idea. You'll have to tell me if you think this one is apodictic." Detective Volario stepped closer to the professor as if he were about to grab him and shake him. The professor took an involuntary step back. "We think he's going home. He grew up in Seattle. We think he's headed back there. What we don't know is why. He no longer has any family there. His parents moved to the Bay Area when he was twelve. They live right over in Hayward. I doubt he'd still have any friends there. That was almost ten years ago and none of his phone records indicate that he's kept in touch with anyone from that state. So why do you think he'd run there, Doc?"

Professor Locke thought hard before answering. They'd come for his professional opinion both as a forensic psychiatrist and criminal psychologist and as someone familiar with the suspect. If he feigned ignorance they'd immediately suspect him of covering something up. If he told them everything, then Joseph would be arrested and put to death, his reputation as a criminologist would be forever tarnished and he'd never get a chance to test his cure.

The professor had his own reasons for wanting to cure Joseph. If he were able to treat the young man's murderous addiction with serotonin inhibitors it would be a major breakthrough in the treatment of sexual predators, a breakthrough that could inject new life into his career. The rule of the blackboard jungle was publish or perish and he hadn't published anything groundbreaking in years. A paper on the treatment of serial killers with medication would put him on top of the heap, and if he could both prove that the serial killer phenomenon was caused by viral transmission and document a cure for it, he'd be almost assured a Nobel Prize. Too many possibilities to put it all in the hands of two ignorant cops. But he had to think of a suitable lie.

They were obviously offtrack. They hadn't yet discovered the connection between Miles and Damon Trent, the serial child killer. So they wouldn't be looking for Joseph in Tacoma, where Trent was locked up. They naturally assumed he was on his way back to the city he was born in. All the professor had to do was reinforce that belief to keep them on the wrong track.

"There are many reasons why he might be headed back to Seattle. There's the possibility that his delusions are actually centered around a particular childhood fantasy, a person that he was attracted to who he perhaps fantasized about eating. During puberty he could have easily gotten his sexual urges confused with his hunger response. Perhaps it was a babysitter who wore a particular fragrance that reminded him of food and triggered a Pavlovian response. Maybe a waitress at a restaurant his family frequented. It could even have been the cashier at the local donut shop."

"Then he would be going back there . . ."

"To live out that fantasy, yes. He would be going back to eat her."

"Okay, that's one theory. Why else might he be going back?" Montgomery asked.

"He may also have suffered a schizophrenic break

and could be regressing back toward childhood. He might be fleeing back to a time when things were safer and simpler. Back to a place where he felt safe. This behavior isn't unusual for signature killers. If I were you I'd warn whoever now lives in the house he grew up in. If he gets there and doesn't find his mommy and daddy like he's expecting, things may turn violent."

"We've already contacted the family and we have the house under surveillance," Detective Volario responded.

"Well, I'm afraid that's probably all you can do."

"What about his virus theory? Could he be going to Seattle to search for a cure? Maybe there's a clinic or something there he'd go to?" asked Detective Montgomery. His eyes were narrowed, as if he suspected the professor of hiding something.

"If he really did cook and eat that guy in Oregon, then it's probably safe to assume that he's no longer interested in a cure."

Professor Locke hoped that this wasn't the case, but that response seemed to satisfy the two detectives.

"Okay Doc, if you think of anything else we'll be around."

"Around here?"

"Yeah, just in case he shows back up."

"But you just said he was in Washington?"

"No, *you* said he was *probably* going to Washington. All we have is the very strong suspicion that he was recently in Oregon killing a man he may or may not have kidnapped from the Bay Area. They may have just gone on a camping trip and he came right home once he was full. We've alerted the Washington and Oregon police departments, and if they catch him then we'll drive up there to claim him. Until then we're staying right here."

The detectives didn't smile when they shook the professor's hand. They whispered to each other and repeatedly glanced back at him over their shoulders as they walked up the aisle and out the back door. Professor Locke suspected that there would be a car in his rearview mirror when he drove home tonight and perhaps a milk truck filled with surveillance equipment and bored undercover cops parked across the street from his house. He hoped that Joseph wouldn't call him again until he could figure out how to shake the suspicion off of him.

Professor Locke left the lecture hall and dashed out into the misty steel gray morning. The damp early morning fog crept beneath his clothing and chilled his skin as he made his way toward the Sociology Building where Professor Douglas was just finishing classes.

"Douglas."

"What's up, John?"

"Those detectives were back in my classroom today."

"What did they want?"

"It looks like Joseph has killed again. They found a body in Oregon roasted on a spit. It was a guy from the Bay Area. That black detective said the guy had frequented the same website that Joseph did and that they had more than likely met each other there. It was a cannibal website."

"Jesus! Roasted alive?"

"Apparently so."

"And do they have anything positively linking Joseph to the crime? Any DNA or forensic evidence?"

"Not that they indicated, but who knows? They probably wouldn't have told me anyway."

"Did you tell them about your theory? That you think he's going to Tacoma to confront Damon Trent?"

"No. And I'd like to ask you not to mention it either."

Professor Douglas's eyebrows rose in surprise. "Oh, and why not?"

"Because I think I can cure him. I've been doing more research on serotonin reuptake inhibitors and I think this will work."

"Yeah, that's if he really does have an impulse control disorder. If he's just a sick fucker and it isn't some addictive disease then it won't do a damned thing and you'll be guilty of harboring a fugitive, and possibly aiding and abetting. You might even find yourself an accessory to murder if he kills again while in your care. And have you thought of the possibility that you might be putting yourself in real physical danger by confronting him? The kid is huge. How do you think you'd stop him if he decided to add you to his menu?"

"I don't think that will happen, and just in case, I'll be armed."

"This is starting to sound real sketchy, John. You're going to go out armed with a gun to confront a murder suspect whom you've already aided by deliberately misleading the police? I want no part of this."

"Before you say that, think of what would happen if we were right. What happens if the inhibitors work and we cure him? Think about offers of tenure from Ivy League universities. Think about making history. Thousands of dollars on the lecture circuit. Magazine articles. Think about the Nobel Prize."

"The Nobel Prize? Really?"

"It's that big. We would go down in history if we could find a cure for the pathology of serial murder. And think of how many lives we'd save. They estimate that more than three hundred people a year are killed by serial murderers. That's nothing compared to the thousands that are killed every year in this country by drug gangs and street violence, but consider that that's more than the murder rate for the entire country of Great Britain. Consider all those families who have to live with the image of their loved one spending their last minutes on earth being tortured and mutilated by some lunatic stricken with a mental disease that we could have cured. Think about Joseph Miles out there adding to the body count when we may have the power to stop him."

"Okay, John. I'll keep my mouth shut."

"I need more from you than that, Douglas. I need your help in capturing Joseph. I can't do it by myself. You've got some vacation time coming up, don't you? Let's go to Washington."

"You're crazy. There's no way I'm going to actively participate in this."

"I need you, Douglas. When was the last time you took a risk and did something daring? No guts, no glory. You lecture about the hero's journey in mythology every day, but you're unwilling to take that journey yourself? We're not getting any younger. Soon the most heroic thing we'll be able to do is sign a 'do not resuscitate' order so that our loved ones don't have to watch us waste away in a hospital bed for months on end. This might be it. Our last chance to make a mark on the world."

"I don't know, John."

"Come on. The Nobel Prize, man! No guts. No glory!"

"All right, you got me. Where do we start?"

Thirty-eight

Alicia lay shivering atop the bloodstained mattress with Joe lapping the blood off her exposed rib cage. Her blood pressure was plummeting. She was going into shock.

"You said you wouldn't hurt me. You promised," she gasped as she watched the big predator chew and swallow the last of her once voluptuous bosom. His body shook with an orgasm. Some of his semen landed on her face and she licked it from her lips as it dribbled down her forehead onto her mouth. She still relished the taste of him. She still loved watching him cum. Despite her feelings of betrayal, she loved the fact that it was her flesh that had given him this pleasure. Some twisted part of her still loved him, even though she knew that she would be dead soon if she didn't get to a hospital. She was losing a ton of blood.

Her voice seemed to snap him out of his rapture. He looked down at the ruin he'd made of his beloved Alicia and his heart crashed to the floor like a stone.

"I-I . . . I didn't mean to. I didn't want to—to . . . I'm so sorry."

His eyes filled with tears.

"I'm dying."

"But you can't. You can't die!" Joe's eyes were wild with fear as he realized that he could see her exposed rib cage. No one could live in that condition.

"Get me to a hospital." Her voice was weak, barely more than a whisper.

"Okay. Okay. I'll do it. Hold on. I'll take care of you."

Alicia blacked out. Her eyelids slammed shut with the finality of a stage curtain at the end of the final act. Joe scooped her up in the blood-soaked blanket and carried her limp body out to the van. He knew exactly which hospital he would take her to.

Minutes later, Joe pulled up outside the state hospital. He sprinted across the parking lot and into the emergency ward with Alicia cradled in his arms, shivering from the massive loss of blood and fading in and out of consciousness.

"Help! I need help!"

Two nurses came rushing from behind the desk and an orderly raced down the hall pushing a gurney.

"What happened to her?" asked a petite young Asian RN as she rushed to Joe's side.

"She was attacked by two pit bulls right outside our apartment. They almost tore her apart."

"Get her into surgery! She's lost a lot of blood."

"Is she going to be okay?" Joe asked, careful to keep his curiously sharpened, bloodstained teeth tucked behind his lips lest he immediately make himself a suspect. Alicia was now lying on the gurney with blood still pumping steadily from the massive wounds in her chest. The other nurse, a tall formidable-looking black woman with shoulder-length hair extensions and a wandering eye that made her look almost sinister, pressed two handfuls of gauze and a towel to Alicia's chest in an effort to staunch the flow of blood. Alicia's eyes rolled up in her head and she began to convulse as she went into hypovolemic shock. Saliva foamed from her lips and sweat bulleted down her face.

"Oh no! No!" Joe reached for her and the slight Asian nurse seized his wrist and managed to turn him completely around with almost no effort at all. She then placed an arm on his shoulder in a reassuring embrace as if to conceal the fact that she'd just used a very effective aikido move on him that had almost shattered his wrist.

"You just wait here. We'll take care of her. We need to contact the police and you're going to have to file a report."

"Okay, just take care of her," Joe replied, a look of genuine concern on his face even as he rubbed his wrist.

Joe backed away as they rushed Alicia down the hall and into surgery. He hadn't meant for it to happen like this. It wasn't supposed to be her.

His plan had been to tear into a stranger and to use her or him to gain access to the hospital, but seeing Alicia lying there looking so delicious, he had lost control and grievously injured, perhaps even killed, the one thing in this world he truly loved. He was completely out of control now and even more convinced that he didn't want to spend the rest of his life this way. He was becoming little more than an animal. Even now, with his heart collapsing beneath the weight of his guilt and sorrow over the harm he'd caused Alicia, he was still sizing up every nurse who passed, imagining how the meat of their triceps, the fat of their hips, the muscle and sinew on their thighs and buttocks would taste as he tore it from their quivering bones. Even as he mourned he could feel the monster awakening.

He hoped Damon had done his part and gotten himself admitted to the hospital as well. The only thing left to do now was for Joseph to find him and get him out of the hospital where they could have their heart-to-heart and he could rid himself of the curse and love Alicia as a man was supposed to rather than as the monster he'd been since puberty.

There was only one elevator that went to the third floor. That's where Damon had told him that most of the in-house patients were treated. It sat at the end of the hall and you had to pass another reception desk to access it. Two overweight nurses sat behind the desk wearing hardened impassive expressions. As soon as the nurses took Alicia away, Joe slipped into the elevator and rode it to the third floor. Joe's pulse rate increased, his heart drumming against his chest as the elevator ascended.

The third floor was pandemonium. Shrieks and cries reverberated as the insane vied for the attention of the nurses and doctors while fighting the voices and phantoms in their own heads.

How far am I from winding up in a place like this? Joe wondered.

An obese elderly man took off naked down the hall, drooling like a rabid dog, and tackled a pear-shaped middle-aged nurse. From his thighs to his shoulders his entire back was covered in feces as he mounted the wide-bottomed nurse and began thrusting his pelvis furiously against her. The security guards rushed to restrain him and Joe stepped out of the elevator.

Joe strode purposely down the hall, peeking into each room, wincing at the foul cocktail of odors wafting from the mad denizens within. Medicine, disinfectant, vomit, urine, excrement, and blood. More than the smell of the sick, it was the stench of insanity, the noxious perfume of the shattered mind. Joe's nostrils flared and a growl roiled deep in his throat. He wanted to latch onto it and rip it to shreds, to kill the disease in each of them, just as he sought to murder the disease within himself . . . to murder Damon Trent.

Some of the doors on this floor were locked, but most of them stood wide-open with their occupants unrestrained. He suspected that the patients who had been locked in were those with a history of violence. The average schizophrenic or jolly old child molester had free reign of the place. Joe wondered how many of them just up and walked out.

"Hey! What are you doing up here? No civilians are allowed on this floor."

Behind Joe, a small nervous-looking orderly who looked like he was fresh out of high school advanced on him with a mop in his hand, wielding it like he meant to brain him with it.

Joe looked around to make sure the security guards were still busy with the naked guy, then across the hall at the maintenance closet the man had just stepped out of.

"Do you hear me, man? You've got to leave this floor before I call security."

Taking one last look around, Joe charged across the hall and tackled the diminutive orderly, driving him into the maintenance closet. He clamped a hand over the orderly's mouth and the other around his throat and squeezed until the man's eyes bulged out of his head.

The man struggled and tried to bite Joe's hand. Joe bit back, tearing the man's throat out with jagged teeth that sank all the way down to the cervical vertebrae. When he jerked his head from side to side, ripping through the esophagus and larynx like a shark in a feeding frenzy, he nearly decapitated the man. Joe sat for a moment as the ecstasy of his fresh kill washed through him in staggering waves. Even killing out of necessity brought an immediate sexual thrill.

Joe thought about what Trent had said about losing that lush and delirious sensation if he managed to cure himself, yet still longing for it, seeking one weak substitute after another in an effort to reclaim this feeling. He remembered when he used to stalk the sex clubs before the urges got out of hand and he would see the jaded libertines who had so dulled their senses with excess that it took electric shocks, whips, and blood play just to get them aroused.

He remembered an old guy named Jack who used to hook wires to his nipples and send shocks through himself while being beaten with a two-by-four in order to get an erection. Joe didn't want to be like that. He knew that for him it wouldn't be what he needed to do to himself in order to get off that would reach such extremes, but what he needed to do to others. Right now he maimed and occasionally killed, but it was just for the taste of the flesh. He killed to eat. The killing and the pain was just an unfortunate side effect of his appetite. He had no real love for torture and murder. But what would happen if the flesh lost its appeal? Would he then kill just for the sake of killing? Would he cut into his victims just to hear them scream and beg? Would their pain be the only pleasure left to him?

What if this works? What will life be like for me without this . . . this passion?

Joe stopped in the middle of his preparations, unable to continue further. Blood from the orderly's ravaged jugular and carotid artery continued to spurt from the hideous throat wound, creating a dark pool around his convulsing corpse. Joe stared in a daze at the fountain of blood as if mesmerized by it. It was beautiful and stirred his appetite anew.

His hunger rose, growling and snarling in the pit of his stomach like some demonic alter ego, but it wasn't his hunger that stalled him. Despite the power and fury of his ravenous lust, which had grown exponentially in the last few days until it was now the most dominant drive in his body, it was the question that worried him. *How do I live without this high?* Now, so close to ending the tragedy his life had become, Joe had doubts. *Do I really want the curse to end?*

The tremendous human predator who had murdered and eaten his third person in less than two weeks was thinking about living without ecstasy, without the narcotic rapture of the flesh. He was afraid he might be making a mistake.

Joe slipped down into a dank mire of self-pity and fear. He imagined a life of boredom. The passionless existence of the mediocre. He thought of husbands and wives fucking once a month in short ten-minute bursts, rushing toward orgasm in their eagerness to be done with the chore. He thought of chemically castrated rapists staring in impotent rage at their former prey, lamenting the loss of their rabid libidos, hating their victims for their inability to arouse and eventually seeking to avenge themselves by washing in their blood. These seemed like his only options: wasting away, a sedentary erosion, or trying to recapture his current rapturous highs through ever increasing acts of violent sadism. Then he remembered the look in that librarian's eyes when he locked his teeth onto her labia and began to devour her sex and the look on Alicia's face as he indulged his violent perversions on her breasts. He had no choice. He could not lurk in the shadows forever preying on the very beings he loved.

Joe felt tears well up as he recalled the look of terror and betrayal that had so recently scarred Alicia's lovely features when he'd once again let his appetite overwhelm him and he'd attacked her as she lay helpless in bed. The tears flowed freely, dripping into the pool of blood at his feet. He imagined Alicia in surgery, fighting for her life. He tried to imagine life without her and found that more cold and unappealing than he'd imagined life without his hunger. He hardly knew her, yet still he could feel that she was the one. The one he was meant to be with. The only thing that could make him strong enough to resist the curse.

She probably hated him now. If she survived she'd never love him again. He was certain of it, but still it didn't matter. He didn't believe that love conquered all but he knew that he would do whatever it took to win her heart. And that if he didn't break this curse he would never know any happiness but that of the flesh. Love would forever be an impossibility. There was no way he could continue on like this. It was either break the curse now or wait until he started to sprout fur and a tail and was locked up in a freak show somewhere. Even if he wasn't actually turning into a werewolf or a vampire he was becoming a monster. He was not human in any recognizable sense of the word. Whatever was happening to him, he could feel himself changing more and more with each kill. He looked down at the orderly's broken body and at his own blood-soaked palms. His lifeline was a river of red. He could feel the hunger gaining momentum, gaining ever-increasing control. Reason was slowly becoming little more than a tool of his appetite.

There was nothing left to decide. If he didn't destroy Trent now and reclaim his humanity he would wind up as some mindless puppet motivated only by hunger and lust. Joe went back to work on the orderly. The man's body had ceased its spasms and lay still. His facial features had flattened and deflated as his life force had spilled out, relaxing into an expression that was more idiotic than serene. Blood continued to flow from his carcass but with his heart now at rest it steadily dripped, rather than the vivid eruptions of red previously spraying from his wounds.

Joe tried to remove the man's hospital scrubs for a disguise, but the amount of blood pouring from the corpse had been so tremendous that they were soaked almost immediately. Even if he had managed to salvage them, Joe was easily twice the orderly's size in both height and weight. There was no way that the clothes would have fit. Instead, Joe rolled up the man's clothes and stuffed them under the door to prevent the growing pool of blood from pouring out into the hall and alerting others to the location of his kill. Then he looked around for something else to disguise himself with.

He located a soiled lab coat and a couple of green hospital pants stuffed in a corner. The pants were too small but the lab coat was a good fit. He slipped it on and stepped into the hall, trying to position the orderly's clothes so that they would still form a dam to hold back the growing tide of blood. He had only minutes to locate Trent and get him out of there.

Out in the hallway the security guards had gone back to their posts and the naked fat man was once more back in his room. Joe was now far enough down the hall to be out of the guards' sight. He continued looking into the rooms as he strode down the hallway with his back to the guards. He was careful not to seem too obvious. Midway down the hall he located Trent's room. The door was open but Trent had been strapped to the bed with leather restraints that held him fast to the bed rails.

"Well, glad you could make it."

"Shut the fuck up," Joe sneered. The fat child killer lay on the hospital bed with a TV remote in his hand and his thick vulgar lips smeared with what Joe hoped was chocolate pudding.

"What did you do to your teeth? They look wonderful! Very sexy. And I see you've had a snack recently. Tell me about it, would you? It's been so long."

"We don't have time. I need to get you out of here."

"We've got a little time. The guards and nurses will be taking lunch soon. They go in shifts. Half of them stay behind while the first shift goes downstairs to the cafeteria or down the street to that Mexican place on the corner. That's the best time for you to try to sneak me out. That way if they try to stop us they'll be less of them for you to contend with."

"You mean 'us,' don't you?"

"I'm a lover, not a fighter." The fat pedophile leered at Joe and licked his tongue across his fat lips. Joe finished unbuckling his restraints and snatched him out of the bed by his throat.

"Don't test me, fat boy. Now hurry up and get dressed."

"I told you there's no hurry. Look at your watch. We've got another hour before lunchtime. You might as well get comfortable."

Thirty-nine

Night slipped into the unmarked Chevy Cavalier and wrapped itself around Detective Montgomery. His eyes peered like lasers out of the shadows as he stared intently at Professor Locke's modest home. Something was going on.

The professor had seemed more than annoyed when Montgomery and his partner had approached him earlier. He had seemed scared, guilty, and he'd been lying. At almost every question the detective had asked, Locke's eyes had slipped up and to the left, accessing the creative side of his brain in search of a response, in search of a lie.

Montgomery had followed him as he rushed across the campus to visit his friend and fellow suspect Professor Martin Douglas. He'd watched them argue while seated on a bench facing the professor's office window. Then he'd watched as they appeared to reconcile and shake hands over some secret pact.

It was nearly an hour later when the two of them stalked across campus to the medical building. They smiled and backslapped with the head of the psychiatry department and left with what appeared to be a prescription. They then continued on to a nearby

pharmacy and then to Locke's home in Protrero Hill.
Now he could see their silhouettes behind drawn
shades, filling a bag with supplies as if preparing for
a hunting trip. Montgomery was pretty sure that was
exactly what they were doing, going to hunt a predator named Joseph Miles.

Hours after being confronted by the two detectives,
Professors Locke and Douglas crept out to a waiting
car carrying two suitcases and a duffel bag filled
with handcuffs, duct tape, chloroform, a .45-caliber
Taurus semiautomatic loaded with Glaser Safety
Slugs, and several packs of powerful serotonin sup-
pressors.

"It feels like we're carrying a murder kit."

Locke smiled at his colleague in bemusement.
"What do you know about murder kits?"

"I've listened to your lectures before. Murder kits
are the tools that serial killers carry with them to their
kills. Duct tape, handcuffs, add a ski mask and leather
gloves and it would be almost identical to the stuff
they found in the trunk of Bundy's car the first time he
was arrested. I mean, what are we doing here?"

"Going to stop a killer. And to cure a young man
with a possibly treatable impulse-control disorder
that is ruining his life and the lives of everyone he
comes in contact with. That's what we're doing,
Douglas."

"Serotonin inhibitors. Could it really be that sim-
ple?"

"It might be. It just might be."

"And if it isn't and he keeps killing?"

"Then we turn him over to the police. Either way
we're both heroes."

They dropped their luggage into the trunk and enjoyed one last look around the safe, sane neighborhood before stepping into the car to begin their journey into madness. Professor Locke slipped behind the wheel of his six-year-old BMW and pulled away from the curb. The vehicle crept to the end of the block, crawling slowly as if hesitating. At the end of the corner it seemed to recommit itself, turning the corner and accelerating toward the freeway.

Detective Montgomery took off in silent pursuit, following nearly a block behind them as the professor's BMW climbed the freeway on-ramp, headed toward Washington.

"What the hell are you two up to?" he grumbled as he watched their headlights charge off into the night. He then picked up his radio and called in to the station to let his captain know that he would be out of state for a few days in pursuit of a suspect.

Forty

The urge to kill the obese pervert was almost unbearable. Joe sat staring across at him with a murderous lust pulsating through his veins with every heartbeat. Only this time it was less sensuous, black as death and sin; born of hatred rather than desire. This was the man who'd made him what he was: a monster. It was his fault that he'd nearly killed Alicia. His fault that he'd killed all the others. He was the one who'd cut him, raped him, and scarred him within and without. It was his face that he still saw in his nightmares.

"Has anyone ever told you that you look like Superman? I mean, not like Christopher Reeve, but I mean the real Superman . . . from the comic books. You look just like that son of bitch!" Damon chuckled in amusement.

It took a Herculean effort to keep from taking him right there in the hospital. Joe desperately wanted to see the man bleed. He had no desire to feed on him. This wouldn't be killing for food. For the first time it would be killing for the pure enjoyment of ending another human being's sorry existence.

If it weren't for all the noise the fat bastard would

make, squealing like a stricken hog, he would have tried to end it right there and take his chances getting back out of the hospital. It would have been easier to get out without the fat freak in tow anyway, Joe thought. The discovery of his body would even act as a perfect distraction to allow him to slip past the guards. But there was also the possibility that they'd lock the whole place down as soon as the body was discovered and he'd be trapped.

"Shut the hell up before the nurses hear you. Do they check the patients before they go on break?"

"Only the terminal ones and the ones who can't control their bowel movements. There's a schizophrenic spree killer at the end of the hall that they keep a pretty tight watch on. He's always going on about 'The High Score.' See, the record for the most people killed in a single murder spree is twenty-one. This guy killed about thirteen when he went off on a rampage at a supermarket in Seattle. But he was trying to crack twenty-one, beat the high score. He still wants to do it and he makes no secret of it. Says he's on a mission from God or some shit. So they watch him very closely. They don't come in here too often, though." Trent snickered in his high-pitched squeaky voice. "I think I make them nervous." His smile seemed to rip his face in half like a reopened wound.

Despite his masquerade of cool composure it was obvious that Trent could not wait to be free, to feed once more for the first time in over a decade. He seemed to have forgotten that Joe was not just there to set him free but to kill him, to tear the curse out of his flesh and dash it to the wind. He was practically vibrating with anticipation as he sat on the edge of the bed, glancing repeatedly at the clock on the wall like a kid waiting for a turn on his favorite amusement park ride. But Joe was even more excited.

For him it was not just about the cure anymore. Seeing the fat pederast again had reawakened all the old anger and fear. And now he wanted to make Damon feel some of what he had felt as a little kid, locked in a dark basement, being tortured and fed upon by some grotesque monster. He wanted Trent to scream.

"How much longer?"

"I'm not sure. It should be any minute now."

The more Joe thought about it the more he thought it would be better to try to kill Trent right here in the hospital. Getting him out past the guards would be too hard and he'd almost forgotten about the janitor who was still evacuating his body fluids in the maintenance closet. That body would be discovered soon too and then they'd definitely lock the place down and probably start searching rooms. He needed to end this now. The problem was how to do it quietly.

"I'm going to need to put those restraints back on you."

"But . . . but why?" Fear leapt instantly into Trent's eyes. Only then did he seem to remember Joe's true motivations.

"I had to kill someone to get in here. They might do a room check before they leave for lunch if they find his body. I can always slip under your bed but if they see you without your restraints on they might search the room and find me."

This explanation seemed to appease Damon, but only slightly.

"Which one was it? Was it that fat nurse with the

red hair and the big hooters? I'd kill for a taste of her. Who'd you get?"

Joe seized Damon's wrists and began tying him back down to the bed. "I killed one of the janitors, I think. He might have been an orderly."

"That creepy little skinny guy with the receding hairline and the great big eyes? I hate that guy. He's always bugging me for stories about how I killed those kids. He says he wants to write a book about me, but I think he just goes into that closet and jacks off over it."

Once Damon's wrists and ankles were secure, Joseph walked over to the door and looked up and down the hall. Other "resident patients" were wandering the halls, pestering nurses for more medication and gibbering to themselves. The RNs were all gathered up by the reception desk checking their watches, ignoring the insistent cries of their haunted and tormented patients, and gathering their purses. Several of the guards were there as well. Joe watched as they piled into the elevator and began their descent toward the cafeteria before slipping back into the room and shutting the door behind him.

"Why are you closing the door? What are you doing? You aren't going to kill me, are you? You can't! They'll catch you. Help!"

Joseph punched Damon hard in the gut, driving the oxygen from his lungs and turning his complexion red and purple. Damon's eyes went wide and his tongue shot out of his mouth. Joseph waited until Damon stopped coughing and caught his breath before leaning in and clamping a hand over his mouth.

"If you scream again the next punch will break your sternum and puncture your lungs. You'll die slowly as your lungs collapse and fill up with blood, drowning you. Do you understand?"

Damon nodded. Joe withdrew a scalpel he'd stolen from the maintenance closet and placed it to the fat man's chest. Then he began to cut.

"Please. Please don't kill me. I didn't mean to hurt you."

"I don't care anymore. I only care about getting the cure."

"Killing me won't cure you."

"It's worth a try."

He sliced a long line down the unctuous pervert's chest, cutting so deep that he could feel the blade bounce over the fat man's rib cage. Damon's pallid flesh opened up, revealing thick yellow globs of adipose tissue smothering the ruby red muscle fibers surrounding his ribs. Damon cried out despite the warning.

"Arrrrgh! Stop! Stop!!! Hellll!"

Joe smashed an elbow down into Damon's solar plexus, shattering his xiphoid process and rupturing his lungs. Damon wheezed and choked, gagging as the blood filling his thoracic cavity and crushed his lungs. Blood bubbled up from between the pervert's lips as he struggled to breathe.

"This won't cure you. I didn't make you what you are," Damon wheezed in an exhausted whisper.

"I would have been normal, just like any other person, if you hadn't passed this disease on to me!" Joe struggled to keep his voice down as his entire body vibrated with rage. His cold blue eyes were livid with half a lifetime of shame and anger.

Damon began to laugh. A hideous gurgling sound

issued from his lungs and blood sprayed from his lips as he wheezed and cackled.

"You were made long before I came along. Why do you think I picked you as my first? You were made by the same person who made me years before. The disease was already in your blood. Just like the legends say, you have to kill the original vampire, and I wasn't the first one. I was just a victim, like you. I was made into a monster."

"By who?"

Damon's voice was growing fainter as he continued to try to breathe through his collapsing lungs.

"Haven't you guessed it already? There is no curse. It's all in the genes."

"What the fuck is that supposed to mean?"

"You figure it out. You know. Deep down, you know. You've known all along."

Joe leapt onto the mattress, straddling the child killer's bloated stomach, and plunged the scalpel deep into the wound he'd made in Damon's chest. In a near frenzy, Joe began ripping the obese pederast apart. He cut chunks of flesh out of the man's torso, slicing deep into his fat and muscle and then digging his fingers down into the meat and jerking it free with both hands. Pulling off his pectoral muscles with a wet sticky *riiiiiip!*

He stripped the meat from the man's arms and legs, wrenching loose his flabby biceps and triceps from his humerus and tossing them to the floor, tearing his huge fat enclustered vastus muscles and hamstrings from his femur as Damon tried to force a scream up through his blood-clogged larynx. Damon passed out from the pain, blood loss, and shock of seeing his body so recklessly unmade, yet Joe continued to rip into him with the scalpel and his own bare hands until large hunks of warm wet meat lay all over the floor around the bed.

The room was now a gruesome abattoir. The sterile white walls and ceiling ran red with Damon's depleted life. The mattress upon which his savaged carcass lay was a blood-drenched sponge that squished beneath their weight, leaking more blood down onto the tiled floor. Joe's anger began to ebb. He stared down at the ruin he'd made of the corpulent pederast and felt muscles uncontracting and relaxing for the first time all over his body, as if he'd been flexing for years and hadn't been aware of it. Joe let out a long sigh and it felt as if he'd been holding his breath for a decade. He stabbed the scalpel down through the pederast's rib cage, impaling his heart, and then climbed off the bed, continuing to stare at the corpse as it voided its body fluids.

The floor was littered with flesh. Blood poured from the mattress in long sheets, covering the linoleum in a shimmering blanket of burgundy-wine red. Joe had never seen so much blood come from a single person. It was as if all the blood the child killer had sucked from his victims' wounds had still been in him and had only now been freed. He imagined the souls of all the children Damon had consumed pouring out of his bloated corpse on that endless river of dark plasma.

Joe stared intently at Damon's face as the pederast's life fled his mutilated carcass, hoping to see some sign that the curse was over. He half expected the man's body to collapse into ash like the vampires in the movies, but instead the fat freak simply expired. Joe studied the man's features for a while longer, recalling the long hours he'd spent cringing in a damp basement as that pudgy face leered at him from behind a mask of Joe's own blood. He didn't know for sure if the curse had left him, but he had no desire at all to feast on Damon Trent's fat vulgar corpse. He walked out of the room, quietly shutting the door behind him.

Part III

Forty-one

Joseph was drenched head to toe in Damon's blood. The lab coat he'd appropriated now looked like a butcher's smock. It was plastered to his skin, the blood already beginning to coagulate. Joe had to peel himself out of it, as if he were removing the skin from a particularly wet and juicy piece of tropical fruit. Blood-soaked meat always reminded Joe of mangoes and ripe peaches, when you opened it up and it flooded your mouth with its sweet nectar. Joe thought once more about Alicia as he dropped the lab coat to the floor. She had been the sweetest fruit of all. He had to find a way in to see her. But they wouldn't let him anywhere near her saturated in blood, especially once the two corpses were located.

The polo shirt Joe had been wearing underneath the lab coat had already been red, but now the darker, truer red from Damon's arteries stood out clearly against it and even more so against his blue jeans. Somehow he had to get a fresh lab jacket or something to cover his clothing.

Joe walked into the bathroom and stared into the mirror. Even though he had not fed, his face was covered in blood from where Damon's severed veins and arteries had sprayed him as he worked the meat free from his bones. The eyes that stared out at him from that grisly crimson mask were feral, the eyes of some ravenous beast. Joe ran water into his cupped palms and splashed it over his face again and again. He lathered his arms, face, and hair with liquid hand soap and washed it away until his handsome Clark Kent face reemerged from that gory fright mask. He took a deep breath and watched as all his features settled down, the beast within him slipping away, leaving him alone in the bathroom of a hospital room with a child murderer's eviscerated corpse bleeding out on the mattress and his own clothes still dripping with blood.

"I've got to get the hell out of here."

He slipped out of the bathroom and out of Damon's room, casting one last look at his mutilated corpse before shutting the door behind him.

"Rot in hell, you son of a bitch."

Before anyone could notice his grisly hulking form tracking blood across the immaculate hallway, Joe slipped into another room directly across from where Damon's corpse lay bleeding out onto the floor in great bucket-loads. He was lucky to find an obese elderly woman lying catatonic in her hospital bed. With considerable effort, straining beneath the weight of rolls of billowy fat, Joe rolled her over so that he could remove her hospital-issue dressing gown.

Suppurating bedsores had leaked their pus onto the mattress, forming a gooey adhesive that stuck her loose, moldy flesh to the even moldier bed. There was a wet, sticky, ripping sound when Joe peeled her off the bedspread, leaving bits of her flesh still clinging to it.

The back of the dressing gown was caked with pus and gore and stained with urine and feces. Joe peeled it off of her. In this filthy gown he would fit right in.

Joe faked a lumbering stagger as he made his way down the hall. There was an emaciated teenager with tufts of hair missing and black scabs all over his scalp where the hair had been yanked out by the roots. He staggered down the hall in a similar fashion just ahead, and Joe caught up to the disoriented youth and linked arms with him. Together they made their way up the hall toward the reception desk.

The kid smelled as bad as the dressing gown Joe was wearing and his eyes were dull and flat as if his mind had long ago fled and his body was merely following a preprogrammed ritual back and forth through the antiseptic hallways. The only indication that he was at all aware of Joe's presence at his side were the occasional giggles, his left hand firmly planted on Joe's rock-hard buttocks, and the erection growing beneath his gown.

The guard was no longer in front of the elevator. The nurse was not at her station either. Joe heard a radio squawk and an excited voice shouting breathlessly.

"We've got a 187 on the third floor! Officer needs assistance!"

Joe stumbled down the hall and looked down the adjoining hallway where he had left the janitor's body. He could see that the blood had seeped out into the hallway, which had no doubt alerted someone that there might be something amiss in the closet. The door was open and two corrections officers were kneeling in the blood, leaning over the body as if there were anything they could do for him now. Three nurses, including the one from the front desk, stood around gasping in horror and chatting in excited whispers as they peered in at the janitor's corpse, unable to resist their own morbid curiosity.

The guard was looking up and down the hall, searching for something out of the ordinary. A suspect. Joe clutched the haggard teen tighter as they continued past. The guard had luckily looked right past him, assuming he was just another patient. As soon as they reached the other side of the hall and were out of sight of the guards and nurses, Joe let go of his teenaged camouflage and sprinted for the elevator. He pressed the down button and the door opened right away. The hallway was still empty when Joe slipped quickly inside the elevator. The mauled and murdered janitor was apparently too fascinating for the guards to tear themselves away.

Joe tried to catch his breath as he rode the elevator back down to the first floor. Adrenaline dumped into his bloodstream, lighting his nerves on fire. His muscles were bulging through his clothes as if he were about to burst out of them like the Incredible Hulk. He looked completely insane. If the doors opened right now, anyone with half a brain would know he was a killer. He had to calm down.

The elevator descended to the first floor and Joe closed his eyes and took a deep breath. He let it out slow and willed his muscles to relax. He let the satisfaction of finally avenging the loss of his childhood seep into his body. When the doors opened he was the picture of serenity.

Hospital guards and policemen were running everywhere. Joe slipped unnoticed from the elevator.

By taking Damon's advice and waiting until half the hospital staff was on lunch break, the big muscle-bound predator had found just the right amount of wiggle room to get in and out of the hospital's detention wing unnoticed. Now he had to do something even harder. He had to get out of there with Alicia.

Alicia was still in Emergency following her surgery. Her chart showed her listed in critical condition. Joe slipped into her room and knelt down beside her bed. Her chest was covered in bandages. There was a morphine drip feeding into a pulsating vein behind the elbow on her left arm.

"My God. What have I done to you?"

There was no way he could take her out of the hospital in this condition without causing her further pain or death. He would have to leave her.

"I'll be back for you. Don't worry. I won't leave you like this."

Joe thought he saw a smile creep across her face at the sound of his voice.

He removed his bloody smock and walked out the front door of the hospital as police officers began to swarm the place. He stalked across the parking lot and slipped behind the wheel of his van. Minutes later he was back at the motel listening to the prostitute next door get her head banged against the wall by her latest trick.

Forty-two

After driving for hours without stopping, Professors Locke and Douglas pulled up outside the state hospital only to find it swarming with police and news media. They were too late.

They parked the car in a parking lot across the street from the hospital and walked across the four lanes of slow-moving traffic, making their way through the crowds of onlookers and newshounds to get to the police officers. Professor Locke ran up to the yellow crime scene tape, ducked under it, and seized the nearest officer. Professor Douglas was right behind him.

"You there! Officer! What happened here?"

"Who the hell are you? Get back behind that barricade!"

"I'm Professor John Locke and this is Dr. Martin Douglas. We're here looking for a murderer."

"Well, take your pick. There's about a hundred of them locked up in that hospital. Now please step back."

"What's going on here?"

"Nothing that concerns you. Now get the hell back behind that tape!" The exasperated officer began forcibly pushing the two professors back into the crowd.

"I need to know what happened. Has there been a murder? Has someone been arrested?"

"If you don't step back, your ass is going to get arrested!"

"But we may know something that could help you," Professor Douglas spoke up.

"I'm really not interested in what you know."

"Oh, but I am." Detective Montgomery stepped forward, flashing his gold shield. The faces of the two professors fell in defeat.

"Is your captain around?" he asked the flabbergasted patrolman.

"Uh, yeah. Who are you again?"

"My name is Detective Montgomery of San Francisco Homicide. I'm here investigating a series of murders that I believe may involve your fair city. I also believe these professors may be material witnesses. Now, would you please do me a favor and arrest these two gentleman for withholding evidence and interfering with the course of an investigation and whatever else you can think up, then take me to see whoever's running this show?"

"I'd be happy to," the officer said, glaring at the two professors with an ever-widening grin.

"We haven't done a thing wrong! You can't detain us!"

"Yeah? Well, we'll see about that. I want them to be available for questioning. There's a killer on the loose and I think they know where he is."

Another officer took Montgomery to meet the captain in charge of the investigation. He was a stocky, middle-aged man of medium height, with thick, weathered skin from too much time in the sun. His eyes were hard but jovial. He looked like an old cowboy or farmhand, like he would have been just as at home on a horse as in a squad car.

"Captain Marshall. This is Detective Montgomery of San Francisco Homicide."

They shook hands and leaned back against the captain's vehicle.

"So what brings you all the way up from San Francisco?"

"I'm looking for a man named Joseph Miles. He's killed two people that we know of and he's going to kill a lot more if we don't stop him. I have reason to believe that he might be here in your town and that he might be responsible for whatever happened here tonight. Uh . . . what exactly did happen?"

"A janitor was killed. He had his throat ripped out. The ME says it looks like his larynx was bitten through and the bite marks look human. We've also got a dead inmate. He was carved up, vivisected. There's pieces of him all over his room."

"Are there any pieces . . . uh . . . missing? I mean . . . is there any evidence of cannibalism?"

"Not as far as we can tell." The captain's eyes narrowed in suspicion. "Maybe you'd better tell me what you know about all this."

"Unfortunately, I don't know a hell of a lot, but the two professors that I followed up here might. They're with a couple of your officers right now awaiting questioning. I have a feeling they know a lot more than they're telling. One of them used to be a profiler with the FBI. At the very least he may have a theory."

"I think we'd better go talk to them then. Oh, and

there's something else. You said your boy was a cannibal?"

"Yeah, his last two victims were both partially eaten. One of them he roasted alive."

"Well, a woman was brought into the hospital earlier today in critical condition. The man who brought her in told the emergency room nurse that she had been attacked by pit bulls. He disappeared before he could be questioned. Both of her breasts were missing. Bitten off. The surgeon that treated her said the bite marks looked human."

"Christ."

"Her ID says her name is Alicia Rosales . . . from San Francisco."

"Has anyone questioned her yet?"

"She's still in critical right now. We'll talk with her as soon as she regains consciousness."

"Was the nurse able to give a description of the man who brought her in?"

"Yeah. That's the funny thing. She said that he looked just like—"

"Superman?" Montgomery asked knowingly.

The captain paused, staring at Montgomery in disbelief and what looked like disappointment. "Shit. I was hoping you were wrong about all this. Yeah, she said he looked just like the comic book character. I guess this really is your boy we've got here. Looks like we'd better see what those two eggheads have to say."

The two professors were still seated in a patrol car with the officer who'd arrested them, doing his best to ignore their whining when Captain Marshall and Detective Montgomery approached the car.

"Get them out of there!" the captain barked.

"Now see here! You can't hold us like this! We haven't broken any laws!" Locke was yelling almost at the top of his lungs. His face had turned a bright pink and thick blue veins pulsed in his forehead.

"Then tell us how you knew that Joseph Miles would strike here. Why you two drove all the way from San Francisco straight to the scene of your student's latest murder? You're either witnesses or accomplices. It all depends on how you answer our questions." Montgomery stood nose to nose with Professor Locke, glaring at him as if he were a schoolyard bully shaking him down for lunch money.

"I don't have to answer a goddamned thing!"

"I think we'd better tell them what we know," Professor Douglas croaked meekly, the unlit mahogany pipe dangling from his trembling lower lip.

Locke whirled on him, eyes blazing with righteous indignation. "We don't have to tell them shit!"

Captain Marshall stepped up beside Montgomery, almost knocking him aside in his eagerness to confront the two professors. His face was beginning to color from the effort of holding in his mounting temper. It was obvious that Locke's self-righteous attitude was rubbing the grizzled lawman the wrong way. He shoved his finger into the professor's chest as if he were trying to stab him with it.

"Let me tell you something, Professor. There's a serial killer loose in my town—*my town!* He just snuck into a hospital and tore apart an inmate and a janitor. There's a girl in there fighting for her life with her breasts eaten down to the rib cage. Eaten! By the man you two are protecting! So I don't care what laws I have to stretch or even break. I'm going to find out what you two know and you both will rot in a jail cell until I do."

"Put him back in the car," Montgomery said, pointing to Locke. "We'll talk to Dr. Douglas here."

"Don't tell them anything. You hear? We can do this ourselves! We can still do it!"

Douglas shook his head, staring at his friend with a newfound understanding and pity. The man was desperate for his one last great act, his last chance at fame and immortality, and he was willing to risk lives to do it. Dr. Martin Douglas wasn't quite so desperate.

"What do you want to know?"

"How did you know Joseph Miles would show up here?"

"The patient he murdered . . . his name was Damon Trent, wasn't it?"

"And how the hell would you know that?" Marshall asked.

"Because Damon Trent is the man who assaulted Joseph when he was a child. Trent kept him locked up in his basement for three days, raping and torturing him repeatedly. Joseph was Trent's first victim, the only one who survived. Joseph believes that Trent was some type of vampire or werewolf or something and that he passed his curse on to him when he attacked him. He thinks that by killing Trent he'll cure himself of his own homicidal impulses."

"A fucking whacko!"

"Well, Captain . . . maybe not."

"What are you saying? That Trent really was a vampire?" Montgomery tried his best to stifle the smirk wriggling its way onto his face. Sarcasm leaked into his voice despite his best efforts.

"I know it sounds far-fetched . . ."

"Fucking loony is what it sounds!" the captain interjected.

"That's what I thought. But you'd have to understand how the human brain works. I'm not a scientist. Actually, Dr. Locke could explain it better if he were so inclined. But basically there is a specific area of the brain that controls our rage impulse responses, our sex drive, and most of our animal instincts. If a virus were to attack that area of the brain and create an imbalance of some sort, it could cause the type of confusion of the rage impulse and the sexual impulse displayed by sexual sadists and murderers. Not exactly causing someone to grow hair and fangs, but effectively turning them into a monster."

"Is there such a virus?"

"Right now it's only a theory, but that's why we wanted to study him. To prove the existence of the virus and to find a cure for it."

"What if this theory's wrong and this guy just tore you apart like he did those in there?" Captain Marshall asked. "Did you two geniuses ever consider that?"

"Okay, so enough with all the bullshit. If you know where he's going now then you'd better give it up."

Douglas looked from Montgomery to Marshall to Locke, whose eyes were pleading with him to remain silent. He let out a huge sigh and his shoulders slumped as his eyes swept the ground.

"I honestly have no idea. If he thinks his cure worked he might disappear forever. He might disappear even if it didn't work. Shut himself away from the rest of society and live as a hermit or something. I'm not a psychiatrist. That's John's field of expertise.

I'm just a professor of sociology. Any ideas I have would be based on history and cultural myths and legends, which would make them not a hell of a lot better than yours."

"Get him out here too!" Captain Marshall barked in obvious exasperation, pointing at Locke, who still sat handcuffed in back of the squad car, straining to hear what was being said between the two policemen and his colleague.

The uniformed officer opened the door to the patrol car and helped the professor out of the backseat.

"We want to know where you think this lunatic will strike next," the captain barked.

"Who says he'll strike anywhere next?"

"Come on, Professor," Montgomery said, calmly draping an arm over Locke's shoulders like they were old pals. "We know all about Joe's little theory. We know that you guys came up here on the hopes that he wasn't crazy and there really is a virus that creates these monsters. Now, if I arrested you for withholding evidence you'd probably beat it, but think of all the damage it would do to your reputation. What would your colleagues think if they knew you were protecting a serial killer? If you don't help us, then we'll make sure that everyone knows it. Now, you know as well as I do that killing Damon Trent ain't going to do shit for Joe's pathology. Those old urges are going to start coming back to him any day now. What I want to know is what he'll do when they do come back."

"He'll feed on whatever's handy. Wherever he might be at the time. And my guess is that his appetite will be much worse this time. I don't think you'll have any trouble recognizing his handiwork."

"But how can we catch him *before* he attacks again? Where is he going now?" Captain Marshall interrupted.

"I'm a psychologist, not a mind reader. But maybe if I could speak to that girl he brought up here from San Francisco. She might know quite a bit about what's going on in Joseph's head. It seems that he's taken quite a liking to her."

"Why do you say that?"

"Because she's still alive."

Forty-three

Joe sat on the blood-soaked bed, hugging his knees to his chest and rocking back and forth. The room was completely dark. Headlights from passing cars spun shadows around the walls like a puppet show. Joe's thoughts were also dark and spinning madly along the inner walls of his skull. He knew he wasn't cured. Killing Damon had done nothing to assuage his hunger.

The pants, groans, and passionate shrieks and cries from next door were awakening the big predator's murderous libido. He could smell the thick musk of semen, sweat, blood, and stool from the aggressive anal penetration taking place beyond his bedroom wall. In Joe's pants, the monster rose and stiffened. It was hungry again.

The hooker's ecstatic outbursts continued in rhythm with the pounding of her skull against the headboard. The animalistic grunts of her brutal trick were making Joe jealous. Another predator intruding on his turf. Joe squished his toes in the blood still leaking from the saturated mattress. Alicia's blood. The outline of her body was clearly visible as a rust-colored stain. A tear ran down Joe's cheek as he rose from the bed, gnashing his terrible teeth, and headed for the door.

The whore hadn't bothered to close the blinds to her apartment and Joe could see her being crushed into the mattress by a long, lean, muscular body saturated in sweat, muscles taut and straining with each violent thrust. The man's eyebrows were knitted together in concentration. His lips curled into a ferocious snarl. His eyes stared straight ahead at the bedroom wall. The look on his face resembled fury rather than pleasure. He didn't look like a normal trick. There was something too possessive about the way he handled the whore and something too passive about the way she received him; not struggling despite the violence being done to her by his savage lovemaking.

One of his long, muscular arms had snaked beneath the transvestite's chin and was squeezing tight, choking off her screams of pleasure as he punched his engorged penis deep into her bowels. The whore's tongue lolled out of her mouth, struggling for air, gasping like a newborn wrapped in an umbilical cord.

Joe could see that the man's thick organ was coated with blood from the whore's chafed and torn rectum. The monster strained in his pants, swelling with blood, eager for a taste of the transvestite. It was ravenous now. Joe kicked in the door.

The whore screamed and tried to disengage from her trick's cock. The large black man calmly withdrew his blood- and shit-stained penis from the transvestite's anus and leaned across the bed, groping for his pants. The whore snatched a pillow from the bed to hide her penis in a bizarre show of modesty. Still trying to maintain the illusion of femininity even in the face of a hostile intruder.

The black guy wasn't groping for his pants in order to put them on. Joe saw that the man was trying to free something from one of the pockets. Something big and silver. Joe sprang onto the bed and almost landed on top of the little transvestite, who let out a squeal and scrambled out of the way. Shirtless, his muscles rippled, taut with violent energy.

He reached down and grabbed the black guy by the wrist, removing the hand from his pants pocket and easily snapping it. The handgun discharged into the floor just before it slipped from the man's fingers. Out of the corner of his eye he saw the whore try to run for the door and he leapt up and dragged her down by her hair and back onto the bed. The black guy took the opportunity and snatched up the gun with his uninjured left hand and brought it up to aim at Joe. The big cannibal charged and tackled him. A bullet ripped his earlobe in half and shattered his eardrum as he drove his shoulder deep into the trick's solar plexus, knocking the wind out of him. The guy fell to the floor with Joe on top of him, and this time Joe reached down and bit into the man's forearm, tearing out a large portion of muscle and disabling his hand completely. The gun was now useless to him.

Through the entire ordeal the man had not cried out once. His eyes were hard and cold and stared at Joe with a murderous hate as he continued to struggle beneath the weight of the big cannibal. They were predator's eyes. Joe knew right away that this guy was no trick. He was more likely the whore's pimp.

Sweat dappled the pimp's ebon skin as he used his
bloodied arm as a club, trying to beat Joe off. Joe
could not help but admire the man's tenacity. He let
the guy land a few more strikes so that he could die
like a warrior before the powerful predator leaned
down and tore the man's throat out with his sharpened canines. Instantly Joe felt that familiar rush of
endorphins, that tingling at the base of his cock, and
finally the explosion as an orgasm ripped through
him. Nothing had changed. He had traveled all this
way to kill Damon and end the curse, yet the monster remained inside him.

The whore was still screaming. She had jumped
up off the bed again and was heading for the door
when Joe rolled off of the convulsing corpse of her
panderer and seized her by the foot. He noticed with
curiosity that the transvestite had managed to slip on
a pair of lacy underwear while he'd been struggling
with her boyfriend and that, despite the fact that the
undergarment was just a few wisps of fabric short of
being a thong, the whore's penis was not visible at
all. He dragged the screaming transvestite down to
the floor with him and strangled her silent. Joe
squeezed and twisted until the prostitute ceased all
resistance. Then he twisted harder, wringing her
neck like a dishrag. For a man, her neck was as thin
as a bird's leg and snapped just as easily.

Joe continued to twist the prostitute's neck until
her shattered cervical vertebrae pierced through her
skin and her head was facing the opposite direction.
Then he pulled harder until the flesh began to tear,
the veins, arteries, and tendons popped one by one,
and her head started to separate from her shoulders.
He had to use his teeth but finally Joe succeeded in

decapitating the whore. In a frenzy, he continued to dismember the corpse, using only his bare hands and teeth. When his bloodlust finally abated, the whore was little more than a torso.

Joe stood holding the remains of the transvestite's corpse and staring at the blood spattered around the room. Semen leaked down his leg from where one orgasm after another had erupted as he'd dissected the whore's carcass with his teeth.

"I'm still a monster," Joe mumbled as he let the limbless, headless thing slip from his hands into the pool of blood at his feet. He left the apartment, nearly tripping as he tried to walk on legs that still shook from multiple little deaths.

"How do I stop this?" he wondered aloud, wiping blood and scraps of flesh from his lips. But he knew. He'd known all along. Damon had been right. The only curse was the one in his genes. The one he'd been born with.

Forty-four

Alicia was extremely thirsty when she awoke. Her head was pounding and there was a dull ache in her chest. Her thoughts were cloudy and sluggish from the painkillers coursing through her veins.

"Water," she croaked, and an old man leaned forward with a Styrofoam cup. He placed the cup to her lips and the ice-cold water splashed into her mouth like a blessing. Alicia gulped it down in a few quick swallows.

"Thank you. Where am I? Who are you?"

"You are in a hospital. You were attacked. My name is Professor John Locke. I'm a psychiatrist. I'm here to help you. Can you remember anything about what happened?"

Alicia looked around her. She was in a hospital room surrounded by cops. "What are all these police here for?"

"They are looking for the man who attacked you. Can you tell us who he is?"

"Don't hurt him. He's sick. He didn't mean to—"

Alicia thought about the last few days she'd spent being terrorized by the big cannibalistic serial sex-murderer named Joe. He'd chewed off her nipples, kept her chained in his apartment, murdered another woman in front of her and ate her while Alicia watched helplessly. He'd dragged her all the way across the state in the back of a van, cooked a man alive and forced her to eat human flesh, and then he'd . . .

"Oh my God! My breasts! He ate my breasts!" Alicia lifted the covers and stared at the bandages wrapped around her chest. They were completely flat. Her breasts were gone.

"Who? Tell us who did this to you. Who don't you want us to hurt?"

Despite all of this Alicia still could not bring herself to betray him. "I can't remember."

"Do you remember how you got here? To Washington? Were you kidnapped? Did he bring you here against your will?"

"I can't remember. I can't remember. I can't remember!" She pounded her fists against the sides of her head and tears leaked from the corners of her eyes. Soon she was openly sobbing. A black cop who looked like a detective stepped forward in front of the professor.

"Okay. Okay. We'll leave you alone. But if your memory returns, here's my card. Give me a call."

Alicia turned away and continued to weep into the pillow. "My breasts are gone. They're gone. He ate my breasts!" She began to scream.

The detective dropped his card on the nightstand and backed away just as the nurses rushed into the room.

"Sorry, but I'm going to have to ask you to leave. You're upsetting the patient and she's still in guarded condition."

"We were just about to leave." The detectives and the two professors stepped out into the hall with the captain.

"That was quite a show," Professor Locke offered.

"You think she was faking that? Did you see the look on her face when she realized that she'd lost her breasts?"

"That part may have been real but I don't believe for a second that she doesn't remember who attacked her. She's protecting Joseph."

"Protecting him? But he's the scumbag who ate her titties off," Captain Marshall added, with his eyebrows raised quizzically. He looked both exhausted and overwhelmed, as if he would fall over at any second.

"Ever hear of Stockholm syndrome?"

A sea of blank stares looked back at him.

"It's when a prisoner begins to identify, even to sympathize and, in extreme cases, to fall in love with his or her captor. Who knows how long Joseph had her or what he told her. His is a pretty sympathetic tale if you look at it from his perspective. Here's a kid who was attacked by a serial killer and horribly tortured and raped for hours. He survives only to grow up and discover that this serial killer passed some disease on to him that's turning him into a killer too and the only way he can cure himself is by murdering the man who gave him the disease."

"So you think she bought all this bullshit?"

"It may not be bullshit. As I said before, there is a possibility that such a disease could exist. That's what brought us out here. We just need to convince *her* that it's bullshit. That's the only way we're going to get her to cooperate."

Captain Marshall's cell phone rang and he excused himself to answer it. When he hung up, his face was set in a hard line that told everyone in the room that the night was not yet over.

"You think this will convince her? We just got a call from a motel manager a few blocks away. There are two bodies down there torn to shreds."

Marshall walked briskly out of the hospital followed by Montgomery and the two professors.

"I guess you two eggheads had it right. He's on a rampage now. It's only been a few hours since he killed Trent and the janitor."

"He didn't feed on them, Captain. He must have been hungry when he got home. Not to mention his disappointment when he found that his cure wasn't working," Professor Locke offered.

"Well from what my officers are telling me, he should be pretty damn well fed now."

They piled into two separate squad cars and raced the two miles to the motel where Joe had been just hours before. They slipped past the barricades and police tape and into the room where the dismembered bodies lay strewn around the room like wet red confetti.

"Jesus!" the two professors cried out in unison.

"Oh my God! He did this? How could anyone do something like this?"

"You tell us, Doc. Does this hold with your little theory? You still think you can cure him with a few little pills?" The captain was feeling surly. He didn't like the idea of a serial killer in his town and he liked it even less that these two had known he was coming and hadn't said anything. If they had thought to drop a warning there might be four people alive right now and one lunatic behind bars. But instead they had tried to play heroes. It was all he could do to keep from knocking one of them down. He knew exactly which one it would be too.

"I'm even more sure of it now than ever," Professor Locke said, elevating his chin to look down his nose at the policeman. "This escalating pattern of violence is consistent with the pattern of addiction. He's developing a tolerance for it so he needs more. More victims, and more violence. If we don't get him into treatment the victims will just keep piling up."

"That is unless we shoot him down. Or lock his ass up."

"That would be one solution. At least to this problem. But what about all the other killers out there? This is bigger than one man and a handful of victims. We could possibly put an end to this type of sexual/rage killing forever."

"Get off your soapbox, Doc. I ain't buyin' it. Now wait in the car while we search this place. You're contaminating my crime scene."

The captain and Detective Montgomery cleared everyone else out of the room except for the CSI crew. They immediately went to work photographing, bagging, and tagging everything they found that looked even remotely like it might lead them to the killer. There was more than enough physical evidence to tell them who the killer was and even to practically guarantee a conviction—his DNA and fingerprints were all over the place. But there was nothing here to suggest where he might have gone.

"What about the telephone?"

"This one?" the captain asked, lifting the receiver from a cradle that was tacky with blood.

"No. The one in the apartment he was renting. Let's get the phone records and find out who he was calling."

"That's no problem. There's a police liaison at the phone company who does traces for us."

They were both more than a little relieved to leave the murder scene.

"Where's that manager?" the captain asked one of the officers standing nearby.

He pointed to a short, paunchy, balding Mexican with guilty, fidgety eyes. The man stepped forward, looking from side to side as if frantically trying to plan his escape. He had the look of an ex-con with the crude tattoos to match.

"Which one did Miles stay in?"

"Right next door . . . uh, sir."

"Well, then open it up! We need to check it for evidence."

They paused in the doorway of the apartment, taking note of the handcuffs attached to the bed and the wide bloodstain that saturated the mattress and sheets. This is where Alicia had been held, where Joe had performed his radical mastectomy on her. The big burly police captain froze and turned to look at the young black detective with stunned, exhausted eyes.

"What the fuck are we up against here?"

"A man. Just a man."

The captain picked up the phone and dialed the operator. Minutes later they had their information. He set the phone back in the cradle and let out a sigh of relief.

"Well, it looks like Joseph Miles is *your* problem again. The last number he dialed was back in the Bay Area. Hayward, California. A Mr. Lionel Ray Miles. He's going home to Daddy."

Lionel Ray Miles stood on his porch, cradling the Mossburg pistol-grip shotgun in his arms and peering out into the darkness. He knew he'd heard something out there. Maybe one of the neighbor kids was playing a trick on him, but he was sure he'd heard the sound of glass breaking. And it had sounded like it was coming from his garage. He crept around to the front of the garage and saw that two of the windows had been smashed and there was a huge dent in the aluminum, as if something big and heavy had crashed into it. He heard shuffling noises coming from inside.

Lionel Ray jacked a round into the chamber and crept around to the side service door. He didn't make a sound. He was not about to give whoever had dared break into his property any warning. Lionel didn't want to scare them away. He wanted blood. He imagined himself creeping up on some teenaged crackhead or speed freak and opening up on them with the shotgun. One less junkie, sneak thief, shoplifter, burglar, purse snatcher for the over-burdened court system to worry about.

The service door on the side of the garage had been smashed in too. It looked like someone had used a sledgehammer on it. That door had cost Lionel Ray two hundred dollars at the home-and-garden store.

Not to mention the time it had taken him to install it and paint it. That alone was enough to justify him blowing away the intruder.

There was a shadow in roughly the outline of a human body standing right beside Lionel Ray's prized '69 Lincoln Continental. The Lincoln was Lionel Ray's dream car. Not a Cadillac or a Mercedes, but a Lincoln with its sleek lines and suicide doors had always symbolized success to him. He'd purchased it on eBay with money from his 401K. Had it driven all the way from Texas. And that speed-freak intruder was using it as a shield.

The Lincoln had all its original chrome bought straight from the factory and shined to a high gloss. Brand-new black leather upholstery. White-walled tires. Lionel Ray had spent countless hours restoring the car to mint condition. It was his pride and joy and there was no way he was going to risk a shot in the dark that just might spray the old girl with buckshot and ruin the new eight-hundred-dollar paintjob he'd just put on it. If need be he'd just walk over there and throttle the bastard with his bare hands.

Lionel Ray Miles was tall with thick muscles from years of hard labor rather than months in the gym. He had no fear of the intruder attacking him before he could squeeze off a shot.

But the guy was big. A lot bigger than he'd expected. Too big to be a junkie or a crackhead, though that still didn't rule out a teenaged jock or a frat boy pulling some kind of prank.

If this sonuvabitch tries to charge me he'll wind up getting his neck broken just before I blow his damned head off his shoulders, Lionel thought. *I just want a better look at him so I can aim properly.*

Lionel Ray reached over and pulled the chain on the little keyless light that dangled from the ceiling overhead. The sudden burst of radiance dazzled him and he quickly raised the shotgun in the direction the figure had been standing, afraid that the intruder might try to attack him in the seconds it took his eyes to adjust to the light. The guy wasn't moving, however.

As Lionel squinted through the harsh glare of the naked 100-watt lightbulb, he began to recognize some of the intruder's features. The man was even bigger than he'd appeared in the dark, bigger than Lionel himself. He had short, neatly cut black hair parted down the middle. Crystal-clear blue eyes. A strong chiseled jaw. High cheekbones and a smile filled with rows and rows of perfectly straight white teeth—teeth that had all been filed to sharp points. His body was armored with thick muscle rippling beneath the yellow polo shirt he wore.

"Joey? Is that you, boy? What the hell are you doin' breakin' into my garage? Why ain't your ass in school?"

"I came to ask you a question."

Lionel Ray lowered the shotgun and stared at his son with that angry, disappointed, and somewhat bemused expression he used to get just before he would slap Joe around when he was a kid.

"Boy, it is way too late for games. What is this, some college prank or something? Some fuckin' frat boys dare you to break into your dad's garage, smash up my door and dent the damned garage door? I hope they've got money to pay for all of this or else it's coming right out of your hide!" Lionel Ray growled.

"How soon after they found me bleeding to death in the park did you realize that one of your chickens had come home to roost? How long did it take you to recognize Damon Trent as one of your victims? I guess he was one of the unfortunate bastards who managed to survive, wasn't he? How many were there? How many kids have you killed?"

Tears streamed down Joe's face. His father just looked annoyed and slightly amused.

"Well, you finally figured it out, huh? I tried to tell you before, but I didn't think you could handle it. It looks like I was right. Look at you, standing there crying like some old woman. I can't believe we're the same blood. But we are, aren't we? You've got my blood coursing through those veins, don't you? My curse."

"How many were there?"

"There were dozens! I don't know."

"What did you do to them? Tell me everything."

Lionel Ray cocked an eyebrow at his son. "Are you sure you want to know, boy?"

"Tell me! I want to know what I am."

"I would pick them up at parks just like that Trent kid picked you up. Sometimes I'd offer them a ride home or tell them that their mommy had sent me to bring them home. Sometimes I'd just snatch them. After a while it became easier to just snatch them off the street. Less exposure that way. Then I'd take them home. Yeah, right to this house. Down in the basement. I'd cut on them for a while. I didn't do sex with them. I wasn't into all that. I'd just cut on them. I liked to hear them scream."

"Did you drink their blood?"

"What? No! You mean like that fat freak who did

you? I wasn't some pervert. I just liked to hear them scream."

"Did you kill them?"

"Some of them. Most of them, I guess. But I let a few of them go too. Mostly the really young ones I let go. I knew they wouldn't be able to tell the police enough to send them after me. Most of them were too scared to say anything when I was done anyway. And if I was really worried about them talking I'd just cut their tongues out or put out their eyes or both. I should have cut Trent's eyes out."

"But why, Dad? Why did you do it?"

"For the same reason you tore apart that librarian at your school. Yeah, you didn't think I knew about that, did you? The minute those cops showed up at my door asking questions about you I knew you were the one who did it. Like father, like son. I did it because it feels good, boy! Doesn't it, Son? Doesn't it feel good to prey on those weak, pitiful little things? It feels like your body was designed for it, doesn't it? Like you're fulfilling your purpose in life. Killing off the weak. Culling the herd. They ain't good for nothin' no way except screamin' and dyin'. You happy now, boy? You got all your questions answered?"

"All except one," Joe replied, staring down at the shotgun still leaning against his daddy's leg. He was calculating his chances of crossing the garage floor and disarming his dad before he could raise that shotgun and squeeze off a round. *Maybe he wouldn't even shoot?* Joe thought. *After all, I am his son.* But he doubted that. He knew his dad well enough to know that the man valued his own happiness and preservation above any familial love or responsibility.

He would shoot Joe dead if he thought his life was in danger.

Joe began inching closer to his father. The closer he was when he attacked the old man, the better his chances would be of avoiding a steaming hole in his chest.

"So ask then. What else do you want to know about your old dad?"

Joe was now only a few feet away.

"I want to know if there's a cure for what we are. I want to know how to end this."

Lionel Ray began to laugh. "A cure? You can't change what you are, boy! There ain't no cure!"

"I think there is." Joe leapt forward, springing for his father's throat. Lionel Ray tried to raise the shotgun to shoot his only son. He was too late. The blast went over Joe's left shoulder. Joe noted without emotion that his dad had been aiming for his head.

A few shot pellets lodged in Joe's shoulder, bicep, and chest, slowing him a bit but not stopping him. He tackled the elder Miles. His entire body slammed into the old man with the mass and velocity of a stampeding horse. They collapsed onto the hard concrete floor with a wet smack as the back of Lionel Ray's head cracked against the cement. Joe bared his fangs and clamped them down onto his father's throat. There was something terribly satisfying about hearing the man's screams.

Forty-five

Detective Montgomery had called ahead to his partner to meet the Hayward police at the home of Lionel Miles. He then called the Hayward police chief and gave him a rundown on the situation.

"If he's heading home I doubt it's to reminisce over old times. He's got a major bloodlust going and if we don't get there fast you're going to have a body to clean up—and believe me, Joseph is quite a messy eater."

The detective set his phone in the charger and waited for the chief to call him back with what would hopefully be some good news for once—like, that they'd captured Joseph Miles. He stared out his windshield, barely aware of the traffic, barely even seeing the road, thinking only about the big, man-eating college kid as he raced down the highway back toward California. He'd been on the road for over an hour when he finally got the call.

"We missed him. He must have gotten there just a few hours before us."

"So what happened? Did he kill his father?"

"He did more than kill him. Much more." The previously robust voice of the Hayward police chief faded to a faint whisper. Montgomery recognized the symptom. The man was going into shock. Whatever he'd found at the home of Lionel Miles must have been more horrible than the detective had been able to prepare him for. Montgomery stomped down on the accelerator as the chief filled him in on all the ghastly details. Six and a half hours later, he pulled up outside the home of the late Lionel Ray Miles.

If Montgomery hadn't prepared the police chief for what he might find at the home of Lionel Ray Miles, he had prepared himself even less.

"Jesus Christ!"

Lionel Ray lay on the hood of his prized 1969 Lincoln Continental with his chest torn open and his heart ripped out. The gaping chest cavity had been filled with garlic and a rosary lay atop the piles of fresh cloves. A wooden stake, driven through the spot where his heart should have been, pinned him to the hood of the car. His head had been removed and lay on the floor at his feet, stuffed with cloves of garlic. The body was smoldering from where his murderer had tried to set him on fire. The Hayward police had arrived just in time to douse the fire before it did much damage. The entire street smelled like roasted garlic and barbecued pork. The most disturbing thing was how delicious the aroma was. It made the detective even more aware of the fact that he hadn't eaten in almost twenty-four hours.

Montgomery knew that the arson had not been an attempt to destroy evidence but rather a way to ensure that this demon would never rise again. He walked over and looked down at the sizzling corpse.

"You poor bastard. What did you do to deserve this?"

"Detective!" A young officer, who looked like he was fresh out of high school, ran into the garage with his eyes wide. He was sucking in breath in big gulps like a guppy in an empty tank.

Montgomery turned around quickly, recognizing the excitement in the young rookie's voice. He knew that excitement. It meant they had found something unexpected.

"What is it?"

"We found more bodies. Lots of them! In the basement."

"What? Show me."

The young officer led the detective quickly out of the garage, around the back of the house, and into the basement. There a big German shepherd from one of the K-9 units was busily digging up the dirt floor. Two other officers were down there beside him with brooms and shovels, uncovering a skeleton. There were already two others partially exposed.

"How many are there?"

"I don't know. They're piled on top of each other. Some of them are pretty old."

"They—they're children!" Montgomery started to get woozy.

"How old did you say the suspect was?" one of the officers asked. "Because these bodies look pretty old. Look at the clothes. I haven't seen shoes like those since the eighties."

Montgomery stared down at one exposed leg wearing an old pair of British Knights. He had owned a pair of sneakers just like them years ago—back in 1992. That would have made Joseph around ten years old. These weren't Joseph Miles's victims.

They were Lionel Ray's. That's why Joseph had come back here, to destroy the real source of the curse.

His own father.

It took them several days to unearth all the bodies. When they were done the count stood at twenty-five, ranging in age from six to sixteen. The oldest corpse was at least a decade old. They had all been cut to pieces. A slash across the throat was the killing blow. None of them bore any of the marks of cannibalism, confirming the detective's theory that the senior Miles had been the culprit rather than his son. It looked as if Joe had done the world a service by taking out his father. But where was he now?

Forty-six

Alicia winced as the hot water sprayed from the showerhead onto her raw, pinkish skin. It had been months since her ordeal with Joseph Miles and she had only been out of the hospital a week. She was scheduled to see a plastic surgeon at the end of the month to discuss prostheses to replace her stolen mammary glands. She had already gone through six surgeries, painful skin grafts to cover the gaping hole in her chest where her breasts had been. Now they were going to see if they could give her some kind of implants to make her chest look more normal, more like it had looked before her abduction. Alicia scoffed as she watched the water cascade down her smooth, nippleless chest. She had no illusions. She knew she would never look the same.

She stepped out of the shower and appraised her scarred and disfigured torso. Her chest was now little more than a thin veneer of skin stretched over a rib cage. She could almost see her heart beating beneath it. She began to cry. The man she had fallen in love with had done this to her.

"Why didn't he just kill me? Why leave me like this?"

They still hadn't captured Joe, but there had also been no more cannibal killings. He appeared to have just disappeared. Either that or the cure had worked. In a way she hoped that it hadn't. Every night she prayed that he would return for her. To finish the job he had started.

She heard a noise coming from her bedroom as she gently wiped away the bathwater and tears with her towel. It sounded as if someone had opened her window. Minutes later she heard the unmistakable sound of footfalls.

"Hello?"

She clutched the bath towel to her vandalized chest and peered into the room. She was not surprised at all to see Joe standing in her bedroom.

"You got my note? On the message board?"

"Yes." His expression was almost sad.

"Then you'll do it? You'll do what I ask?"

"Are you sure you want this?"

"I'm sure. I've got a ton of pain pills from the hospital. I'll take a whole handful. I won't feel a thing."

"I've missed you, Alicia." A tear drizzled down his cheek.

"I missed you too."

"I even set us a table."

Joe turned toward the little kitchen, and indeed a large table, way too big for her tiny apartment, stretched from the kitchen into the little dining room nook area and partially into the living room. The table was solid oak and looked expensive. It was set with a silver serving tray, big enough to hold a large pig and one dinner setting at the head of the table. A large carving knife sat on top of the tray.

"The table's an antique," she said. "I bought it just for this occasion. Just in case you came back."

"I love you, Alicia."

"I know you do. But I can't live like this," she said, gesturing toward her chest.

"What about plastic surgery?"

"Look at me." Alicia dropped the towel, revealing the hideous scar that transversed her chest. Joseph sucked in a breath, shocked at his own savagery. "They can't fix this."

"This may take a while. My appetite isn't what it used to be."

Alicia stepped back into the bathroom and opened the medicine cabinet. She had a few Fentanyl patches they had given her at the hospital to replace the morphine drip she'd been hooked up to after her last surgery. She peeled one of them out of the box and stuck it on her neck. There was also nearly a full bottle of Darvocet and a half bottle of Percocet. She scooped them off the shelf and took a whole handful of each and went back into the bedroom. Her legs began to wobble as she turned and staggered into the kitchen. The room spun just before she lay down on the table. The Fentanyl was kicking in.

"I want you to eat all of me. Don't leave anything. I want to be a part of you forever."

The Percocet and Darvocet kicked in now and Alicia could no longer feel her own body. She felt like she was floating.

Joe was crying when he raised the knife. He was still crying when he began to cut through her soft plump flesh. And tears still fell as he slid the blood-moist meat between his lips and swallowed it down. She tasted just like he remembered.

It took him a couple of days to completely consume her. She was awake for the first few hours, telling him how much she loved him. How happy she was to bring him so much pleasure. How she'd wanted this all along. And, despite himself, Joe did feel those familiar jolts of ecstasy as he chewed and swallowed her soft muscle and fat. She passed away that same night, yet Joe had continued eating as he had promised. He ate until her entire body had been consumed—skin, muscle, organs, fat, her brain. He even sucked the marrow out of her bones. He could feel her life inside of him as he walked out of the apartment with his stomach distended, fighting back nausea. He could feel her love coursing through him. He barely noticed the police cruiser until it was right on top of him.

"Freeze! Stop right there! On your knees! Hands behind your head!"

The cop was muscular, middle-aged, and scared. His partner came from the other side of the car looking even older and more scared. Joseph hadn't showered and was still covered with Alicia's blood, but that wasn't the only reason the men were scared. Joe had seen their car across the street three nights ago when he'd first snuck into Alicia's apartment. They had both been behind the wheel, fast asleep. They had been assigned to protect Alicia and they had failed. Joe didn't care anymore. He watched with curious detachment as they handcuffed him, cursing and praying at the same time.

"We fucked up big time!"

"What did you do to the girl? Go check on her, Nate. I've got him. Fuck! Man, we're going to be crucified when they find out we lost a witness!"

"At least we caught the bastard. Who knows, they might even call us heroes."

The middle-aged cop looked at his older partner and shook his head. "I doubt that. I seriously doubt that. See all that blood? It ain't his. And you know what he does to his victims."

The older man's eyes went wide. He ran up the walkway and into the apartment. Less than a minute later he was back out on the sidewalk, throwing up into the gutter.

"Bones! There's just bones up there! He ate her! He ate all of her."

Joe watched the man regurgitate and tried to hold his own enormous meal inside of him. He concentrated on digesting his meal. He knew that they would want to pump his stomach and he wanted to keep as much of her inside of him as he could.

They were just putting him in the backseat of the squad car when another car pulled up. A black detective that Joe thought he recognized was behind the wheel, and next to him sat Professors Locke and Douglas. The two professors sprang out of the car before it had even come to a complete stop and ran over to him.

"Don't worry, boy. We won't let anything happen to you. We're going to help you. We're going to cure you." Professor Locke's eyes were beaming with joy. It looked like he had just won the lottery.

Epilogue

Joe sat behind the glass partition, staring across at the petite young lady who'd come to visit him. It was the model from his art class. The one who'd purchased the painting from him.

"How are you doing, Joseph?"

"I'm fine. You don't have to keep coming here, you know."

"I know. I like seeing you, though." She smiled at him in a practiced, seductive way meant to communicate that she wanted to do more than just see him.

Joe noticed that the woman had begun putting on weight. Her breasts, thighs, and hips all looked fuller, almost plump. She caught Joe looking and smiled.

"Do you like it?" She stood up and turned around so that Joe could get a good look at her ass, which had also increased in size. It was still small but now it had some jiggle to it.

"You look good."

"Good enough to eat?"

Joe didn't reply.

"What do you want?"

"I just want to make sure that you're being treated

well, that you're comfortable. I heard they were experimenting on you?"

"Yes. I volunteered for the experiments. They are using serotonin inhibitors to suppress my urges, to help me with my addiction. Professor Locke is heading the experiment. He thinks it will get him a Nobel Prize if he can cure me."

"So? Is it working?"

"I don't know. I guess so. I don't have the urges anymore. Not often, anyway. But then they keep me locked up and isolated all the time. No outside stimuli. Nothing to bring the urges on. Except for you. You're my only visitor outside of doctors and media."

"Do you get urges when you look at me?" There was an obvious excitement in her voice when she asked the question.

"Yes," Joe replied without looking at her face. His eyes continued to roam her body. She was starting to look good. No longer the anemic waif he'd first met at his art class months ago. She'd obviously been studying up on him, learning more about the type of women he liked. A few more pounds and she'd be almost irresistible.

She'd started writing to him after the trial. At first there had just been questions and then the letters had turned almost pornographic, describing all the things she wanted to do to him and all the things she wanted him to do to her. She'd asked him to marry her on more than one occasion. She claimed she was in love, that she had been ever since the day she saw his portrait of her. Now she'd started putting on weight to make herself more appealing. And it was working.

Joe's eyes landed on her breasts. That's where the

most dramatic change in her appearance had taken place. When he'd first seen her she'd had little or nothing up top but now the extra weight had caused her breasts to swell two or three cup sizes. They looked good, but something was wrong with them that Joe couldn't quite grasp.

"I brought you something. Something from me. To show you how much I care for you. How much I love you." She reached into her purse and pulled out a napkin. It was folded over to conceal something inside of it and there was blood soaked through it. The woman then reached over the glass partition and shoved it into Joe's hand. He didn't even bother to look at it. He opened the napkin and dumped the contents into his mouth as the guards charged in to separate the two of them. They dragged the young model out of the room and tried to pry Joe's mouth open, suspecting that she had passed him some type of narcotic.

One of the guards had his arms around her waist, lifting her off the floor and carrying her out of the room. Her shirt came up as she tried to wriggle out of their arms. Joe suspected that she'd done it on purpose. Exposing herself for him. She wasn't wearing a bra, which gave the other inmates a quick glimpse of her pert medium-sized breasts. Their howls and cat-calls were cut short as they noticed that one of her nipples was missing.

An orgasm ripped through Joe's loins as he chewed up the small pink lump of flesh and swallowed it.

JOHN SKIPP
AND CODY
GOODFELLOW

Pastor Jake promised his followers everlasting life…he just
didn't say what kind. So when the small-town televangelist
and con man climbs out of his coffin at his own wake, it
becomes Judgment Day for everyone gathered to mourn—
or celebrate—his death. Jake is back, in the rotting flesh,
filled with anger and vengeance. And accompanied by demons even more frightening than himself. What follows is
a long night of endless terror, a blood-drenched rampage
by the man not even death could stop.

JAKE'S WAKE

ISBN 13: 978-0-8439-6076-1

L. H. MAYNARD
& M. P. N. SIMS

At an old manor house on a remote Scottish island, six managers of a large corporation arrive for a week-long stay. Within days they will all suffer horrifying deaths and their bodies will never be found. The government assigns the case to Department 18, the special unit created to investigate the supernatural and the paranormal. However this is no mere haunted house. The evil on this island goes back centuries, but its unholy plots and schemes are hardly things of the past. In fact, while the members of Department 18 race to unravel the island's secrets, the forces of darkness are gathering . . . and preparing to attack.

BLACK
CATHEDRAL

ISBN 13: 978-0-8439-6199-7

BRIAN KEENE

They came to the lush, deserted island to compete on a popular reality TV show. Each one hoped to be the last to leave. Now they're just hoping to stay alive. It seems the island isn't deserted after all. Contestants and crew members are disappearing, but they aren't being eliminated by the game. They're being taken by the monstrous half-human creatures that live in the jungle. The men will be slaughtered. The women will be kept alive as captives. Night is falling, the creatures are coming, and rescue is so far away. . . .

CASTAWAYS

ISBN 13: 978-0-8439-6089-1

To order a book or to request a catalog call:
1-800-481-9191
This book is also available at your local bookstore, or you can check out our Web site www.dorchesterpub.com where you can look up your favorite authors, read excerpts, or glance at our discussion forum to see what people have to say about your favorite books.

☐ **YES!**

Sign me up for the Leisure Horror Book Club and send my FREE BOOKS! If I choose to stay in the club, I will pay only $8.50* each month, a savings of $7.48!

NAME: _____

ADDRESS: _____

TELEPHONE: _____

EMAIL: _____

☐ I want to pay by credit card.

☐ **VISA**   ☐ **MasterCard**   ☐ **DISCOVER**

ACCOUNT #: _____

EXPIRATION DATE: _____

SIGNATURE: _____

Mail this page along with $2.00 shipping and handling to:
Leisure Horror Book Club
PO Box 6640
Wayne, PA 19087
Or fax (must include credit card information) to:
610-995-9274
You can also sign up online at **www.dorchesterpub.com**.
*Plus $2.00 for shipping. Offer open to residents of the U.S. and Canada only.
Canadian residents please call 1-800-481-9191 for pricing information.
If under 18, a parent or guardian must sign. Terms, prices and conditions subject to change. Subscription subject to acceptance. Dorchester Publishing reserves the right to reject any order or cancel any subscription.